My Christian Penis

R. Tyler

This is a work of fiction. All of the characters, organizations and events portrayed in this novel are either products of the author's imagination or are used fictionally. The opinions expressed are those of the characters and should not be confused with the author's. Any resemblance to real events or actual persons is purely coincidental, with the sole exception of Sam's mom. Any resemblance between Sam's mom and the author's mother-in-law is probably more than coincidental.

ISBN-13: 9780615887388
ISBN-10: 0615887384

Thanks to everyone who made the 2010 Fringe Festival performance possible. I thought I'd have to put it on with puppets, but no: Actors came along and for that I'll always be grateful. Another thanks to my family and friends who came to watch it performed. Finally, a special thanks to the stranger who sought us out after a show to say it was "funny and profound." Without that bit of audience feedback, my perspective wouldn't have been the same.

CHAPTER 1

She saw it happen as if in slow motion. The blue PT Cruiser in the far lane of oncoming traffic inexplicably pulled into an already-occupied lane. She almost started to laugh, but the PT Cruiser kept veering, its driver oblivious. Cars collided and spun out of control. When the PT Cruiser careened across the double yellow line and into her lane, she froze, knowing a crash was inevitable.

As the other car entered her space, its intimate details were all too visible—individual grooves in the grill, a ding on the bumper, and a slight bend in the license plate. Then everything was dark. The darkness parted way for one final image of the car floor, like a freeze frame in a movie: stray hair, lint balls, and a thick pool of red. Then it was dark again.

Soon after, a bright tunnel of dazzling light appeared. A silhouette appeared in the light, moving toward her, closer and closer, and … Jim!

Everything would be okay. She bathed in acceptance and warmth. "Mary! Mary! We're back together in Heaven, my love," Jim said. She was speechless, overcome with emotion.

Then, Jim reacted to something behind him, and he turned away from her. "What is it, Julio?" he asked, mildly irritated. He spoke to someone beyond Mary's line of sight. So she waited, still bathing in the light.

She didn't know how long she waited—maybe twenty seconds, maybe five minutes—before she finally said, "Jim?"

Jim turned to face her again. His expression had changed.

CHAPTER 2

*"And when you pray, do not be like the hypocrites, for
they love to pray standing in the synagogues and on the
street corners to be seen by men." (Matthew 6:5)*

It was Thursday. It was 3:30 pm. That meant Crazy Man was
outside.

Crazy Man stood on top of a milk crate and screamed into
the Square. He was reasonably well-dressed and didn't appear to
be homeless. In fact, he was probably gainfully employed in some
manner, dental plan and all. Only the actual words coming out of
his mouth gave him away.

"Earthquakes? Droughts? Hurricanes? Scientists may try to
explain them, but the Bible reveals the truth. God smites those
who displease him, and oh how we've displeased him."

Technically, he was standing on the property of the college
and everybody knew he wasn't a student. However, no one ever
bothered to make him leave. The street behind Crazy Man wasn't
very busy; perhaps two cars a minute would drive past, mincing

their own business. Sam and Anne sat a cautious distance away, on a picnic blanket with their backpacks, behind fifteen or so other college kids enjoying the show. Crazy Man had been yelling for about 10 minutes now, and his rant was picking up steam.

Sam felt sorry for the American flag propped up next to Crazy Man. The flag had to be embarrassed. It did nothing to deserve this, absolutely nothing. It was just for sale and this asshole bought it.

"We've handed over control of our government to the Muslim Brotherhood. We've taken God out of schools, and Christ out of Christmas. Now we've ignored God's instructions about marriage. You watch: next, people will start marrying horses and pigs. *Of course* the Earth is groaning under the weight of our sins."

"Preach it, brother, preach it! God's not going to take it and neither am I," Manfred said. Of course, Manfred always paid rapt attention to Crazy Man.

"Muslim Brotherhood, marrying horses … I'm kicking ass over here," Anne said.

"I'm getting nowhere," Sam replied.

A car drove past very slowly on the road behind Crazy Man. "Fuck you, cocksucker. Hey, cocksucker: fuck you," the passenger bellowed theatrically as the car inched by. "Go home and suck some more cock!" Sam figured Crazy Man was hottempered enough to take the bait, but he didn't seem to notice the taunts. His input jack had been disabled long ago; nothing could get through anymore.

"God doesn't want homes to stand, not when the foundation upon which our families are built is so cracked. I predict … I predict … on September 17th … a great tsunami will destroy the

Pacific Northwest, and this will be ..."—he struggled with the emerging vision inside his head, one hand covering his face while the other reached out to the crowd— "the first sign the Rapture will come on ... January 5th of next year. Yes: January 5th."

Anne and Sam stopped laughing long enough to note the date of the upcoming Rapture. It was worth writing this one down.

"Now, if I can pray hard enough," Crazy Man boasted, "this tsunami *won't* come in September, but only if I pray hard enough."

"Check it out," said Anne, glancing up from her bingo cards, "a narcissistic excuse for why the Rapture won't come: it's already lined up and ready to roll on January 6th. *This guy* will have saved us from it by the power of his prayer."

"What a deluded, pompous asshole," Sam said. "Blasphemer, too, when you think about it ..."

"But it depends on what the government does, too," Crazy Man continued to expound. "Do you know what our *oh-so-great* government is scheming now? They're planning to force people to hand over babies up for adoption to Muslim and queer couples first, and they'll provide taxpayer subsidies to do it. Normal families aren't good enough anymore. No one asked us if this is okay. They'll make us bend over and take it!"

"BINGO!" Anne shouted.

"Ugh. What did you get?"

"I was one away from winning on three different cards." Anne was delighted with herself. "I finally won with five across: 'lamestream media,' 'sodomite,' 'socialist,' 'abstinence,' and 'bend over.'"

"You had all the good cards," Sam said as he scanned Anne's cards. "My best card was still two away. I was missing 'judgment day' and 'porn addiction.' When has he ever not said 'porn addiction?' It's usually what gets him all titillated for the opening."

"I love it when you can tell he's fighting off a boner, because he's thinking about his big old stash o' porn at home," Anne said.

"Yeah, I think he's tamer than usual today. I wonder what's wrong. I'm almost concerned for him. Wait … stop … listen …"

They focused on Crazy Man, who was plumbing new depths. "They're trying to tell Little Suzy and Little Johnny we're descended from a bunch of gay monkeys. Well, my granddaddy was no gay monkey. No sir. Maybe Obama's granddad was a gay monkey, if you know what I mean. But mine wasn't."

"Gay monkeys?" Anne said. "We should add that to the cards." They started laughing again. Sam's hand landed on Anne's, and he let it lurk there for a moment. She didn't recoil.

The hand thing was a breakthrough with Anne, but Sam could always count on Manfred to ruin the moment. "Gay monkeys! Gay monkeys! Gay monkeys!" he chanted. "Obama's granddad was a gay monkey who had sex with another gay monkey and they had a gay monkey baby!"

Of course, Anne didn't notice Manfred. No one but Sam ever heard him.

Anne slowly extended her little pinky toward Sam and gently touched his arm with the tip of her finger. "Gay monkeys," she breathed, as she grazed over him. Sam smiled and imitated her. They both laughed softly at the weirdness of what they had just done. An awkward silence followed, as they stared at each other.

Maybe this is going to work out.

Then, Manfred opened his mouth/whatever. "This is what I'm talking about, Sam. If we keep letting the liberals get their way, they'll make us bend over for their gay monkeys."

Well ... maybe this isn't *going to work out.*

Manfred required some of Sam's undivided attention. Sam spotted his chance when the Three Women with Unshaven Armpits entered the Square, ready to rumble. Equally outspoken and temperamental as Crazy Man, they'd show up most weeks to trade insults and shouts. This scene would keep Anne entertained for a while. "Speaking of monkeys," Sam said, "it's after four, so I'm going to buy a couple of half-price bananas."

"What? Are you crazy? You'll miss the Three Women with Unshaven Armpits. Besides, the street vendor really seems to hate you," Anne said.

"He doesn't hate me," Sam responded. "He's just kind of aloof."

"He's not aloof with me," Anne replied.

"That's only because you're a girl."

"Well, if you're leaving, hurry back," Anne said. With that, Sam left, turning once to glance at Anne and chuckle at the commencing verbal street brawl. These moments were great—the women screaming at Crazy Man, Crazy Man giving it back, the sheer decibel level remarkable. As soon as Sam turned the corner, he looked down at his crotch. "Manfred! You need to shut up down there. You're driving me nuts."

"It's America, Sam. I have a God-given right to free speech!" Manfred replied.

"No, you have a *constitutionally*-given right to free speech, and you're not saying anything worthwhile. You're just trying to needle me into a response. Knock it off."

"I can't help myself. I love that guy! Everything he says makes so much sense."

"Homosexual monkeys having sex and producing human offspring within two generations? What part of that makes sense to you?"

"Earthquakes, then?" Manfred fired back. "You want to explain? How come there's been like, six-hundred mini-tremors in Arkansas during the past year? What do you think is causing it? The wheels are coming off the bus in terms of American values. The earthquakes are no coincidence."

"We don't cause earthquakes, Manfred. Hollywood doesn't cause earthquakes, either, except on movie sets. The president doesn't cause earthquakes. You're not actually that fucking stupid." Sam paused to gather his next thought. "Let me run this one by you: if God is attacking the United States because he's mad about gay marriage or whatever, then why the hell is he attacking *Arkansas*, which would be on his side? Why does *Vermont* emerge unscathed? Why doesn't he smite the entire Northeast corridor?"

"Duh, the Northeast did get attacked. Do you remember 9-11, or do you not care about our country enough to remember that horrible day?"

"So, God is part of al-Qaeda now?" Sam asked, starting to laugh. "Did he get brainwashed by the bin Laden recruitment tapes? Did God train in a terrorist camp in Saudi Arabia? I'm totally lost!"

"Yes, you are lost, sinner," Manfred retorted. It was one of the cleverest things Sam could remember Manfred ever saying.

"And you'll be *really* lost when Jesus Christ returns to Earth. You shouldn't be blaspheming like this. God is not a terrorist."

"Hey, you're the one who said God caused 9-11, a terrorist act, and earthquakes, to punish us. *I* don't make this shit up. *You* make this shit up. You and that shithead on the milk crate."

Manfred's tone grew smug. "Logic doesn't work in these situations. Only faith works."

Sam was angry at himself for having another one of these conversations with Manfred. Well, "conversation" wasn't the right word for it. It's not as if they were really talking. Sam thought words at Manfred, never opening his mouth. Sam's private thoughts were still private, and presumably Manfred had private thoughts of his own (though Sam wasn't entirely certain of that). To Sam's dismay, Manfred shared Sam's powers of sight and hearing. Sam would love nothing more than to be able to see and hear in peace, without Manfred's commentary.

Annoyed that he was standing there internally arguing with his dick instead of hanging out with Anne, Sam said, "Manfred, it's only important for you to have faith in one thing: if you mess up my relationship with Anne, I promise you …"

"You don't and won't have a relationship with Anne."

"Yeah, I will. I know she likes me and as long as you don't go all homo on me, it can happen. Just try being straight once, Manfred. You may like it." Sam only hoped the suggestion Manfred was gay would make him feel the need to prove himself.

"I'm not a fag! You're the fag! I don't have a fag bone in my body."

"You don't *have* any bones in your body." It was a cheap response, but Sam couldn't resist.

"Oh, shut up, Sam. Do you realize we passed the street vendor? Aren't you going to get your half-price bananas? You've been waiting all day for half-price bananas, you cheap-ass Jew."

Since his mid-teens, Sam had no longer felt the need to think of himself as Jewish simply because his maternal great-grandparents did, but he didn't feel compelled to correct Manfred, either.

"Nah, that guy hates me," Sam responded. "Don't start. You know why. I'm lucky I'm not in jail because of you."

"I do what I can to spread the gospel," Manfred replied haughtily.

"Spread the gospel? That's what you call your bullshit? Your so-called gospel spreading would be more impressive if you ever did anything good or kind. You don't even think charitable thoughts. Good luck convincing God you deserve to be in Heaven."

Manfred's tone intensified. "Heaven isn't something you earn. All that matters is you accept Jesus Christ into your heart. But since *you* won't get baptized, *I'm* going to burn in a Lake of Fire because I'm stuck on your godless ass."

"Listen, Manfred," said Sam, attempting a firm but sympathetic tone. "God isn't Hannibal Lecter. He won't torture you in Hell because you didn't have voodoo water thrown on your head while someone said magic words. Don't worry like this, man."

"Whatever, Sam. Either you have the faith or you don't."

Sam appreciated the silence that followed. He reflected on how incredibly tired he was. He was tired of having to listen to medieval views about science, about women, about politics, about nearly everything. He was tired of having to excuse himself to go fight with his dick, because sometimes it was too difficult to mult-task an internal, spoken-only-in-his-mind fight with Manfred while simultaneously trying to have a normal conversation with someone else.

A baptism was likely the path of least resistance. He had come close to it about a year ago, because Manfred asked nicely and Sam figured: why not show Manfred that courtesy gets rewarded? Baptisms are meaningless, free, and possess a magic power to put worried minds to ease.

Sam had looked at some church listings and picked the one that seemed the kindest and most reasonable, but the subsequent conversation with the pastor was unbearable. He hated lying and wasn't any good at it. After a few minutes of spewing out bullshit reasons for his fake conversion to Christianity, Sam's thoughts fell apart. Was he there because he was crazy? Was he imagining Manfred and taking instruction from his subconscious? Was he the only person on Earth who had internal conversations with his penis? No one else admitted to anything like Manfred. Or did other people hear the voices of their bodies in less threat-ening ways, thinking of them as their "conscience" or "soul" or "intuition" without even knowing they were speaking to different organisms living inside them?

Sam had no one to ask, no one to confide in. He pretended to open up to the pastor about how he had seen God's light or some shit like that, but he found himself genuinely wanting to reveal his relationship with Manfred. The pastor seemed like one of the "good ones," someone who spent his time helping people, not manipulating or scamming them.

In the end, Sam had been too scared to open up, and for a few minutes, all he managed to do was stare at the ground in silence.

He eventually left without a baptism. Thus, the hassling from Manfred continued.

Sam walked into a 7-11 and bought a pair of bananas. "Ooooh, look at you, paying full price!" Sam ignored Manfred and walked to Anne.

To Sam's surprise and before he even had a chance to sit down, Anne announced her boredom with the Crazy Man vs. Women with Unshaven Armpits battle. She explained that while he was gone it had inexplicably devolved into an argument about the British Royal Family, at which point she lost interest. Before Sam could respond, she told him she needed his help with something on her computer.

CHAPTER 3

*You, God, know my folly. My guilt is not hid-
den from you. (Psalm 69:5)*

Sam's mind raced as he followed Anne across campus to the dor-
mitories. He was pretty sure the computer thing was a ruse. Or at
least he hoped it was. He just wasn't entirely sure what to do about
it. This had never happened to him before.

He was extremely nervous as she unlocked the door and led
him into her room. It looked like every other dorm room on campus, with two single beds and two identical gray desks. A bookshelf with lots of books and small trinkets was opposite the beds,
as was a simple table with a television on top. He'd only been in
her room twice, for a few minutes, and both times Anne's roommate was there. So his first move was to covertly survey the room
and determine the roommate wasn't there.

As if reading his thoughts, Anne said, "Andrea went home for
the weekend." She closed the door.

Sam was 60% sure she was being suggestive, signaling to him he was free to make a move, but that still left a 40% chance she was simply providing information. He couldn't take that chance, so he stood there stupidly. After what seemed like an eternity of silence, he finally managed, "Something's wrong with your computer?" *Smooth*, he thought.

It was reassuring when Anne reacted as if she had no idea what he was talking about. Maybe he was imagining things. Then she said, "Oh, that. You know what? We can work on the computer later." She was looking right into his eyes. She wouldn't do that unless she was waiting for him to make a move, right? He was up to 90% certainty now.

When he opened his mouth, dumb words tumbled out. "So, if you don't want to show me your computer, what do you want to do?" She half smiled. She had to think he was a total idiot, which bumped him down to 85%.

It felt like a miracle when she reached for his hand. At last, he decided it was time. He took a step closer to her, with his eyes averted. She looked at him expectantly, but he didn't have the courage to do anything else. He took yet another tiny step closer. "That's it," he said with discomfort. "That's all I have."

Mercifully, Anne took over, reaching one hand to the back of his head and pulling his mouth down to hers. *Holy shit, this is happening*, he thought. He had never kissed anyone before.

It took Manfred a moment to catch up. "I thought we were coming here to fix her computer," he said. But as Anne's lips met Sam's, Manfred went apeshit. "No, Sam. Don't you dare! I swear, Sam, don't you even think about it."

Sam had been too absorbed in his own nervousness to consider Manfred's perspective. It had all happened so fast. He didn't have a chance to negotiate for Manfred's good behavior.

"What's wrong?" Sam asked Manfred. In the excitement of the moment, he had accidentally spoken *aloud*.

Somehow Anne took it in context, apparently thinking she had given off some signal (as opposed to assuming he was talking to his dick instead of her). "Nothing's wrong," she breathed into his ear. "It's just that I've wanted this for so long."

And he said, "So have I." Anne was merely the start. He wanted the entire concept of being a normal person. He longed for meaningful human interactions; he wanted what Pinocchio got when he became a real boy. How wonderful it would be, not to be alone all the time … not that he *ever* was entirely alone, because there was always Manfred, but how rewarding would it be to have an actual relationship?

"What is she doing? Sam, what is she doing? What is she doing?" Sam was racking his brain to understand Manfred's problem. He needed Manfred now more than ever. Why would his penis, of all people or things, have a problem with this prospect?

Sam's knees started buckling and he fell onto Anne's bed (he hoped it was Anne's bed and not her roommate's), and Anne came down on top of him. Her hand landed on his chest and slowly worked its way down to his pants. He kicked off his shoes.

"You stop her NOW!"

Fuck, Manfred! He thought. *Why are you doing this to me now?* At that moment he realized Manfred was terrified.

Anne undid the button on his jeans, and started pulling down the zipper. He was frozen, unable and unwilling to move as she reached her hand inside. This was awesome, but then: "You have about 10 seconds to tell this woman she cannot touch me, not under any circumstances. Now, Sam. Right this instant!"

Sam didn't know what to do. He didn't want to do anything; everything was going swimmingly, so why change? He decided to hope Manfred would fall in line. Amazing things were about to happen to him if he would give it a chance.

Manfred didn't even give him 10 seconds. "Forget it, Sam. I'll take care of this problem myself."

Anne had pulled Manfred out and had him in her hand. Sam felt something happening, a familiar sensation, but he didn't quite realize what it was until he heard Anne's voice.

"What ... what are you doing?" Anne asked. "Oh my God ... are you ... *peeing?*"

Sam opened his eyes and lifted his head off the bed in time to see the end of it. Anne still had Manfred in her hand, fully erect, pointing straight up to the ceiling. He was spouting pee like a volcano, the urine shooting three or four feet into the air before coming down in all directions. Anne's shirt and face were all wet, and so was the bed. Sam couldn't think, he was so astonished by the sight.

Anne was stunned, too. After it stopped, she was still sitting there, trying to come to grips with what had just happened. Sam knew if you touch a live electrical conductor, you should use the back of your hand because otherwise the electricity makes your hand curl up so you can't let go. Well, that's how Anne was now, her hand seemingly convulsed into a tight grip she couldn't shake loose.

She half cried and half screamed, "Holy shit, you son of a bitch!"

Then he felt himself ejaculate—in a ridiculous, unprecedented quantity. As soon as the first bit of semen hit her hand, Anne snapped out of her frozen shock and yanked her hand away. The remainder of the semen landed on her thigh. She jumped up, the load dripping off, some on the bed, some on her foot, and some on the floor. She jerked away and Sam fell back on the bed, landing in a warm pool of urine. Normally he would have jumped up too, but at that moment he was incapable of movement.

"Anne ..." his voice cracked.

Anne had recovered from the initial shock and was in full freak-out mode. "You peed on me? Does my bed look like a toilet? You think this is hot? It turns you on to piss on people?"

Then, fully realizing the situation, she cried, "And what is ... what is ... how ... you came right after you peed? Wait, you were peeing with an erection! Is that even biologically possible? How can a man piss and cum all within five seconds? What the fuck? You freak loser! Weirdo! Get the fuck out of my room, fucking freak asshole!"

As much as Sam wanted to somehow make everything right, he also wanted to do precisely as she commanded and get the fuck out of her room. Escaping proved difficult. When he pulled himself off the bed, warm urine dripped down his hair and back. He recoiled clumsily, causing his unfastened pants to slip down around his ankles. He tripped and fell onto the throw rug between the two beds, his hand landing in a pile of cum.

Manfred hummed in self-satisfaction while Anne cursed at Sam. Her individual words merged into a single, extended, high-pitched shriek, which confused Sam, rendering him immobile, until she yelled with clarity, "Get the fuck out!"

Sam got up off the floor and pulled up his underwear and pants. There was pee all over both. Before he could zip his pants she had yanked the door open, repeating, "Get the fuck out!"

Sam didn't want things to end like this, so he stammered, "Look, Anne, I don't know what ..." But as he started talking, he realized there just weren't any words for this sort of thing. Sam made his share of apologies over the years, but he didn't have one for this particular situation.

"GET OUT!" She was using every bit of her strength to shove him out the door. As she pushed him, he lost his balance and crashed into the bookshelf. A couple of books fell, as well as a box of some sort with roughly 1,000 pieces in it. Did she have a marble collection or something? Small pieces bounced around the ground, scattering. When he stepped on one of those small objects, it occurred to him his shoes were still on the floor next to her bed.

"My shoes ..." he managed.

"Out!" she yelled, pointing into the hallway. Three girls and one boy were standing in the open doorway of the room across the hall, staring. They may as well have had a bucket of popcorn. One of them was Andrea, Anne's *supposedly* out-of-town roommate.

Anne retrieved his shoes and backpack and threw them at him. There was a pool of cum inside one of the shoes. He turned back to look at her one last time and saw the mix of horror and fury on her face. There was no way to make this any better. New onlookers were gathering in the hallway, attracted to the sound of hostilities like flies to shit.

Without thinking, he bellowed, "Manfred!" as he fled. He could only imagine what Anne and the rest of his audience thought that meant. Dripping with bodily fluids, shirt half-open, and carrying semen-encrusted shoes, he plowed through the throng of people.

He stopped in the stairwell, plopping onto the floor. He put his shoes on, and Sam recoiled as he heard his heel splat down on the semen inside. Semen should be seen and not heard.

Someone was coming upstairs towards him, and he sped up, skipping steps on the way down and hiding his face.

All the while, Manfred hummed his jolly tune.

CHAPTER 4

*Without wood a fire goes out; without gossip a
quarrel dies down. (Proverbs 26:20)*

All Sam could do was pray to whatever God Manfred believed in that his roommate Darren wouldn't be home. As if in answer, when Sam stepped into his room, he found himself alone.

In the quiet of his room, force of habit took over. He sat at his computer, jiggled the mouse, typed in his password, and opened his email. No new messages. He bent over and, calm as Mister Rogers, began taking off his shoes.

The drying white goo running down the outside of his shoe brought everything came back to him. Sam became frantic. He leapt out of his chair, remembering his pants were covered in urine he had now transferred to the cushion. Realizing the pee and cum on his socks was getting all over his floor, he started dancing, battling in vain to keep his feet in the air to avoid further contamination. It looked like the potty dance of a toddler, except the last thing Sam needed to do was pee. After firing enough urine to rival the Mississippi River into Anne's face and all over her room, he figured it would be days before he needed to pee again.

He thought about the clean-up job Anne would be facing. He had transformed her room into Chernobyl. It would take her hours to clean. He felt terrible and wanted to help, but he was pretty sure her response wouldn't be one of gratitude. More likely she would club him over his head with her chair. His blood would mix well with his other bodily fluids now flooding her room.

Thinking about Anne's plight got his attention off his own problems, and he calmed down. There was nothing he could do for her moment; the best course of action was to get himself clean.

He noticed his framed portrait of George Washington Carver atop his dresser. The slave-turned-scientist was an odd choice for a framed portrait in a dorm room, but Sam had always counted Carver as a personal hero: overcoming insurmountable odds, becoming the epitome of resourcefulness, scientific genius, and artistic ability. What a man! Now this hero was just staring at him, probably disapproving from beyond the grave. Grabbing a towel to serve as a barricade between his disgusting hands and the rest of the universe, Sam opened the top drawer, pushed in the portrait, and closed the drawer.

There was no way George Washington Carver would want to see this shit.

Sam used the towel to pull off his socks and wipe his shoes. He soon realized he'd never be willing to put his feet inside those shoes again. He calmly stepped into the bathroom he and Darren shared with the two kids in the next room, and, without taking off his clothes or even waiting for the water to heat up, he stepped into the shower.

He pulled off his soaking wet clothes and pushed them to the corner. Half a bottle of body wash later, Sam felt clean enough to get out of the shower, although he didn't know if he would ever feel truly clean again. Still naked and wet, he pulled a plastic bag from under the sink and stuffed in the sopping wet clothes. Then he went back into his room and added his towel, shoes and socks to the bag. He wanted to burn it all in a giant bonfire. But since he didn't have access to a giant bonfire in his dorm room, he decided the dumpster would have to do. He decided to carry out this disposal plan the next time he left his room ... when it was safe to go out in public again ... in ten years or so ...

If those people leering in the hallway hadn't witnessed the denouement of the scene in Anne's room, maybe Anne would keep his disgrace a secret. Perhaps she wouldn't give anyone the ugly details. Who wanted to admit they had been peed on? He even considered the possibility Anne liked him enough to forgive him. She was freaked out right now, but it was conceivable she'd cool down and be receptive to a heartfelt apology later.

It was six o'clock, still light outside for another hour or so, and Sam hadn't eaten anything except a banana. But he turned out the lights and decided to go to sleep. Hopefully he could sleep until this whole incident blew over.

Of course, he couldn't sleep. His mind drifted back to the conversation with the pastor, when he lied and lied about wanting to get baptized, when he really wanted to tell the truth.

If he was nuts and Manfred was imaginary, then Sam was beyond crazy. He was also a twisted, sick bastard, because if Manfred wasn't real, then *Sam* was the one who wanted to pee on Anne, and he made this "Manfred" fabrication do it for him. All the ridiculous, destructive, silly, spiteful, idiotic things Manfred had coerced him into over the years: they would be Sam's own doing. Most of Sam's self-respect was derived from thinking he was a decent human being. Manfred had better be real—or else Sam was scum.

But, didn't the events of the last 90 minutes refute that hypothesis? He didn't predict Manfred's reaction; in fact, he got it thoroughly wrong. If Manfred was just a part of his deranged mind, then why would his reaction be so unexpected? He would have invented it, therefore he would have anticipated it, right? Well, unless it was a split personality deal. But then he wouldn't even know about Manfred. Or maybe this whole thing was the result of being gay and in denial about his sexuality. What if his subconscious fabricated a massive heterosexual charade, from which "Manfred" rescued him, just in time?

Ridiculous. He'd know if he were gay. He never experienced sexual attraction to other men. The feelings he felt for Anne were real, and he sure as hell enjoyed making out with her before Manfred ruined everything. Something was going on. He was unique. He had to be the only man on the planet Earth who could effortlessly urinate with an erection, and ejaculate immediately afterwards. Sam decided his best bet was to assume he wasn't crazy and wasn't gay. This left only one place to go for an explanation.

"Manfred ... Manfred, why did you do it?" Sam was very calm and measured as he asked. He was too numb for fury.

Manfred had been quiet since returning to the room, with the exception of a somewhat muted version of his typical chatter when Sam washed him in the shower. It took a second for Manfred to respond. "I did what I had to do. I wasn't going anywhere near that ugly skank."

"She's not an ugly skank," Sam countered. "And you know that." Manfred made a sort of snorting noise, but didn't otherwise respond.

"Here's the thing, Manfred: you seemed ..." Sam had been about to say *petrified*, but he figured that could be a confusing choice of words when talking about an erect penis, so he settled on, "You seemed terrified."

Again, Manfred was silent for a few seconds before responding, "I was *not* terrified." It was a sharp retort that would have been more convincing without the three-second delay.

Sam let the delay go and said, "Then what was it?"

"I just don't think it's right," Manfred said. "You were on your way to having premarital sex, and the Bible is pretty clear on that one."

"I don't get it, Manfred," Sam said. He honestly *didn't* get it. "If Jesus died for your sins and you go to Heaven regardless, then what difference does it make if you commit a biblical sin?"

Manfred responded with a hint of anger, "Except you won't get us baptized, so we're going to Hell for our sins."

"Yeah, but if I don't get us baptized, then we're hellbound no matter what, right? So why does it matter if we engage in premarital sex? I'm not trying to fight with you here. I honestly don't understand."

"It matters," was all Manfred said.

"But it doesn't matter if you do other sins? You're fine with disrespecting our mom. You're fine with bearing false witness. You're fine with stealing bananas and chips from a street vendor after calling him a towelhead. You're fine with a host of other horrible things, but you draw the line at premarital sex?"

"Oh, get real. Disrespecting mom isn't a sin!" Manfred laughed in disbelief.

"Damn straight it is. Honor thy Mother and Father. I'm agnostic and I know more about the Bible than you. How sad is that?"

"Knowledge means nothing without faith," Manfred quipped. "Good deeds mean nothing without faith. Good minus God equals zero. That's what's left when you take out the G-O-D out of the G-O-O-D, just a zero."

Sam laughed at Manfred's earnest attempt at clever wisdom. *He tries so hard sometimes*, Sam thought. "Um, actually, if you remove the G-O-D from G-O-O-D, you're left with the letter O, which is entirely different from a zero. One is a letter, and the other is a number. This is the letter O. As in, 'O', say can you see?'"

Manfred pivoted to the didactic, condescending tone he assumed whenever he went to his pre-packaged talking points. "Sam, we're talking about the moral fabric of society."

"Since when do you care about the moral fabric of society?"

"It's a slippery slope once you cast away the boundaries of God's law," Manfred said. "Orgies, prostitution, all sorts of sick, perverted things. When the moral fabric of society crumbles, you're left with anarchy. Humankind will devour itself."

Well, how do you argue with that? wondered Sam. Arguments are built on logic and critical thinking, and when those are gone … well, back around the maypole we go. He reverted to what had—briefly—worked before going to Anne's room. "You know what I think? I think you're saying all these things to deflect from the fact you're gay. You have no problem with my man hand, but when the possibility of a woman comes into play, you panic."

"That's ridiculous, Sam," Manfred sputtered out. "I love vagina as much as the next penis. If you need me to prove it to you, I'll prove it."

"Great, Manfred, I'd love for you to prove it to me," Sam said. "Only you already humiliated me to the point where no woman in this hemisphere will be interested in me. Maybe we can move to New Zealand, and you can prove it to me there."

"Things aren't so bad, Sam," Manfred said soothingly. "You'll see."

For some irrational reason, Manfred's words provided reassurance. Despite it being so early in the evening, Sam began to feel exhausted from the day's events and fell asleep for the night.

When he woke up, it was 10:30 a.m. Well, that was some solid sleep. He looked across the room and saw no sign of Darren, so he must have slept through his roommate's return and departure.

Sam then realized he had missed his organic chemistry lecture. He could probably handle missing that class; he was doing pretty well in O-chem. He scored 57% on his last test. For some reason, unlike any other class he had ever taken, O-chem had a ridiculous curve where getting 20% of the answers right amounted to a C+, so Sam was in good shape. Friday mornings were light. His next class wasn't until 1:00.

Sam was still wearing the clothes he put on after his desperate shower the evening before. They were clean, relatively speaking. He still needed to do something about his hair, but he really felt the need to venture outside his room for a moment first. He needed a brief re-entry into society to make him feel ready for what would be—no doubt—a rough day.

He smelled the urine in the plastic bag containing yesterday's clothes, but as he bravely poked his head out the door he was overcome by a much more powerful stench of urine. Squishy carpet made Sam reflexively jump a few feet into the empty hallway. A large yellowish stain was now befouling his door and the industrial-grade carpet in front of it.

The smell was so strong, Sam concluded multiple guys must have taken turns pissing on his door while he was asleep. *Well, that's karma for me*, he thought.

He stared at the door trying to figure out what to do. The janitorial staff would take care of it … someday. Still, there was something embarrassing about that: the cleaning people would learn one of the residents of Room 344 was a hated loser. They might not know if it was him or Darren, but that didn't really matter.

He should probably clean it up himself. He knew why this happened. It wasn't a random event. It wasn't the cleaning staff's fault. Cleaning this pool of strange piss seemed like a bizarre form of justice for what he did to Anne.

He jumped over the pool and removed the pee towel from the plastic bag destined for the dumpster. No reason to ruin another towel. He ran it under the sink for a few seconds and then wiped the door and patted it against the carpet. Then he grabbed some paper towels from the bathroom as well as a container of Soft Soap, the most powerful cleaning agent in his possession.

As he jumped over the pee and into the hallway, a disheveled Darren strolled toward him. *Strolling* really was the word. When Darren saw Sam, he said, "Dude, guess who got his name crossed off the book of virgins last night?"

No guessing needed there.

Sam was about to offer Darren some perfunctory congratulation when Darren sniffed the air a couple of times and curled his lips, asking, "Dude, what the fuck happened here?"

Darren was one of those people who started every sentence with "Dude," but was otherwise as good a roommate as Sam could have hoped for. He was friendly and, more importantly, didn't spend much time in their room. Sam figured Darren thought of him as a social leper, but at least he was kind about it. He had been terrified of having a roommate in college, and indeed things had worked out very poorly last year when he was a freshman, but so far living with Darren was going fine.

"A bunch of people peed on our door last night," Sam explained.

"Why would they do that?" Darren asked, disgusted.

Sam was relieved Darren didn't know the story of his misadventures. He went for misdirection without an outright lie when he replied, "Don't ask me."

Darren hesitated before asking, "Dude, need some help?"

Sam gave him the answer he was clearly looking for. "No, don't worry about it. I'm almost done. Just make sure to jump over this spot on your way in."

Darren backed away. "No, that's all right. I'll come back after class. See you later, dude." He turned around and walked back down the hall.

As he got back to work cleaning, Sam smiled to himself, glad to know at least one person hadn't heard about the farce.

But then he heard girls laughing hysterically from the common area around the corner where Darren had just gone.

"When it was all over, she said he screamed 'Manfred!' at the top of his lungs."

He heard a couple of girls laugh, and another said, "Oh my God, do you think Manfred is the name he calls his dick?"

"Ha Ha Ha, Manfred's his penis!" one of the girls laughed. "That's a classic. It wasn't *me*. It was my dick Manfred who peed on you. Bad Manfred!"

A hive of about thirty girls must be out there, Sam figured, judging by the volume and variety of laughter. Finally, they simmered down until it was quiet enough for Sam to hear one say "Poor Anne" in a softer voice.

"I don't know why she had anything to do with that weirdo in the first place."

He tuned out the rest of their conversation and quickly finished scrubbing the door and floor, and then went back inside his room. One of the guys in the room next door was using their shared shower, but Sam walked into the bathroom anyway, washed his hands, and ran a brush through his hair for a couple of strokes. It didn't really help, but Sam figured if people were going to laugh at him today, it wouldn't be because of his hair. He put the brush down and walked out the door, passing the common room on his way to the cafeteria.

Those girls were still there, and started laughing even harder when they saw him. He walked past them without glancing in their direction. This was just how things were going to be for a while.

He picked up a muffin and some hash browns from the food line, ignoring everyone but the cafeteria staff—there was no way *they* could know, was there?—and took a seat in the corner, as far away from anyone else as possible.

There was no one he could talk to, except Manfred, who wasn't exactly sympathetic. Darren was a nice enough guy, but they weren't really friends, just roommates. Sam surely couldn't talk to him about *this*, much less the bigger problem.

He looked up again, searching for a friendly face, but instead saw a table of frat boys laughing at him. "You the man, Sam!" one of them hollered. Yesterday, he would have been shocked if any of those guys even knew his name. Today, the whole damned school apparently knew his name and his shame.

Sam placed his untouched plate on the conveyor belt and walked out of the cafeteria. On an impulse, he decided to blow off his Friday classes and go home for the weekend. He walked to his room to gather his stuff, so he could get the hell out of there.

Upon arriving at the door to his room, he was relieved to find no one had applied a new coat of piss. But what did disappoint Sam was the note, posted to the door: "MANFRED'S NOT THE DICK. YOU ARE!" Someone outlined the note with a crude penis drawing in pink glitter. Sam let his forehead rest on the door for a moment, took a deep breath, and then pulled the note off the door. Glitter got onto his hand in the process, which he wiped on his pants without thinking. He went inside and picked out some clothes for the weekend.

He couldn't get to his car fast enough.

CHAPTER 5

I searched everywhere, determined to find wisdom and to
understand the reason for things. (Ecclesiastes 7:25)

The room looked like someone picked up a random assortment
of 1970s décor items: mustard yellow chairs, moss green pillows,
and a piece of macramé on the wall. It was the sort of stuff a
family might put in their yard sale, hoping—but not *optimistically*
hoping—it would inexplicably be purchased. The room seemed
like a museum of decaying American history, but Mary liked it. It
made her think of her childhood and, for that reason, she found
it comfortable. Why should a place like this, the basement of the
town community center, spend money on superficiality? The interior displayed a proper set of priorities where resources were
concerned. As a practical person, not to mention a taxpayer, Mary
couldn't ask for more.

Several couches and chairs—none of them remotely matching
the others—were arranged in a circle, with room for twenty-odd
people. But there were plenty of open seats tonight. Besides Mary,

the group consisted of eleven other people: six women and five men who, four months ago, before crashing into an out-of-control PT Cruiser, Mary would have dismissed as delusional.

A coordinator named Alvin led the group. Mary thought the name apt, because if she squinted her eyes just right he kind of looked like a chipmunk. He was a short man with glasses, brown hair, and a full beard. He wore a bow tie, probably for the sole purpose of letting everyone know he was the coordinator.

Alvin kicked off the meeting by saying, "Thank you, everyone, for coming to this support meeting of NDE survivors. Here, we discuss our Near Death Experiences without prejudice. No fears. No one will judge you. No one will think you're crazy or weird. Many people ignorantly associate us with the occult or mysticism, but no one makes that mistake here. We know we experienced something important. We may not understand precisely *what* it was, but it was meaningful.

"My NDE happened six years ago," he continued. "I was on vacation with my wife, in Cozumel. My wife was on the beach while I swam in the ocean. To this day, I don't remember how it happened, but something hit me on the head and knocked me unconscious. When I opened my eyes, I was someplace bright and warm. There didn't seem to be any walls or structure. My father and my brother were there, and said it was time to join them, and they began leading me toward an enormous gateway. They looked the same as they did when they died almost forty years ago." He seemed lost in the memory for a moment, and then snapped out of it. He concluded, "But before we reached the gate, I woke up on the beach with a crowd of people surrounding me."

This was Mary's third NDE survivors meeting, and each time Alvin opened with his own personal story. Mary always wondered how his father and brother died—judging by Alvin's appearance, forty years ago he and his brother must have been children. She figured that maybe Alvin's family had been in a car accident with some early ancestor of the PT Cruiser.

Some of the people were new, but she remembered most from previous meetings. Across from her was Judy, an elderly woman with all-white hair who had lost her husband to a stroke a decade earlier. Unlike Mary, Judy didn't see her husband in her NDE, but rather, "Our Lord, Jesus Christ, opening his arms."

A college-aged man named Colin sat to Mary's right, and she noticed he was the only person in the room younger than her. Last week, he explained that he found himself in paradise, standing on a beautiful beach. A voice behind him made a greeting, and he turned to see who it was, but awoke in a hospital bed before seeing the speaker's face.

As today's meeting went on, Mary heard more people tell their tales. A black woman named Shontay (Mary had no idea how to spell it) revealed that when she almost died she saw her parents, who had been waiting for her a long time. Another middle-aged woman said she found herself in a room filled with people she didn't know, all wearing dazzling white robes. An older man to her left talked about colors he couldn't describe, colors outside the normal visible spectrum. It was very difficult for him to explain, but the colors radiated security and love, even if they weren't accompanied by a person.

After several people spoke, the coordinator interjected, "You see, none of us saw exactly the same thing, but several common themes arise. We all experienced something beyond, and it's probably fair to say we all felt comforted by it. The Unknown doesn't have to be The Empty."

Mary fidgeted and scowled slightly. The coordinator noticed. "Mary? How about you? Are you ready to open up with the group?" Sensing her reluctance, he added, "No pressure, if you're not ready."

She had been dreading this moment. Everyone else's NDE had been standard fare, exactly what she'd expect to hear, before she had her own. As Alvin pointed out, they were all somewhat different but unified by a theme of comfort. She believed their stories. But that just made her experience much stranger.

She decided it was time to get whatever answers she could, and her nervousness turned into anticipation as she began. "Well, yes, um, hello. I'm not sure if I've said my name before. I'm Mary Franklin. I had a near death experience. But ... I don't know. My story is weird."

She cleared her throat. "It started off the way that many of your experiences did. I was in a car accident. I saw lots of blood, and I blacked out. The next thing I knew, there was a bright light. I was looking at the light when the outline of a man approached me. It was Jim, my husband."

She paused to collect her thoughts. She thought she should go back and explain how Jim died of cancer two years ago, at a mere 35 years old, but it occurred to her that none of the other people explained how their loved ones died. She didn't know if there was a reason for that, some rule she had never been told, but she decided to follow suit and forego details about Jim's passing. She continued her story.

"Jim called my name. He told me he loved me. I was so excited to see him, and he seemed just as excited to see me. We were so happy. So happy ..."

Again she paused to collect herself. She longingly remembered that one perfect moment. "But then things took a strange turn. Jim … he turned to look back and off to the side, like he was responding to someone I couldn't see. I didn't hear this other person, or being. I only saw the way Jim reacted. He turned away from me and started mumbling, 'Mary, it's not your time. You have more work to do on Earth.' Then he turned back to whoever was behind him and he didn't look at me again. The bright light faded and everything went dark. I woke up in an ambulance.

"I started to wonder what it all meant. Am I not worthy of Heaven? Did Heaven just reject me? Or maybe I have some grand purpose on Earth? If so, no one told me what that grand purpose was! Afterwards, I no longer felt the warm acceptance or unconditional love everyone seems to talk about."

She saw the sympathetic faces all looking at her. Alvin looked like he was about to say something when Mary decided there was one last detail she needed to mention.

"There was one other thing," she said. "Right before telling me I had more work to do on Earth, Jim looked annoyed and made the most random, bizarre comment. He said, 'Mary, I'm so sorry. Julio …'"

Mary stopped, trying to decide whether she wanted to say the next part aloud in front of all these people. Alvin made a gesture to continue, so Mary said, "We're all adults here, so I'll just say it. He said, 'Mary, Julio fucked up.'" She looked around the room with embarrassment.

"Now, I don't know who in the wide, wide world Julio is. I've never known a Julio, and Jim never mentioned anyone named Julio when he was alive. And Jim hardly ever used profanity. What do you think it means? Does anyone have any ideas? I don't know who else to ask."

Quiet. All the other people were staring at her in silence. Even Alvin seemed at a loss for words.

CHAPTER 6

I am hard pressed between the two. My desire is to depart and
be with Christ, for that is far better. But to remain in the flesh
is more necessary on your account. (Philippians 1:23-24)

Manfred's strategy was, apparently, to pretend nothing happened.
If anything, his loquaciousness was on high, as if he thought banal conversation would fill a void otherwise open to hostility. He
laboriously spelled out all the personalized license plates, making
Sam curse their shared power of vision. Manfred was fascinated
by license plates from distant states. "Idaho? What are they doing here?" He was particularly vocal about a car with two bumper stickers, one commanding "Fight Mass Vaccinations" and the
other asserting "I Support Public Schools." Sam had limited interest in the arguably incongruent positions held by a random driver.
For Manfred, the stickers provided fodder for about 15 minutes
of ranting. Sam didn't take the bait or provide any encouragement.
Right now, the last thing he wanted to do was to try to detangle
Manfred's passionate yet unintelligible opinions.

The ordeal of one-sided road chatter ended once they arrived home. He hadn't been looking forward to opening the front door. He parked out of sight of the house and took dilatory walks around the block a couple of times, until he realized it was best to metaphorically rip the bandage off.

"Who's there?" asked Sam's mom with alarm.

"It's me, Mom," answered Sam.

She leapt out from the kitchen, wearing her worried expression. "Sam? What are you doing home?"

"Oh. I decided I'd just come home for the weekend."

"When did you decide that? You didn't mention it to me. You always tell me when you're coming home. Did something happen? What happened, Sam?"

"Calm down, Mom," Sam said in a voice as soothing as he could make it. "I just wanted to come home for the weekend."

Sam's mom was unconvinced. "Why didn't you tell me before you left? Don't get me wrong, I'm glad you're here, but I get worried when you start acting … impulsive."

Sam's mom was a world-class worrier, especially regarding him. She was certainly right in this case: something was wrong. Sam's entire college life had come crashing down on top of him. He was here because he didn't know if returning to school was an option. He really had no idea what to do next. Spending a couple of days with his mother wasn't ideal; she'd just keep asking questions. But, given the alternative …

Now that he was getting the third degree from his mother, he realized there was only one person on Earth he *did* want to talk to.

"Hey, I think I'm going to put my stuff down and visit Andy, okay?"

"Now hold on, Sam," his mother cut in. "You can't just come home unannounced, not tell me what's going on, and race out of the house."

"It's still my house too, right?" Sam instantly regretted his tone. His mother leveled one of her stares at him. As always, he was powerless under that stare. He tried to reboot. "Sorry, Mom, how are things?"

"You're asking how things are with me? Things are the same as ever with me. That's not important. What's going on with you?"

Sam wasn't confident of his ability to convince her everything was fine. As her only child, Sam had always taken up much of his mother's attention, so it was very hard to hide anything from her. But he also wasn't ready to talk about this problem with her, of all people. Was there any good way to tell your mother that your talking, willful penis decided to piss and cum all over the girl you like, while the girl was holding said penis in her hand? Maybe a semi-humorous greeting card existed to describe the scenario.

"Mom, it's nothing big. What if I promise to tell you everything at dinner?" he stalled. She always had dinner ready at precisely 6:30 pm, leaving him about two hours to figure out what the hell he would tell her. "But I'd like to see Andy right away."

She relented, much to Sam's relief. She told him to be back by 6:30, and she was holding him to his word that he would tell her everything. Only then did her worried aura fade. She stepped forward and gave Sam a hug. "I don't know why you're here now, but I'm glad to see you," she said. Then she let him go and headed back into the kitchen. Sam slipped out the front door.

—m—

Since elementary school, Andy Lopez and Sam had been friends and neighbors. When they were in middle school, Sam and a couple of other kids in the neighborhood would play Dungeons & Dragons, and Andy was the Dungeon Master. Sam enjoyed the role playing aspect of the game, but Manfred thought it was a competition and just wanted to get the most bad-ass weapons and magic items. Sam and Manfred usually agreed Sam was permitted do the role playing, provided the role was that of a self-absorbed weapon and magic item hoarder. If Sam didn't play the way Manfred wanted him to, he would prattle non-stop, pee, or get an erection until he got his way.

Once they reached high school, they stopped playing Dungeons & Dragons (by then, Manfred declared the game was for fags, anyway). Andy was reasonably popular and outgoing in high school, a time when Sam was just the opposite. But unlike most cool kids, Andy remained friends with Sam despite any damage it might have done to his social standing. It wasn't easy being a longtime friend to Sam. Thanks to Manfred's hidden influence, Andy had tolerated a cumulative ocean of weirdness over the years.

By default, Andy was probably Sam's best friend. In turn, Sam figured (or hoped) he might have a spot in Andy's top-10 list of friends. He likely wouldn't make it into Andy's future wedding party, but he'd at least count on being invited.

While Sam had gone off to college a few hours away from home, Andy stayed with his parents and enrolled in the community college. The Lopez family was close-knit. Sam couldn't imagine Andy dreading a conversation with Mrs. Lopez the way Sam did with his own mother. Though, of course, Andy (so far as Sam knew) never needed to explain to Mrs. Lopez how he wanted to drop out of school because everyone thought he was a perverted freak with a penis that rivaled Mt. Saint Helens in both the volume and unwelcomeness of its ejecta.

Sam rang the doorbell at Andy's house. No one answered, but Andy's car was parked out front and the lights were on. He re-rang the bell, had a moment to wonder if he was being too insistent with the multiple rings, and was turning around to leave when Andy finally appeared in a T-shirt and boxer shorts.

"Oh, hey. Sam," Andy said absently. He seemed in no way happy to see Sam.

Sam had come to talk with Andy about the incident at school, but Andy's expression was clear: here was someone not looking forward to this conversation. Why would Andy not want to talk to him? There was no explanation, unless …

"Did you hear about what happened?" Sam asked. Somewhere in the back of his mind, Sam realized there was no way Andy could possibly know about it … at least not until Andy's reply.

"I didn't need to hear about it. I was right in the middle of it."

That didn't make any sense. Andy was here, four hours away from Sam's college. How was he in the middle of it? "Wait, you know Anne somehow?" he asked, panic blocking logical thought from making its way from his brain to his mouth. "You know about the mess? I cleaned up. Well, not the first part, but I cleaned the second part, the part not in Anne's room."

Andy looked at Sam as if he were nuts, held that stare for a few seconds, and let loose his response. "What the hell are you talking about? I'm the one who fucking cleaned it. And what second part? Did he kill someone else?"

The part of Sam's brain that had been trying to tell him Andy didn't know anything broke through, and Sam felt like an idiot. Manfred, who hadn't made a peep for thirty minutes, told Sam,

"You really are a self-centered prick sometimes. Do you know that?" There was a certain irony in *Manfred* being the one to call Sam self-centered, but in this case Manfred had a point.

Still, Sam dismissed Manfred and replied to Andy, "Sorry, I guess we're talking about different things. Something happened at school, but it sounds like you've been having your own problems."

Sam more or less invited himself inside. Typically, Andy would have immediately invited him in and offered something to eat or drink, but obviously he was distracted right now. They made their way to the living room, where Andy took a seat on the floor and Sam on the couch.

Andy's parents weren't around, probably still at work. They were both hard-working people, a trait Andy shared. In addition to taking a full set of classes at the community college, he worked twenty hours a week as a janitor at the mall.

Andy was a fourth-generation American. His skin color and surname were the things marking him as Hispanic, and he enjoyed playing into Hispanic stereotypes ironically. That's why he had taken the janitorial job: he vaguely had fun with it (as much fun as anyone *could* while cleaning shit, anyway). He always delighted in laying on a thick accent for his boss and pretending not to speak English whenever mall patrons would ask him anything. "*No hablo inglés*," he would tell people. Those were the only words Sam had ever heard Andy say in Spanish.

Andy's enjoyment of playing into stereotypes started one day when he and Sam were both in high school. Andy had been raking leaves in the yard when a BMW pulled up in front of the house. The driver rolled down the window and said to Andy, "When you're done here, I need to get my lawn mowed. Do you think you can get it done today?" When Andy stared at him blankly, the guy actually added, "*Trabajo.*" Andy politely responded, "Sorry, I'm not a landscaper. I live here." The man replied, "Whatever. When you're done with this job, I have another one for you, right down the street at the corner of Landover and White Oak ..."

Even though Andy derived some twisted enjoyment from the janitor gig, it was definitely temporary. He saved good money by living at home with his parents and going to community college. Now he was nearing the end of his second year, and planned to transfer to a four-year college to finish his degree. Sam spent plenty of time hoping Andy would come join him upstate for college, but now the timing seemed cross-purposed.

They sat there silently for a couple minutes, both consumed by their own thoughts. Sam realized he was back to thinking only about his own problems, and remembered Andy had problems, too. "So, what happened to you?" he asked.

As Andy told his story, Sam realized his own issues weren't that big of a deal. Andy had finished three consecutive classes starting at 8:00 in the morning (in contrast, Sam had learned in his second semester to drop any class starting before 10:00) and went to work the lunch shift at the mall.

But today things went badly. A deranged man had come into the food court with his wife and child. For whatever reason, the man had decided it was a good idea to bring a gun into the mall. Then he thought a second good idea would be to shoot both his wife and child before shooting himself. Sam later discovered the wife's name was also Anne. It had been a rough 24 hours for people named Anne.

Andy had been in the supply closet getting a bundle of napkins when it happened. He heard the booms and came out carrying napkins, which turned out to be completely inadequate.

The food court, understandably, had erupted in chaos. Andy's co-workers, Yanny and Ana Luiz, were both eyewitnesses. They were extremely upset, so Andy decided to stay with them while they waited for the police to get their accounts. He figured he'd give them a ride home when they were done.

Once the bodies had been removed and the evidence collected, Andy's manager told him someone needed to clean up the mess, and that someone was Andy. Weren't there specialized trauma clean-up crews for this sort of thing? Or didn't the police do it themselves? Was it legal to even go near it? Well, of course, they had their own staff to gather anything of potential forensic importance. The bodies were long gone. But there was still plenty of blood splattered around.

His nervous, twitchy manager was eyeing his watch, pacing around anxiously, apparently calculating the money they were losing each minute. He wasn't a bright man, but he took his job *very* seriously, and he needed the scene cleaned now, now, now. Lunch was forfeited, but the food court needed to be ready in time for the dinner crowd. It's not like the place was being converted into a crime museum. They were running a business, folks.

Andy balked at cleaning the tables and chairs, using his normal voice with his manager for the first time. He thought the chairs should be thrown away; no one would want to sit on them ever again. So, his manager turned to Ana Luiz. She was old, probably too old to be doing such physical work. But her options were limited, and Andy knew her paycheck was very much needed in her grandchild-infested home. She was in no position to refuse; she couldn't afford to lose her job. She would have to do the final cleaning.

So Andy did the chivalrous thing, grabbing his towels and spray bottle without another word. He tried to hurry through the job, but was unable to do so. By not finishing quickly, he felt like he was postponing the finality of their deaths or something, though that didn't make any sense. White towels turned an ugly reddish-brown as he worked. His manager would no doubt demand the towels be bleached and re-used instead of tossed in the trash.

At the end of the story, all Sam could say was, "Shit."

At some point during the story, Andy picked up a black book, and Sam realized it was a Bible. Noticing that Sam was looking at it, Andy looked at the Bible and mumbled, "I only go to church on Christmas Eve and Easter."

"I know that they're supposed to be with Jesus now," Andy continued. "Yanni kept saying, 'they're angels in Heaven, they're angels in Heaven.' But if that's true and Heaven is so wonderful, then wasn't that psycho just doing them a favor? Why don't we all go kill ourselves right now, if we instantly wake up in a better place with all our problems solved?"

Sam looked at Andy with concern.

As if sensing Sam's thoughts, Andy said, "Don't worry, I won't kill myself. I like being alive too much. It must be a sin to kill yourself, and God must give you a life so you can learn through it, and not just kill yourself right away. But why would it matter? Is suicide a bigger sin than all the others he forgives every day?"

Sam didn't have an answer, although it was probably rhetorical because Andy continued rather quickly, "I just want to know they're all right now, that they're in a better place. But nothing makes any sense. I suppose I just have to believe. That's all I can do." With that, Andy sort of tossed the Bible on the table ahead of him in a gesture of frustration.

Sam didn't necessarily think they were in a better place. He thought they were just dead. *That* was why it was so important to *not* do things like go into homicidal rages in the food court: there was nothing beyond. There was no silver lining, no replay button. He wanted to concur with Andy and say sure, they were in a better place, but he knew he was a terrible liar so he didn't even try.

"Well, Andy, I don't know what to say."

Andy looked at Sam silently for a few seconds, as if considering what Sam had said, even though Sam's combination of words had been devoid of meaning. Then he started to brighten up and gave Sam's arm a squeeze, saying, "Thanks, I know. I know how you feel about it. Thanks." Whatever that meant.

Then Andy asked, "So, you also had a crummy day? What happened?"

At that moment, he wanted nothing less than to add his woes onto Andy's pile. "Oh, it was something stupid. It can wait. I'll be here all weekend, so maybe we can talk later." Sam caught himself just in time before suggesting they should meet at the mall after Andy got off work.

"Yeah, maybe tomorrow or Sunday would be better," Andy said as he stood up. Sam followed and they both headed to the door. As bad as things might be for Sam, they sure could be worse.

CHAPTER 7

It is better to live alone in the desert than with a quarrelsome, complaining wife. (Proverbs 21:19)

"It's a terrible world we live in," Manfred said, just when Sam had started to forget about Manfred's existence. Manfred's tone seemed sorrowful and sincere, arousing Sam's suspicion.

"Society has some evil crazies in it, that's for sure," Sam said, just keeping the conversation moving until he could discover where Manfred was going. Sam walked through the front door of his house and headed directly upstairs to his room.

"At least that man will burn in Hell," Manfred said. Sam was ready with a response, but decided to wait for Manfred to finish his thought. "Just like us," Manfred concluded miserably.

Sam should have known: the baptism thing again.

"What makes you think he's going to Hell? What if he accepted Jesus as his Lord and Savior? In that case, he'll be okeydokey, living it up in Heaven," Sam said.

Manfred seemed genuinely affronted. "Sam, if he were baptized and accepted Jesus, he never would have done such evil."

"Are you saying Christians never do evil things? That's laughable."

"You'll never understand what it feels like to have the love of Jesus inside you," Manfred moaned.

It was a dumb point, but there was no logical way to argue against it, so Sam stayed quiet and waited for the inevitable.

"Why not put us on the winning side?" Manfred asked. "Just get us baptized! Why wouldn't you? What is stopping you? If I'm wrong about this—and I'm not wrong—then it costs you nothing. But if I'm right, then we go to Heaven and you can feel God's love in your heart like I do."

"How is it possible," Sam began speaking very precisely, rather slowly, "you have the nerve to ask me, after what you did to me with Anne, for a big, fat, stupid favor? How is it possible? Not even 24 hours have passed since the worst thing that has ever happened to me—something *you* caused—and you are here, asking me for a *favor*?"

"It's not a favor to me! It's a favor to you, too. You're also going to burn," Manfred pleaded.

"Just shut the fuck up." After losing himself in Andy's story for a while, his own ordeal was coming back with hot anger.

"I'm rattled by Andy's story, Sam. We can die anytime, anywhere, killed by a nutcase. We don't get to control how we go. We can only control how we prepare. We need to get baptized and we need to do it ASAP. I'm willing to give you whatever you want. Let's make a deal, Sam. Whatever you want: let me make it happen for you."

The anger receded as Sam began to recognize the possibilities available to him in such a negotiation. "All right, Manfred," he said, "I'm willing to consider getting us baptized, but I definitely need something big from you."

"Okay, what's your opening bid?" Manfred asked.

"Well, I want to find a way to fix things with Anne," Sam said. Manfred made a noise, the meaning of which was indiscernible, but didn't say anything. Sam continued, "That's probably not possible at this point, but whether it's Anne or someone else, I need you to behave ... *normally*. No more peeing on girls, no more calling them sluts or skanks. I want to be able to talk to, make out with, and even have sex with girls. How's that as a starting point?"

"Well," Manfred said, "you know premarital sex is a sin."

"But if we get baptized, you'll have your get-out-of-jail free card," Sam responded.

"Okay, so I let you have sex with one girl and then we get baptized?" Manfred asked.

"No, maybe one girl, but not specifically *one* girl," Sam responded, "however many girls it works out with. And if I can get you to act right, I can start being a normal person and not some freak no girl would want."

"You're asking for a lot," Manfred said. "You want me to help you engage in premarital fornication indefinitely when all I'm asking for is a one-time thing? I just want to get baptized and confess my sins."

"Oh, you'll confess your sins, too? How are you planning on doing that?"

"With the English language, Sam. I'll create sentences with verbs and nouns and a few adjectives, and these sentences will describe my sins."

"Manfred, has it occurred to you there may be a problem with your plan insofar as—and let me say this slowly so you'll understand—I'm the only one who can hear you?" Sam laughed and added, "Yeah, I can imagine the conversation. 'Father,' I'd say, 'I have someone who would like to confess his sins. He's down here, in my pants.'" Sam thought about that and cocked his head to the side with a quizzical look. "Actually …" he began, but he didn't finish his next thought.

Manfred ignored Sam's performance and said, "One way or another, I need you to get baptized. I don't want to go to Hell attached to you when the Rapture hits and all the gays, Jews, Atheists, and Muslims get vaporized."

"I don't know, Manfred," Sam said. "I think you should hope that if I get vaporized, you get vaporized along with me. What would you do on your own?" Sam used his best high-pitched Manfred impression as he continued, "*Hi, I'm Manfred. I don't have arms or legs or a face or a torso. I'm just a penis. And I'm really stupid, with no redeeming personality traits whatsoever. Come be my friend!*"

"I'm going to rule in the afterlife without you getting in my way," Manfred said softly, ominously.

Unconvinced, Sam concluded his thought: "I think you're better off sticking with me, pal."

"Well, I'd be happy to stick with you," Manfred said, "if we can get baptized."

"Fine, but here's the thing: I'm not doing it right away, because I need proof of your good intentions. Otherwise, I don't trust you to keep your side of the bargain. I'll make it simple: once I'm not a virgin, we'll head to a church and get baptized the next day."

"Yeah, but not a Mormon Church," Manfred interjected.

"Of course not a Mormon Church! Who said anything about a Mormon Church?" Sam snapped.

"And not one of those tutti-frutti Unitarian churches, or one of those crackpot churches that accept women priests and fag priests and …"

"Enough, Manfred," Sam snapped even sharper than before. "We'll go to a church that's in the ballpark of being agreeable to both of us. Do we have the makings of a deal here?"

"Well, if I'm not getting anything for my good behavior except the promise of a future baptism, then I need something more to compensate for the risk I'm taking. We may get shot by a maniac at any moment, before the baptism happens."

"I've asked for something in perpetuity from you, Manfred," Sam said. "I'll keep my promise, as long as you show your good intentions by giving me that first time. What more are you asking for now?"

"Don't worry," Manfred said reassuringly. "It's just a one-time thing. In fact, it's just a tonight thing. I've got plans. Special plans."

Manfred and Sam continued to discuss the deal for the next several minutes. After they had worked out the details, Sam looked up to see the clock change from 6:29 to 6:30.

"Sam, dinner's ready!" his mother called at just that moment.

How does she do that? he wondered as he left his room to join his mother for dinner. He had his deal hammered out with Manfred; now he just had to figure out what to say to his mother.

Dinner was already sitting on the small kitchen table when Sam got downstairs. It was a plate with rice, broccoli, and a pork chop coated in Shake 'N Bake. His mother made pork chops all the time, but for some reason it was never enough to convince Manfred that Sam and his mother were not practicing Jews. The only difference between Sam and his mother was that if Sam was asked what religion he was, he would say

53

"none" (although he remembered calling himself Jewish as a kid, before he realized he didn't give a shit about religion). On the other hand, his mother would say she was Jewish, just to have something easy to say. Sam's great-grandparents were the last ones in the family who were actively Jewish, in the sense of following tradition or believing in the religion. Manfred was probably much more interested in protecting Israel than either Sam or his mother.

Sam's mom started to speak. Sam decided to beat her to the punch. "Mom, did you hear about what happened at the mall?"

"I was just watching it on the news while you were upstairs," she replied. "It's unbelievable, happening right in our backyard."

"Andy was working at the mall when it happened," Sam said.

His mother looked horrified, saying, "I hope he's all right."

"He didn't get shot, if that's what you mean," Sam responded, adding, "He's a little shaken up, but I think he'll be fine." He decided he didn't need to mention Andy's clean-up duty.

His mother gave a disgusted look and said to no one in particular, "How many times does this have to happen before we can get serious about gun control?"

"Oh, here we go again!" said Manfred. "The liberals are showing their true colors and trying to take away our guns. As soon as the guns are gone, you watch: they'll redistribute all the wealth and people are going to be publicly masturbating on every corner. You watch. As soon as they take away the guns. As soon as they take away the guns ..."

Sam had no idea why Manfred gave two shits about guns. It was one of those issues Manfred would work himself into a frenzy about periodically, with all the zealotry he applied to his religion, as if he read the nonexistent passage in the Bible where Jesus said, "Wicked are those who would confiscate your military-grade assault rifle."

After a few minutes of discussing gun violence, in a conversation Sam could recite from memory based on the last seven times he and his mother (and, unknown to his mom, Manfred) had it, Sam's mother moved on to what he had been preparing for. "So, tell me Sam, what are you really doing here? What happened at school?"

Sam decided he wouldn't lie—at least not too much—but he would try to talk around what happened. "I experienced the most excruciatingly embarrassing thing possible," he said flatly.

"What happened?" his mother asked.

"Look, I'm sorry, there's just no way I can discuss it with my mother."

"Did it involve … a girl?" his mother asked. She thought they had the sort of relationship where they could talk about anything. Sam did not share this sentiment.

"Yes, Mom, it involved a girl," Sam said, not elaborating. "And what happened with that girl is now front page news all over campus. I can't show my face."

"What are you saying?" she asked. "Are you talking about dropping out? Because that's just not going to happen."

Sam never thought the words *drop out*, not once in the four-hour trip home during which he kept saying he couldn't go back. But there it was. *Drop out.* "Maybe," he said, "I can transfer somewhere else. Maybe I can …" he couldn't believe he was about to say this, "live at home and go to school locally."

"Well, as much as I'd love to have you here—and believe me, I would—I don't think you should run away when things get tough." Then came the part where she started listing people who didn't run away, and what would have happened if they did. Things like, "what if George Washington had run away instead of fighting the British? We wouldn't even have a country." Then she rattled off a long list of irrelevant comparisons to famous heroes.

"Yeah, and what if George Custer had run away?" Sam muttered.

"What was that?" she asked.

"Nothing."

"Sam, I'll make this nice and easy for you. I've paid a lot of money so you can go to college. I'm not even getting child support, now that you're out of high school. But I'm sacrificing so you can get a quality education. You are not dropping out now. You're going back to finish the semester. Then, this summer, if you want to talk about transferring, we can have that conversation. But you'll finish the semester I've already paid for, and you'll finish at least four years of college *somewhere*. Do you understand?"

"Yeah, I understand. I'll do what you said." What she said made perfect sense. It was exactly what he should do, and he knew it.

He just had to keep his head down for the last six weeks of the semester—it was *only six weeks*—and then he could work on transferring to a place where no one would know his history. He could try to convince Anne it was an isolated event, caused by some treatable and non-contagious medical condition. He'd have to do some research to figure out what medical condition would cause men to uncontrollably urinate and then ejaculate in massive volumes.

Once dinner was over, he told his mom he was going out for a while. What he didn't tell her was that he had a bargain to keep with his penis.

CHAPTER 8

I robbed other churches by receiving support from them to serve you. (Second Corinthians 11:8)

Sam stood at the wall, just staring at it.

"Really? I really have to do this?" he asked.

"We made a deal, Sam," Manfred responded. "Start spraying."

The building was almost certainly empty at this hour, a few minutes shy of 1 a.m. Once in a while, a car would drive by, but headlights never fell on Sam because of the way the building was oriented to the road. Still, he was nervous. It was important for the sake of Sam's personal happiness to keep his deal with Manfred, but that didn't change the fact what he was about to do was risky, unethical, and really dumb.

Sam adjusted his ski mask. He felt silly even bringing it in the car and had walked up to the building without it, but as the nervousness set in, he returned to the car to get it. Now that he was wearing it, he realized just how stupid it was. First, he couldn't see very well. Second, it was scratchy and uncomfortable. Third, it was a warm spring night. Most importantly, he realized it was counterproductive: Without the ski mask, anyone would simply see a guy next to a building and think nothing of it. With the ski mask, anyone who saw him would think, *Holy shit, that man's wearing a ski mask. He must be doing something bad.* But he decided to commit to his decision this time, and he left it on.

Sam stared at the wall a moment longer and steeled himself for what needed to happen. He pressed the button on the can of spray paint and quickly moved his hand to write the letter R. The R came out fuzzy because he had moved too fast and didn't get enough paint where it needed to go.

He made the opposite mistake with the E, as several discrete splotches made it look like he had done a connect-the-dots puzzle. As he sprayed the next few letters—P-E-N-T—he calibrated his spraying. He had it down pretty well by the time he finished the first line, "REPENT NOW." Manfred had insisted on capital letters, because they make the point more strongly.

Sam did have one trick up his sleeve, something to soften the message with irony. The second line of text came out nicely: "THE RAPTOR IS CUMING."

Sam knew there was no way Manfred would pick up on the misspelling. Sure enough, Manfred murmured, "Good, good, *very* nice. The beanie-wearers can suck on this for a while." Then, he added, "Sorry, Sam, no offense."

"I'm used to it," Sam said. As if he still took offense to Manfred's ethnic slurs.

"Okay, on to the freaks!" Manfred said gleefully. It was time for Phase Two of Manfred's Master Plan. Sam made his way to his car at a normal pace, but started to feel exposed, so he broke into a sprint. Then he realized he was fleeing a crime scene in a ski mask, so he stopped running and pulled it off. His car was parked across the street about two hundred feet away, because it seemed like a bad idea to pull into the Synagogue parking lot. He was additionally nervous because the car didn't handle particularly well during the drive there. Nothing would suck more than having it break down while he was engaged in this idiocy.

It was a ten minute drive to the Mormon Church. This was no grandiose temple; it looked like a municipal building from the 1970s. Somehow, this was the least horrifying of the three humiliations. Sam actually laughed a bit. He didn't bother with all the precautions he had taken the last time; he parked right next to the building and left the ski mask behind. He ran out of his car, quickly sprayed "MAGIC UNDERWEAR CULT" on both sides of the wall adjacent to the door, and scampered away rat-like into the darkness. It took all of four minutes. He was getting good at this.

The final stop in Manfred's hate-crime trifecta was the Islamic Community Center, about fifteen minutes away. This one made Sam more anxious, for reasons he couldn't explain without feeling prejudiced. He assumed he was risking his life on this one. It didn't help he had to go into town for this job, rather than remain on the country-like roads where the Synagogue and Mormon Church were located. He took a moment to pick at a stress-related zit.

He parked five blocks away. In fact, the entire operation was going to be conducted at a distance. He walked three blocks toward the Islamic Community Center, and would go no closer. Despite the higher level of general terror, this assignment was technically much easier. After looking around to ensure he was alone, Sam bent down and pretended to tie his shoes. He had his spray paint in hand and drew an arrow pointing in the direction of the community center and spelled out, "THIS WAY TO THE MUSLIM." There was supposed to be an "S" at the end to make it plural, but he ran out of paint before he could finish the last letter. Close enough.

Sam couldn't help but ask, "You had me come all the way out here to write that? You didn't even force me to write an insult."

"Sure I did," Manfred said. "I made you call them Muslims. That's insult enough."

Sam's retort was aborted in the middle of the first syllable. Two high school kids, a boy and a girl, were looking at him from a bench. How did he not notice them before? From their vantage point, it seemed like they could have seen it all. Had they?

Sam's full concentration was now fixed on appearing normal, casual. Convincing these kids he was boring and innocent was top priority. His conspicuous possession of a can of spray paint ran contrary to this goal. He had a quick, clever idea of pretending the can was a tall beverage, so he pantomimed that he was drinking out of it. He could feel a few drops of the red paint landing on his face as he tipped it up to his mouth. He resisted the urge to wipe the paint off. The spilled paint near his mouth probably made him look like a vampire, not that it mattered in the low light. He called the pantomime a success when the kids were no longer looking at him.

CHAPTER 9

A malicious man disguises himself with his lips, but in his heart he harbors deceit. Though his speech is charming, do not believe him, for seven abominations fill his heart. His malice may be concealed by deception, but his wickedness will be exposed in the assembly. (Proverbs 26:24-26)

Sam tried to be as quiet as possible, yet he managed to crash into an accent table near the front door, sending its contents crashing to the ground. The sound of small objects landing on the floor was eerily familiar, and Sam's thoughts returned to the fiasco of leaving Anne's room. Did every female own and prominently display a box of marbles or something like that? Because once again, it seemed like about eight million pieces ricocheted all over the floor. Sam went down to his knees, grabbing blindly with his hands, as if he could somehow go back in time and catch all the contents before they hit the ground and created a carnival of sound.

But the damage was done. As Sam flailed for the objects— he still couldn't tell what they were, but they weren't spheres so marbles were eliminated—his mother's hoarse voice called out, "Sam? Sam, is that you?"

"Yes, Mom," Sam called back. Under his breath, he added, "Shit." Waking his mother was one genie he couldn't easily put back into the bottle.

"It's 2:30 in the morning. Where have you been?"

"I've just been out, Mom." This is why he didn't like coming home. He was in college now; he shouldn't have to answer these questions.

"I didn't even know you weren't here. You're old enough to go out when you want, but please tell me when you do." Sam knew she was being perfectly reasonable, but that didn't make it any less annoying.

"Sorry, Mom, I didn't mean to worry you. Good night."

"Good night, Sam," his mother said. Wait, could it be so easy? Sam expected to be stuck talking to her for half an hour.

Sam slipped into his bedroom and shut the door softly, not flipping on the light switch until the door was fully closed. His room was a time capsule, unchanged from before he left for college, which was to say, it was nothing like his dorm room. He had been hesitant about revealing too much of himself in front of his roommate, so his dorm room remained largely utilitarian, with limited decorations.

But his room at his mother's house showed much more of his personality. Two of the walls were covered in historical maps and one wall was devoted to *Deep Space Nine*. The fourth wall was a painted mural of peanuts from when he was about twelve years old, a tribute to George Washington Carver's agricultural research and peanut-based product innovations that Manfred always described as "gayer than gay sex." Looking at the mural, he remembered the huge fight he had with Manfred about it. "If he wasn't black, no one would talk about him," Manfred said. Sam responded with a list of achievements, and an argument about what a wonderful person Carver was on a personal level. His epitaph, a realistic summation of his life, was, *He could have added fortune to fame, but caring for neither, he found happiness and honor in being helpful to the world.* None of these arguments did it for Manfred, who insisted he was a product of affirmative action a generation before affirmative action was a glimmer in anyone's eye.

When Sam pointed out that Carver was also religious and taught a Bible study group, Manfred decided he could, just barely, tolerate the peanut mural.

Sam stripped off his shirt and pants and went over to the bed. As always, the bed was neatly made in a way Sam never would have done himself. His mother was really passionate about making beds. The sheets were tucked so tightly that no human being could possibly squeeze between them and the mattress. Sam wished he had a crowbar to pry the sheets open. Postponing the bedding battle, he decided to lie on top and relax for a few minutes.

Manfred, meanwhile, hummed a happy tune. Sam sat down on the bed, and said, "I guess you had a pretty good night? Did you enjoy yourself?"

"It was a great night, a magical night," Manfred replied, his voice sounding like a kid describing his time at Disney World. "Can you do one tiny thing for me? I would really love to polish it off with The True Christian Channel. That would make it super perfect."

"Oh, Manfred," Sam hadn't been overly tired a moment ago, but now exhaustion washed over him like a wave. "That shit just brings me down. I hate watching those hypocrites steal money from suckers. Come on, we're better than that."

"You're always badmouthing The True Christian Channel," Manfred said defensively. "When's the last time you watched it with an open mind? Just give it a chance."

Sam relented without much cajoling. "I'll put it on for ten minutes, if it will make you shut up. Watch me be a wizard and predict they'll be talking about sex. Did you hear that? That's my prediction: It will be all about sex."

He picked up the remote and turned on the television, clicking the volume low, as the last thing he wanted was for his mother to hear this bullshit. He pulled up the guide and scrolled to find the right channel. "You don't need the guide! I know it's channel 123. It's channel 123!" Manfred squealed with excitement. Then Sam made Manfred's night by keying 123. Manfred got a boner.

They were immediately greeted with the sound of a soft-spoken Southern gentleman saying, "Contraception is contrary to the teachings of Christ. An attempt to circumvent the will of God should be acceptable to no true Christian."

Sam laughed aloud, not just to Manfred internally. "And the wizard was right!" he said. "The psychic prediction was true. They're talking about sex." A cold chill went through him, as he realized he may have said those three short sentences *aloud*. He desperately hoped his mother hadn't heard.

Manfred ignored Sam. "I know," he seemed to be saying directly to the televangelist, engrossed. "Why would any Christian consider contraception?" Sam thought of the debacle in Anne's room. He had never owned a condom, but could only imagine how much worse that incident would have been if he had tried to put one on.

"Then why," asked the coiffed blonde sidekick, "do so many married couples who attend Church every Sunday fall into the trap of contraception?" Her voice had a saccharine sweet quality. It was vocal syrup.

"Well, Shelley, they apparently don't trust God as much as they claim," answered the televangelist. "They think they can decide these things for themselves. But these are decisions only the Lord can make. God knows how many children he wants you to have. Accept God's will. Don't try to second-guess His plan."

"Is this related to the epidemic of pornography?" the blonde asked.

"Of course it is!" the televangelist responded. Sam was pretty sure the man had truncated the sentence he had originally formulated in his mind: "Of course it is, you stupid bitch."

"Contraception allows people to believe they can engage in promiscuity without consequences," the televangelist said in his Southern drawl. "Do you remember the game Monopoly?" He waited while the blonde dutifully assured him that she did indeed remember the game. "It's a good, wholesome family game, and one of the Chance cards says Get Out of Jail Free. Well, contraception is a Get Out of Jail free card for all sorts of immoral behaviors. This opens the door to many sins, like mutual masturbation and anal sex."

At this point, Sam realized he was honestly delighted they were watching The True Christian Channel. The only thing that dampened his happiness was remembering how much he and Anne had enjoyed listening to Crazy Man on campus together. Meanwhile, the televangelist continued, "The ideal for True Christians is to remove the foul stain of temptation from their lives, to shed any addiction to pornography, and to re-commit to chastity unless they're trying to fill God's quiver of soldiers."

"Oh, Manfred," said Sam. "It's hilarious and all, but I may throw up."

Again, Manfred was too absorbed to notice Sam's commentary. "Mutual masturbation? Anal sex? I can't believe how our society swims in such immorality."

"Oh, you just lead that morality bandwagon, Manfred. Lead it with a bagpipe."

The televangelist wrapped up his little tirade and announced it was time for some words from their sponsors. Afterwards, they could look forward to discussing the commitments everyone should make to Christ. Only then did Manfred clue into Sam's existence. "Morality bandwagon? What are you talking about, Sam? Are you trying to make fun of me again?"

"No, I'm being straightforward," Sam replied. "You're the most immoral person—or whatever you are—that I know. It's pretty rich to hear you complain about the so-called immorality of others. But, you know, I guess we all project our shortcomings onto other people."

"That's ridiculous!" Manfred quickly retorted.

"Really? It's ridiculous? Let's re-cap this April," said Sam. "In a mere 30 days, you tried to get me to start a physical fight with a Hare Krishna—and a good thing I didn't, because that guy looked ripped—and you succeeded in getting me to vandalize some innocent man's food cart and steal a bunch of his stuff. You forced me to masturbate onto an ATM. Some poor soul had to clean that shit up, but probably not before a bunch of *other* poor souls got jizz on their hands. I still don't get the message you were trying to send. If it was some kind of statement about the banks or the concentration of financial power, well, that message was lost on me."

"I just wanted some hand," Manfred mumbled. "The ATM was incidental."

Sam paused. He felt terrible about the things he had done. They may have been Manfred's ideas, but why did he go along? Why did he let his dick think for him like that? Why, why, why? In the heat of the moment, he never seemed able to control the situation and he always went along with the bullshit. Later, in cold reflection, he was so ashamed of his actions.

I can't change the past, Sam thought. *I can only try to be a better person in the future.* With that, he broke out of his self-reflection and continued his list. "Before we put a bookend on April, let's not forget you peed on my almost-girlfriend and got me to vandalize three different religious centers. I'm sure I'm forgetting a ton of stuff, but that was a mere 30 days in the life of Saint Manfred, moral fucking champion."

Manfred countered what Sam had thought was checkmate with a surprisingly effective and succinct response: "Whatever."

"You know, I wonder if you're actually trying to put me in jail."

"Why would I want that?" Manfred asked. He seemed genuinely confused.

"Oh, I don't know, maybe to satisfy your homoerotic impulses." Sam had to work hard to maintain his seriousness. He was almost laughing by the word "impulses." He never thought Manfred was gay or straight or anything else. Sometimes a penis, even a talking penis, is *just* a penis. But the accusation sure did push Manfred's buttons.

"Gross! How dare you make such a suggestion? I am not gay. I have never been gay. I'll wet the bed if you don't shut up."

"Okay, okay, I'll shut up. Don't wet the bed."

Manfred's tone changed, becoming slightly seductive, which would have been revolting if Sam wasn't accustomed to it. "How about you stop being mean and start paying me some attention?"

"If I do, will you promise to shut up?"

"Mmmmm, maybe," answered Manfred.

Usually a little hand calmed Manfred down and allowed Sam to get to sleep, so despite the lack of concrete assurance from Manfred, Sam agreed. He reached into his underwear and started to rub Manfred, who responded almost immediately.

After a few moments of rubbing, Sam was startled by the TV voices, which had returned to a normal pitch after a series of maniacal infomercial salesmen and car advertisements that were not the least bit Christian. "We're back on The True Christian Channel. Thank you for joining us on this blessed night," the male televangelist said.

"Before we took a break, we were discussing the sins of contraception," the blonde began. Sam continued rubbing. He tried picturing the blonde naked.

"You may be thinking God didn't give explicit instructions about contraception," the male televangelist said, steamrolling over her. Picturing the older male naked set Sam back a few seconds; he had to regroup and reset his imagination, this time fantasizing about Anne touching Manfred in the same way he was right now.

"You may be thinking contraception is a modern invention and somehow God didn't anticipate it, making the Bible an outdated work. But that isn't true. The Bible provides us with plenty of clues to let us know, in clear terms, exactly what God would think of contraception." Anne was undressing in Sam's imagination, and he was getting close.

Without warning, the door opened and Sam's mom poked her head in. "Sam, what in the world are you watching in here?"

"Mom!" was all Sam managed to say. Manfred in hand, he tried to slide under the covers. After eventually winning a frantic battle with the super-tucked sheets, he lay still for a moment.

"And it's not hard to guess what the Devil thinks about contraception, either," the female televangelist breathlessly exclaimed.

"Indeed, indeed," the male televangelist concurred. "Children are a gift from God, so it only makes sense the Devil wants to stop them from being born. Satan is the force directly, powerfully, behind the use of contraception."

Sam's mother stood frozen in the doorway. She averted her eyes, staring up at the ceiling rather than looking at Sam.

"That fucking bitch," Manfred said. "Get the fuck out of here so we can finish!"

"Can't you knock?" Sam asked.

"I ... I just heard ... heard the TV and, um, I was ... um, I was wondering ..." her voice trailed off. But she remained fixed in the doorway as what felt like hours went by.

"How else does Satan affect our sex lives?" the blonde asked earnestly, oblivious to the drama playing out in Sam's room.

"Good question, Shelley. You'll find the Devil in Hollywood movies. Hollywood teaches us the so-called fun parts of naughty behavior and sin, but not the moral decay and the affront to God."

Sam's mother finally brought herself to say, "Well, goodnight." Sam was almost proud of her, the way she managed to act like everything was fine and normal. She closed the door behind her.

"Okay," Sam said to Manfred, "let's tack that on to the long list of humiliations you've caused me. Now she thinks I'm an even bigger weirdo. It would have been so much better if she had caught me whacking off to Cinemax like a normal person. Shit, jerking it to C-SPAN or even Animal Planet would have been better than this!" Humiliation aside, Sam grabbed Manfred again and picked up where he left off. He might as well fucking finish at this point.

"Are you saying there's a connection? Contraception, homosexuality, pornography, genital touching … and the Devil?" the blonde asked as if it were a perfectly reasonable question. Sam wondered how it was possible for her to ask without cracking up. Yet there she was, no amusement on her face, simply waiting for confirmation from her dominant co-host, the apparent source of all information inside her head. She seemingly didn't even have the awareness to anticipate what he would say. She just looked at him with wonder.

"Yes! The Devil is behind it all! He tempts us and he tempts us," the man explained patiently.

"Oh, wait, Sam?" called his mother from the hallway.

"What?" Sam responded with exasperation. He let go of Manfred and froze in place.

"He lures us in with his perversion and his good times, and, before we know it, we're forgetting all about the promises we made to Christ," came the Southern drawl. The blonde audibly gasped.

"There's no more syrup. I have to pick some up. So, don't make any pancakes in the morning."

Are you fucking kidding me? Sam thought. He had enough self-control to call back, "Okay, Mom. I won't make any pancakes until you come back with syrup. Goodnight."

The Southern gentleman continued, "And then we're touching genitals, first our own genitals and then someone else's genitals … even the genitals of someone of the same gender."

Sam was exasperated with his mother and with the fact that there was, apparently, available shelf space in the intellectual marketplace for this gentleman's shit. He had been about to cum before his mother entered the room and Satan's sexual agenda entered the conversation, but now he just wanted to be done. He closed Manfred back in his underwear and reached for the remote. He didn't think he could cope with hearing the word "genitals" again.

"You may return to what you were doing before that woman interrupted us," Manfred said in a haughty voice.

"Only if we shut these perverts off first!" Sam exclaimed, clicking the power button on the remote. Once the television was off, he considered turning it back on simply to change the channel to something else, so these people wouldn't be on his TV the next time he turned it on. To clear the browsing history, so to speak. But he just couldn't take three more seconds of that garbage.

"Perverts? Who are you calling perverts?" Manfred asked indignantly. "They're the ones leading the charge against the perverts!"

"Just like I predicted when we turned it on: They were talking about sex. And that's all they talked about. Nothing else. You all got bored with the stuff about being kind to others, and decided to make it all about sex, because sex sells. I guarantee you're not the only one who likes to jerk off to this trash."

Manfred returned to his default position. "You would never understand. Without Christ you have no moral compass."

Sam ignored this and elaborated. "Do you know what the funniest part of that slime was? That contraception is a sin because it circumvents the will of God. Like, God wanted someone to get pregnant, but darn it all, contraception stopped him. He can't overpower that. Yet, somehow, he managed to get Mary pregnant and *she didn't even have sex*. Think about it. Why would anyone think contraception could stand a chance in Hell against the will of God?"

There was a long pause from Manfred. Sam could picture the little hamster wheel going around in Manfred's little penis brain. "Mary," Sam said. "You know? Mother of Jesus? Virgin birth? Any of this ringing a bell?"

"Well, yes, yes," Manfred blustered his way through his equivalent of a brain fart. "But that was a different time. There was no contraception back then. The liberals would have aborted Jesus!"

"Oh, Manfred, I wish you would think and not just speak. We're going to sleep now," Sam announced.

Manfred was mercifully quiet and slowly softened as Sam drifted off to sleep, thinking about a clothed Anne and the fun they had together.

"Hey, Sam. Sam? Sam, wake up," Manfred's voice jolted him back, right as he had mostly faded away.

"What the fuck do you want?" Sam mumbled, half-asleep.

"You know something?"

"What?"

"I'd really like a handjob now. Can you give me a handjob?"

"What? Shit, Manfred. I was getting to sleep. And I just gave you a handjob."

"Well, I wasn't asleep, and you never finished."

"You're an inconsiderate pig, Manfred!"

"Jesus!" Manfred blasphemed. "You'd think I was asking you for a million dollars. I'm just asking you for a handjob."

"You don't wake people up for handjobs!"

"Sam!"

"Fuck off and go back to sleep."

"You're so selfish. Everything's all about you, Sam. The rest of us have needs too, you know."

"Goodnight, Manfred," Sam said. He had a hard time getting to sleep. He remembered the clock reading 4:16. But once he did get to sleep again, it was a sound sleep.

CHAPTER 10

And if your hand or your foot causes you to sin, cut it off and throw it from you; it is better for you to enter life crippled or lame, than having two hands or two feet and be cast into the eternal fire. (Matthew 18:8)

"Sam? Sam, honey?" His mother was waking him up. Maybe she had already made it to the store and the pancakes were ready.

"I'm not hungry. I just want to sleep," Sam murmured.

"Sam, sweetheart? Please wake up," she said gently. Sam looked past her to his clock, which read 1:53. That must be PM. She had let him sleep in. Well, it probably was time to get up. His annoyance at being woken up faded and suddenly pancakes sounded great. He wasn't too tradition-bound to eat pancakes in the afternoon.

He was about to say he would indeed like pancakes, when it finally occurred to him she hadn't said anything about them. He amended his words to, "What's going on?"

His mother put on her bravest face as she responded, "There are some officers here to see you. Please wake up." Her voice was shaky.

"Huh?" was the only response Sam could muster.

Before he knew it, a police officer stepped into his room, a man in full uniform with a gun by his side. Sam tried to piece together the situation, but his mind wasn't keeping up. Did the police know about last night? It didn't make any sense. Even if they did know, wouldn't they wait for him downstairs? They must have been aggressive and followed his mother upstairs, because, here was a cop ... right here in his room ... no, make that two cops, another one walked in.

"Mr. Meyers? Good morning. We need to ask you a few questions," the first officer said in a dry, formal tone. Both cops stepped toward his bed. He couldn't read anything in their expressions, which were All Business. His mother gave him an apologetic look and withdrew to the doorway.

"What's going on?" Manfred muttered as he woke up. "Don't you people know what time it is?" Sam didn't bother telling him it was the early afternoon and these police officers had probably been on the job for at least five or six hours.

Sam hadn't been awake long enough to carry on simultaneous conversations with both Manfred and the police. He sat upright, naked above the waist, in order to begin speaking. However, "um" was about the only thought he managed to communicate.

"We need you to come down to the station with us," the second police officer said. "Please get dressed."

"Um," Sam repeated. "What is this all about?"

"We'll discuss it at the station, sir."

"No," Sam said with a newfound resolve largely based on the fact he was lying in bed, almost naked, and didn't want to go anywhere. "You need to tell me what this is about, or else I'm not going anywhere." At that moment, the only thing in life Sam really wanted was to eat pancakes with his mom.

The police officers looked at each other, seemingly engaged in a silent conversation. The second officer gave a very slight nod to the other, turned to Sam and said, "Sir, multiple instances of vandalism occurred last night."

This is bad ... Sam thought.

"Damn right," Manfred said proudly. "Message received."

The first police officer, obviously not hearing Manfred, picked up where his partner left off: "A patrol car ran the plates of a car parked near the Synagogue where some of the vandalism occurred. The plates belong to a 2001 Ford Taurus registered to your mother."

The second police officer glanced at Sam's mother standing in the doorway and said, "It's standard practice for patrol cars to check the license plates of vehicles parked in suspicious locations." His eyes moved to Sam askance and added, "Just in case."

"Are they here to thank us for our good work?" Manfred asked.

The first officer continued, "Additional vandalism was reported at the Mormon Temple, where a surveillance camera recorded a white Ford Taurus entering and exiting the parking lot."

"We definitely needed to send a message to those cultists," Manfred said.

Sam glanced over toward his mother in the doorway. She had a horrified expression on her face. Sam found himself unable to make eye contact with her and instead he focused on the officers

The second officer continued, "Similar vandalism was discovered a couple of blocks away from the Islamic Community Center, using identical red spray paint."

"Two blocks away because you didn't have big enough balls to go up to the building," Manfred said. "I know how small your balls are; I live right next door to them."

The first officer concluded, "Your mother informed us the car is unofficially yours and she gave us permission to search it. In doing so, we found this empty can of spray paint matching the paint at the scenes." He pulled Sam's spray paint can from a bag Sam hadn't noticed him holding. Sam turned to his mother, who appeared abashed. But he didn't blame her for letting them search the car. She couldn't have expected him to be such a dumbass.

Everyone was silent for a moment. His mother and the officers stared at him expectantly.

Someone had to speak first, and that someone ended up being Manfred. "I can't believe your Jew bitch mother betrayed us!"

That was about all Sam could take. "Well, *shit*," he said. He rubbed his temples and head for a couple of seconds, trying to choose his words. When he realized the words he needed to save himself didn't exist, he started talking anyway. "Look, *I*,"—he pointed at his chest with both hands—"didn't do any of this."

"We will listen to your explanation at the station, sir. Please get dressed and come with us."

Sam shook his head, knowing what he needed to do. He desperately wanted to cleanse his conscience. "It wasn't *me*. It was Manfred! Alright: It was Manfred!"

"What?" came Manfred's voice, hurt and shocked. "You're selling me out?"

His mother appeared hopeful for the first time, allowing herself the possibility Sam was innocent. The first officer asked, "Who is Manfred?" He had his notebook and pencil ready for a paint-by-numbers accusation against the guilty party.

Manfred turtled, retracting as far as possible, and hissed, "Traitor! You sold me out! What's going to happen to me now?"

Sam looked down at his crotch and screamed aloud, "Probably the same shit that's going to happen to me, asshole!"

The officer cocked his head to the side and lowered his notebook. He repeated his question, "Who is Manfred?"

"Manfred's my dick, OK!" Sam screamed. Manfred howled at Sam, but Sam ignored him and stared ahead at the officers. He took one quick glance at his mother, her expression unreadable.

Both officers remained expressionless, but Sam sensed their external calm was the successful result of an internal struggle. "Are you talking about your penis, sir?" one finally asked.

"Yes! Yes, already!" Sam yelled. "Manfred's my penis, my member, my Johnson, my weenie. He's a nightmare. He never shuts up. He ruins my life."

His mother's jaw dropped open. The second officer said, "Sir, the crime we need to discuss with you isn't sexual in nature, so you need to stop talking about your penis."

"Of course it wasn't sexual in nature. Manfred's a closet homosexual. He's a ball of frustration and rage. He can't express himself normally, so of course he expresses himself in lots of stupid, non-sexual ways."

"I AM NOT FUCKING GAY!" Manfred thundered.

Maybe not, Sam figured, but he didn't feel bad about making the accusation. "Here's the deal with Manfred: He's an à la carte Christian, picking and choosing as he goes along. Not to mention, he's a moron. He's terrified of whatever the sleazy talk show pundits have worked him into a lather about most recently. You know what he's been harping on me to do at school? He wants to release a bunch of snakes into the Women's Studies building, because we watched *Snakes on a Plane*, and this dickhead's like, 'Oh, that was so awesome, let's do that to a bunch of feminazis.'" He imitated Manfred with a high, squeaky voice.

"Shut up, blabbermouth," Manfred squealed. "That's my special top secret plan!"

One of the officers moved to the far corner of the room, talking on his radio, possibly calling in for backup. The other officer just stared at Sam. Sam's mother couldn't bring herself to leave, but seemed to be trying to disappear, fading into the paint on the wall.

"You won't believe the crap he makes me do," Sam continued. He jumped out of his bed, not caring that he was only wearing underwear and tube socks. "Did you get the footage of a hooded man masturbating into the ATM? That was him! That was Manfred!" The ATM thing had happened up at school, not here, but Sam didn't let that stop him. "He forced me to make a poop drawing outside a vegetarian restaurant. It said, 'Suck My Meat.' He made me steal a bunch of money being collected for AIDS orphans in Africa. I bet that was reported. He said a bunch of racist stuff and said they all must be gay or degenerate, because only gay people and degenerates get AIDS. Help me deal with this piece of shit! Please! Help me!" Sam's heart was wide open, exposed like it had never been before. It was the first time in his life he ever cried out—shamelessly—for help.

"Mirandize this idiot already! Stop him before he gives away all my secrets!"

As if cued by Manfred's command, that's exactly what happened. "*You have the right to remain silent. Anything you say or do may be used against you in a court of law. You have the right to consult an attorney before speaking to the police and to have an attorney present during questioning now or in the future. If you cannot afford an attorney, one will be appointed ...*"

Sam was in no state to acknowledge the Miranda warning. He continued his rant, his coherency deteriorating, while one of the officers forced him to the ground. "Conspiracy theories ... so-called Global Warming-gate? Manfred has conspiracy theories out the ass for you! Other religions? Oh they suck, but the dickhead can't even name four of the Ten Commandments! He hates women! Hates them! Pissed all over Anne!"

Sam was now pinned to the ground, handcuffed, and still wearing nothing but white briefs (nice and tight because Manfred liked to feel secure) and socks. "Go ahead, take him in!" Sam yelled. "Don't take me in, take him! Chop him right the fuck off! I won't care, I won't miss him!"

"Do you understand these rights as they've been read to you?" one of the cops said loudly, trying to get through to Sam. He was on one knee next to Sam, having put on the handcuffs. The other officer, who had been on his radio moments before, was standing next to Sam's head, staring down at him.

"Get some scissors. There are some in my desk," Sam pleaded, gesturing toward the top drawer with his nose. "Cut him off! Cut him off! Raise the average level of morality and intelligence in the world. Let me get them for you," and with that Sam tried to launch to his feet, pulling himself toward the desk, toward the scissors.

His movement instigated the officers. The one towering over his head said, "We don't want to use more force, sir, but we will if necessary."

Sam kept squirming. If only he could get to those scissors. "Scissors! Scissors!" he bellowed.

The officer kneeling next to him held his legs firmly while the one standing over him dropped to the floor to pin Sam's upper body. Sam kept thrashing on the ground. One snip and everything would be better. Nothing else mattered.

"Oh, Sam, please!" his mother cried. She was squeezing the doorknob, barely able to stay on her feet. His poor mother. She just didn't understand anything. She stumbled and caught herself, and he heard her irregular footsteps scurrying away. She couldn't take it anymore.

Sam's mind was working frantically, trying to figure out how to get ahold of a pair of scissors or a knife or a scalpel. Perhaps an axe. Everything else was a blur.

He couldn't even be sure if what he perceived was truly happening. Without the protective presence of his mother, the police seemed to change, their professional masks replaced by a sadistic, juvenile demeanor.

One of the officers asked the other, "Should we tase him?"

The other laughed and said, "Why do you think I took this job?"

"But, you know who I think really deserves to be tased? This *Manfred* guy."

They laughed together some more. One stepped forward, leaned in, and visibly paused to savor the moment ... then he tased the living shit out of Manfred.

If Sam wasn't nuts before, he was nuts now.

CHAPTER 11

The way of a fool is right in his own eyes, but a wise man listens to counsel. (Proverbs 12:15)

It was a bright, sunny day. Mary and Suzie sat on the patio table in Suzie's newly renovated sunroom. Excited for an excuse to unpack her margarita blender, Suzie made them some drinks.

"So ..." Suzie said expectantly. "You said on the phone you had some big news."

Mary pulled her left hand out from beneath the table, spreading her fingers in front of Suzie. Suzie's eyes fixed on the diamond and she gasped with excitement, but it still felt weird to Mary. It had taken her two years after Jim died to take off the old ring, with Suzie chiding her to do so the entire time.

"Bob asked me to marry him," Mary said, as if it weren't obvious.

"He sure did!" Suzie gushed. "Oh, Mary, that's terrific!"

"The wedding's not for another six months, but I'm hoping you'll be the Maid of Honor."

"Well, of course I will." Suzie exclaimed. "Oh, Mary, this is so exciting." Suzie paused and then said, "How come I'm so much more excited about this than you appear to be?"

Mary hadn't realized her expression was so readable. She loved Bob. He would be a fine husband. But there was something else.

"Suzie," she began, "Friday night, when Bob proposed, I sensed Jim in the room, watching me. Disapproving. I know it's silly."

"Oh, honey," Suzie said. "I know you think you're betraying Jim, but you need to move on. Jim is in Heaven, watching you, and he wants you to be happy. He wants you to move on with your life."

Mary wasn't so sure. She was aware of Jim's presence, somehow, and he seemed angry. She thought she knew why: After all of those unsuccessful, costly trips to doctors' offices for his cancer treatments, Jim had come to despise doctors, and now she was marrying one. But Suzie was probably right. No doubt it was all in her imagination, prodded by her irrational guilt over finding someone new.

"In your near-death experience," Suzie said, "Jim said you had more work to do on Earth, right?" Suzie was the only person outside the support group to whom Mary confided the near-death experience. She hadn't even told her parents. But Mary had told Suzie everything—well, everything except the "Julio fucking up" part. Because, really, that one detail discredited the whole thing and made her seem delusional.

"That's right," Mary said.

Suzie had well-defined ideas of what Heaven was like. Mary wasn't so sure. She didn't remember reading about anyone named Julio in the Bible. Still, Suzie was probably right. Ever since Jim died, Suzie had been there for Mary all the way. After a year, she had gently tried to convince Mary to take off Jim's ring and put herself "back in circulation," but Mary wasn't ready yet. Suzie was understanding and always gentle, always there to console Mary and to help her move on. Suzie was right: there was no way Jim wanted her to give up on life.

"I guess you're right," Mary finally said. She sipped her drink and they sat quietly for a few minutes.

Suzie asked, "So, are you and Bob planning on having kids?"

Mary nodded. She was getting older, and if she was going to have kids, it needed to happen soon. "We'll probably start trying as soon as we're married," she said.

"That's great," Suzie was back to gushing again.

This only added to Mary's sense of guilt. Jim always wanted kids, but she had stalled and told him that she wasn't ready yet. They finally started trying to have a child before Jim was diagnosed with cancer, but stopped so that Jim could focus on the chemotherapy. Then Jim died and here she was without children.

But, as always, Suzie was right. Mary couldn't live in the past. For Jim's sake, as well as her own, she would marry Bob and live a happy life. She owed Jim that much.

Isabelle, Suzie's nine-year-old daughter, ran into the room. Apparently she had been spying on them and she immediately wanted to see the ring. "Oh, that's pretty, Aunt Mary," she said, pulling at the ring in a way no adult ever would. "It's bigger than the one Uncle Jim gave you," she said with the tactlessness of a child. "Was Uncle Jim poor? He must have been a poor person. This is such a nicer ring." Mary winced as she imagined Jim hearing this from the beyond. This would only make his spirit angrier.

CHAPTER 12

You have said, 'I am overwhelmed with trouble! Haven't I had enough pain already? And now the Lord has added more! I am worn out from sighing and can find no rest.' (Jeremiah 45:3)

The next several hours were a blur for Sam. Certain his mother was working hard to get him out of jail, he figured paperwork was in the way. It was a Saturday; administrative aspects of the justice system might not be at full staff.

He found himself in a large holding cell with five other men. The cell was large enough for at least twenty, but he had no idea how many people get arrested and thrown in jail on a typical day.

One of the members of Sam's cohort was about his age, but better dressed ... wait ... he was still only wearing white underwear briefs and socks. *Well, that's just great*, he thought. Man, he had seriously lost it if he hadn't noticed that until now.

Sam tried closing his eyes and opening them again, but everything was the same. Normally, when he realized he was in one of those public nudity dreams, he had the ability to will himself awake. No, this was real, and he was damned-near naked. In a jail cell. With other men.

So, yeah, *just about anyone* was better dressed than Sam at the moment. The point being: the other kid in the holding cell was better dressed than Sam *typically* was. The kid had a terrified expression, his eyes constantly darting around.

Then there were two quiet, older guys who had obviously been through all this before. One had long curly hair and a beard almost as long, with a leather vest and an array of tattoos illustrating his love for naked ladies and motorcycles. The other appeared to be a homeless man missing his paper-bagged bottle of booze. Both had about the same facial expression, which Sam could best describe as, "same shit, different day."

A twitchy, dirty man also shared their cage. Sam could recognize a meth addict when he saw one. He appeared to be engaged in a fight for his life against some imaginary threat in the opposite corner of the cell, and everyone seemed to have enough sense to give him a wide berth. He was thin and frail, but it was anyone's guess as to what he'd do next, if given the choice between his life and that of the invisible beast he was dueling.

Finally, there was the black guy sitting next to Sam, his leg physically resting against Sam despite the many feet of empty bench available. Sam had been afraid to even shift his eyes to covertly glance at this man, but now that he did, there was no longer any room for doubt: he was masturbating. He was about twice Sam's size, in his late 20s or so, with no hair anywhere except for a square inch of beard right at the tip of his chin.

Sam tried to … ignore this, but it was worse than trying to ignore the jerks in middle school. Not only was the man directly touching Sam's leg with his own, but his neck was turned 90 degrees to face Sam. He had a wide smile on his face, with a couple of teeth missing, and a twinkle in his eye. He was purring.

I guess this is how it works, thought Sam. *These things happen and no one cares. They're just relieved the creepy guy is bothering someone else.* He wondered how long it would take the authorities to interrupt an assault.

Manfred had been quiet for all of it. Sam expected a bunch of homophobia, which would have some basis in reality for the first time ever.

When Manfred did speak, Sam found his commentary curious: "Sam? Is it okay to be me? Is it okay to be a penis?"

"I don't … I don't know what you mean. I don't know where you're going with the question … I don't know … what the question means …" Sam was finding it difficult to focus on anything other than the immediate threat posed by the weirdo next to him.

"This guy is touching his penis right here, in front of everyone, and he doesn't care who sees it. He doesn't think he needs to keep his penis a secret. They seem happy together. So, is it okay to be me? Am I okay?"

Under different circumstances, this conversation might have been interesting. They never talked about what it was like to be trapped under clothes 24/7, hidden away from everything as if you were a complete embarrassment. But here—sitting in jail and next to someone who was pointedly jerking off, all because of Manfred's intolerant bullshit—he wasn't inclined to indulge his ignorant, talking penis. His anger towards Manfred flooded back.

Sam lashed out, "No, it's not fucking okay to be you. There's nothing okay about you. You're a piece of shit, a nothing nobody with half a brain. Worthless! Fuckslime idiot shithead fuck, I wouldn't be sitting in *jail* if it wasn't for your dumbfuck ass. I should have gotten the scissors and taken care of business before the cops showed up." Sam paused and realized he was happy with his improvised use of profanity. He screamed his new creation, "fuckslime," four more times in rapid succession.

It had been yet another case of him yelling at Manfred, not realizing he was doing it aloud. The tattooed biker and the homeless man looked at Sam, but only with mild interest. They had seen weirder.

But, the man masturbating next to him stopped and backed away. Sam should have screamed earlier. That said, it probably wasn't something he could fake. He needed to scream from the heart, and only Manfred could make him do that.

Sam remembered seeing an old Western movie in which a pioneer avoided being killed by a hostile Native American by acting like he suffered from a mental illness. Insanity was seen as being "touched by the spirit world" or something along those lines; it had a sacred quality, at least in the screenplay. The man backed away from Sam as if he adhered to that philosophy. Or, like a hawk avoiding sick prey. Eat the meat and you may catch the disease, goes the instinct. *Well, don't eat me*, thought Sam. *This meat is rancid.*

"Sheesh, Sam," Manfred said. "You and your little outburst ruined that guy's good time."

"Manfred, aren't you happy he's leaving us alone? He's probably not going to rape us now. It was touch-and-go for a minute."

"Yeah, yeah, yeah, ruin everyone's good time," Manfred responded.

"Oh, so being raped is fun? Nice, Manfred. Real nice."

"No, but being touched without embarrassment is," Manfred insisted. "He was only touching his penis. Why assume he wanted to rape you? He was already happy with what he was doing. I guess it threatened you, huh? Someone is treating his penis with affection and respect and yeah, you're worried I'll start to get new ideas and big expectations. You better keep me down in my place and make sure I don't witness things like that, right?"

"This is from the same person who worries about public masturbation causing the downfall of modern society?" Sam asked.

"What?"

"Public masturbation," Sam began. "Remember over dinner last night, the whole, 'if the liberals take the guns away, people will be masturbating in broad daylight and on every street corner' or whatever you said? It was super stupid. Do you remember?"

"Of course I remember what I said," Manfred snapped. "What about it?"

"Well, that man was in public, jacking off a spermstorm. That's the face of public masturbation, buddy," Sam said.

"Public masturbation? That guy was just being nice," Manfred countered.

"Now you don't even know what masturbation is? Whatever. Let's give up and agree to what you said," Sam responded, adding under his internal breath, "douche."

That was the extent of Sam's conversation with Manfred—or anyone else—while in jail. Sam did his best to stare at the floor, never looking anyone in the eyes. The other prisoners, including the masturbator, mostly did the same. The only exceptions were the jail veterans, the tattooed biker and homeless guy, who would occasionally talk to each other. Maybe they were old jail friends.

Sam continued to wait ... and wait ... and wait. The well-dressed young man was the first to be released; two officers came by to get him, either to go home or to be processed further into the prison system. Sam breathed a big sigh of relief when the masturbator was pulled out of the cage next. He was replaced by two food service workers, still in uniform. They had evidently been fighting with a third, who was in a different cell across the hallway.

Eventually, one of the officers took pity on Sam and handed him a blanket to cover himself with, and Sam managed to doze off. It must have been some decent sleep, because it wasn't until a man was vomiting in the middle of the floor that he finally awoke. Everyone from the first group was gone and an entirely new group had migrated in. Changing cellmates was about the only way to judge the passage of time. He felt like he was sitting at the DMV and all the other anguished souls got called up before he did.

Another full crop cycled through. When the police officers came to retrieve another of his new cellmates, a Hispanic teenager, Sam wanted to ask if they had forgotten about him. But he worried that by doing so he'd bring unwanted attention to himself, something that might result in a beating of some sort. It was an irrational fear, but in the end he wasn't willing to take the risk. At some point, he managed to fall asleep again, and was awakened by a police officer telling him it was time to leave.

The officer led him to a large, busy room with lots of personnel scurrying about. Sam found his mother sitting at a desk. The officer brought him over and sat him down next to her. She aged since he saw her last. She had a long coat ready for him. He was grateful for the coat but almost felt creepier wearing it, like he'd flash the crowd at any moment.

The next bit also took a long time. There was plenty of paperwork, and a long wait while the officer stepped away to find Sam's personal effects. Sam tried to assure the officer he had no personal effects, but still had to wait for the officer to confirm this by searching the bins.

While the officer was away on his vain quest, Sam worked up the courage to say, "Thanks for getting me out, Mom. I'm so sorry I put you through this."

All she said was, "We'll talk about what happened when we get home. Until then, you should probably keep quiet."

Sam wanted to assure her he wouldn't launch into another tirade about his penis or anything like that, but he thought better of it. He did as he was told and stayed quiet.

Finally, the officer returned and told him he was free to go. As Sam and his mom walked out the door, Sam realized he had no idea where he was. Other than almost two years of college, he had spent his entire life in this general geographic area, but had no idea where the police station was located. It was just something that had never come up before. He wondered if his mother had known where to go or if she had to ask someone.

Sam was shocked it was still daylight. It seemed like he had been in there forever, but apparently it was only a few hours. When he commented on this to his mother, she corrected him: No, it was Sunday morning. He had been in there for about 18 hours. The next bit of weirdness Sam contemplated was that he hadn't noticed a clock inside the police station. He supposed that was an indication of how limited and downward he had kept his gaze.

After he strapped himself into the passenger seat of his mom's car, it took more than 15 minutes for someone to break the silence. "You took my advice one time, Sam, one time. Thank God you did. Doing well in school: That's the only reason why you're here right now." Sam waited for her to elaborate. "I played the good student card. I managed to convince them you were being silly and immature, upset about girl stuff but otherwise a good kid. It was hard convincing them you didn't need to be committed to a mental health facility. I had to assure them you would go to counseling on a regular basis. They were pretty insistent on that."

Sam processed for a while. "What happens now, Mom?" He hated sounding like a little child, dependent on his mommy. But at least she seemed to have something figured out. He didn't have the first clue.

"What happens now is this: You finish the semester at school. It's only six more weeks, and it would be stupid not to finish the semester. You keep your grades up. You sign up for counseling immediately. I'll call the school and get you into their program for now, and I'll also find someone local for the summer. Your trial date will be towards the end of summer. I'll find a lawyer. We can research college transfer options, as well, if you insist that your problems at school are insurmountable." She kept her voice level throughout her speech, but Sam knew it was an effort to maintain control. She looked so exhausted.

Everything his mother was saying made perfect sense. "Okay, Mom," he sighed. "I'll be okay. I can finish the semester. And, you're right, I should start meeting with a counselor right away." He meant every word.

Once they returned home, his mom made Sam breakfast, which he ate ravenously, and then he gathered his stuff and loaded the car, the now-infamous 2001 Ford Taurus.

He went back inside and watched some Sunday news shows with his mom. He had the distinct feeling they would never, at any point in their lives, discuss the stuff about "Manfred the penis." They would mutually pretend none of that weird stuff had ever been said.

Sam did his best to radiate normality. He knew it was working for her a bit; she *wanted* to believe he was okay, and would latch on to any evidence to support her hope. Finally, he announced it was time to head back to school. He said he needed to finish some homework before Monday's classes.

"Sam, are you sure you don't want me to drive you back?" she asked.

"No, Mom, I can drive. I don't want you to miss your book group tonight. I'll be fine. Seriously. Don't worry." Telling his mother not to worry, especially after what she had witnessed, was like telling a fish not to swim. Could he be trusted to take a long drive by himself, so soon after displaying such bizarre behavior?

"Mom, I promise. I'm okay. I feel better today than I have for a while. As stupid as it sounds, a night in jail did clear my head. Also, I love taking long drives. It's relaxing. Don't worry, Mom, I'll be okay."

They looped through a long dance of uncertainty and hesitation and assertion, until she relented.

As he started his car, she came to the passenger-side window, which he rolled down so she'd be able to say whatever she was going to say. She always had one more thing to say.

"Sam, please call me when you get there so I know you arrived safely, all right?"

"Okay, Mom," he said, pulling out of the driveway.

CHAPTER 13

Behold, I shall corrupt your seed, and spread
dung upon your faces. (Malachi 2:3)

Sam gave his mother the customary extended wave goodbye as he drove off. She stayed outside in the driveway while he pulled away, also waving goodbye, but grimacing. Though, other than her facial expression, this was like any other time he had ever left home. She would always stand outside the house, rooted in place until he was out of view. Sometimes he wondered how long she stayed there, imagining that she stood waving for hours after he was gone.

His first stop was 7-11. He picked up some Twizzlers and a fountain soda large enough to drown in. These supplies, along with his radio—his Ford Taurus featured both AM *and* FM!— would get him through the long drive. Manfred delivered his typical response to going inside a 7-11. He took a few minutes to bitch about the "dune coon" running the register, and how lax he considered U.S. immigration policy to be. He followed this by crabbing about the various customers who didn't meet his standards.

The guy with open-toed sandals buying low-fat potato chips really got under Manfred's skin. Sam ignored Manfred, the same way he tried to ignore internet trolling. Nothing new to see.

As he drove, Sam remembered the weird way the car handled during the graffiti incident. Now it sounded as if its various systems were competing with each other to see which one would fail first. But, he decided he couldn't risk his mother insisting on driving him to school, so he rolled the dice the car would be okay.

Now alone, he spent some time thinking about his plan for the next six weeks. It's only six weeks, it's only six weeks, he repeated to himself as a mantra. Things had been toxic when he left. *Literally toxic*, he thought as he remembered the urine all over his door. He wondered if those people pissed on it a second time while he was gone.

He visualized all the details of the upcoming weeks. He would try to avoid other people: just go to class, pick up portable food from the cafeteria and bring it back to his room, and avoid all non-essential public places. He'd have his car, so if things got too bad, fleeing was an option. He thought some more and decided the worst-case scenario was that he'd have to stay in a cheap extended-stay motel. To be prepared, his second stop was the bank, where he made the maximum daily cash withdrawal of $1,500 from his account—which left him with precisely $38.18. He was scraping the barrel.

After leaving the bank, he was on an open road driving through the countryside. It was a nearly magical start: the music on the radio was particularly good, and Manfred was quiet. For some inexplicable reason, Sam was feeling better. Driving back to college felt like a fresh start of sorts, despite returning to a situation that was intolerable roughly 48 hours earlier. But Sam was returning with a nice package of deals from Manfred. It would be bearable. The future was brightening. The worst was behind him. The incident with Anne and the overnight stay in jail were water under the bridge.

After driving for maybe 70 or 80 minutes, he smelled something burning. The car started jerking, and then hesitating. The hesitations started getting longer and the periods of acceleration became shorter. The hesitations won, as the car went from 60 miles an hour to a full stop. The steering wheel froze up, and Sam had to use all his strength to pull the car onto the shoulder of the road. Once the car was stopped, he sat there in silence, watching smoke rising from under the hood.

It was the most predictable outcome of all time: the car was dead. *What a piece of shit*, Sam thought. It was time to get this rolling turd off the road once and for all. No more expensive repairs.

"Cockgoblin motherfucking shit, this asshole car fucked us again!" Sam exclaimed, hitting the steering wheel in a way that genuinely hurt. He now realized his prior good mood had been tenuous. Optimism about long-term prospects started oozing away.

"Please watch your language," Manfred said.

Oh, for fuck's sake! Sam thought. "Really, Manfred?"

"I would really prefer if you didn't use such sinful profanity," Manfred insisted.

"Sinful?" Sam said. "I'm pretty sure the Bible says, 'Thou shalt not take the Lord's name in vain.' But I don't remember it saying, 'thou shalt not say *cockgoblin.*' Though, if God's proper name is Cockgoblin, then it would be a violation. Hold up, you'd know this: is God's proper name Cockgoblin?" Manfred didn't respond. "Well, is it? Is it Cockgoblin?"

Manfred whimpered, "I just don't like hearing those words."

"Yeah, until you do. *You* use profanity all the time, whenever *you* want. Then you whimsically change your mind and decide it's evil when someone else uses it." Sam realized he was unfairly taking out his anger at the car on Manfred. He didn't apologize, of course, but he cut off his tirade and decided it was time to exit the car. He popped the latch on the hood and examined the steaming engine. Yep. Exactly as he suspected, there were car parts. He kept staring at the parts, as if examining them longer would result in him getting the first clue as to what the problem was and how to fix it.

"Are you sure you can't get it started, Sam?" Manfred asked.

"Pretty damn sure," Sam muttered in reply. A hose that was probably supposed to be attached to something, perhaps the radiator, hung loosely. Shiny liquid was pooled under the car, maybe oil or radiator fluid or even windshield wiper fluid for all Sam knew.

"Can't you at least try?"

"I don't know how to fix it." Sam said. "Do you want to put your abounding automotive expertise to the task? There's a hole right here, I can send you in. It's probably the only hole we'll ever get inside. May as well enjoy it, public spectacle and all. Maybe we can get sent back to jail for public exposure. You loved it in jail."

"That's so uncalled for," Manfred moaned. "You know, you've been a real pill to deal with the past couple of days!"

"Oh, I've been difficult? I suppose you've been a little angel?" Sam asked. He knew he was taking out his frustration on Manfred again, but he didn't care.

"Don't think I didn't suffer. I was tased!"

"All right, all right, shut up," Sam said. "I don't want to hear your voice right now. I need to think." He continued to stare blankly at the innards of the car, but he knew he was procrastinating because he hated what had to happen next.

With great pain, he resigned himself to calling his mommy for help. He reached into his pocket, but his phone wasn't there.

The phone was almost a decoration, hardly ever used, yet he still felt naked without it. He searched through the inside of the car to no avail. Then he got a mental picture, crystal clear, of the phone sitting on the kitchen table at his mother's house. He must have put it down and forgotten to pick it up. He always seemed to forget something, but did it really have to be his phone, on the day his car broke down?

Stranded and devoid of any means of communication, Sam realized there was only one thing to do. He shoved the remaining Twizzlers into his backpack and sucked down the fountain soda, fighting off the brain-freeze.

After doing one last search of the car for anything he might be leaving behind, he closed the door and started to walk away. He hoped vagrants wouldn't car-b-que it before a tow truck came.

He was on a rather lonely stretch of road at the moment, but he recalled a truck stop somewhere up ahead. He had no idea how far away it was—maybe a few miles, maybe twenty, he didn't know.

Walk. He figured he'd just walk. Even if it was twenty miles, he'd manage it.

He walked for at least two miles. He got used to hearing the cars approaching from behind, and the displaced wind blowing as they passed him. It occurred to Sam it would be safer to walk on the other side of the road, so he could see the oncoming traffic and possibly leap out of the way of a texting driver. But he decided he didn't want to risk making eye contact with anyone who might know him. What if someone from school recognized him as he walked along the highway? Or what if he was seen by the same cops who arrested and tased him? Somehow, risking his life was preferable. He enjoyed the anonymity of showing his backside to the closest lane of traffic. Besides, even strangers might laugh at him now, as he was getting red and sweaty from the walk.

Finally, Manfred spoke the first words in about 30 minutes. "Uh, Sam?" he said. "I'm truly sorry to bother you. But it's getting a bit unpleasant down here. Do you think maybe we should, um, lean on the kindness of strangers? Hitch a ride?"

It was never a good sign when he agreed with Manfred, but he had been thinking the same thing. He was wearing his uncomfortable back-up shoes, as his good ones were in the dumpster at school. His feet would transform into a blister colony if he continued much longer.

After a few minutes of working up the nerve, Sam turned around, facing the direction of traffic. He slowly extended his arm outwards with the thumb up … it was an alien motion for his body to perform and it almost physically hurt.

He was wondering what he should do with his face. Should he smile? Or would a smile be creepy? What if he didn't smile? Would he look like some dangerous sociopath? The question of what to do with his face seemed like the biggest quandary he ever experienced, as he was unsatisfied with every facet of every possibility he considered. *My face, my stupid face*, Sam internally moaned. But before he fell deeper into self-loathing, a green Honda Civic passed with brake lights lit. It miraculously pulled over about a hundred feet ahead. He had a ride.

Sam was nervous as he stepped up to the car and opened the passenger door. He didn't know how this sort of thing worked.

"Hello," said the man. He had a slight build and was young, late 20's to early 30's. He appeared to be Indian or Pakistani. Sam had a feeling he had gotten lucky. The guy didn't seem like a pervert. Sam wasn't too sure how to tell someone is a pervert, but he didn't get a pervert vibe from this guy. The man was friendly—but not *too* friendly—as he asked where Sam was heading. After some discussion, Sam determined the man wasn't headed anywhere particularly close to where he needed to go, so he said the truck stop would be fine.

Sam climbed in, keeping his backpack on his lap. "Thanks so much for picking me up," he said. "My white Ford Taurus is a couple of miles back." Then he unnecessarily added, "It died."

"Sam, I know we needed a ride, but can we find someone else?" Manfred asked, and Sam pretended not to hear.

"Oh, I've only had Hondas. They never break down. This one has over 210,000 miles on it. I'll drive it until the wheels fall off," the man said with no perceptible accent.

"I like Hondas," Sam responded. "I can imagine getting one after I graduate."

"Just look at him," Manfred said. "He's probably a terrorist."

"You're in school? Headed back from the weekend?" the man asked.

"Yeah, I needed a weekend away," Sam said. Part of him wanted to tell this man everything—cry on the shoulder of a stranger, and get some impartial advice.

"This is a Muslim. I don't feel safe here," Manfred insisted.

"What are you majoring in?" the man asked.

"I haven't decided for certain yet," Sam admitted. "I'm thinking biochem, but I'm taking a little bit of everything until I can figure out which way to go."

"Sam, this car is probably wired with explosives. We're going to be a suicide bomb." Manfred wouldn't drop it.

Sam saw a sign indicating the truck stop was five miles away. Silently, he told Manfred, "We just have to make it another five minutes."

"I don't think we *have* another five minutes, Sam! I don't want to be a martyr for Allah." Manfred said. Manfred lengthened both syllables and pronounced it like *Ahhhhh-Lahhhhh*. "We haven't been baptized yet. I'm not taking chances."

Sam saw something he figured should assuage Manfred's fears—a strange lion-shaped trinket, gold and red, dangling on a chain draped around the rear-view mirror. Sam knew he had no chance of convincing Manfred that all Muslims aren't evil terrorists, but maybe he could convince Manfred this man was not a Muslim, but rather a Hindu.

"What's this?" Sam asked the man.

"That's Namagiri, the Goddess my family feels the greatest connection to," the man responded.

"Oh, here we go …" Manfred said frantically. "He's saying his last prayers to his Muslim Gods before blowing us up."

And then it happened. Again. All that fountain soda became a geyser of piss erupting from Manfred. Sam tried to push his backpack down into his crotch to absorb as much of the urine as he could.

"She was also the family Goddess of Ramanujan, one of the greatest mathematicians who ever lived. Ramanujan had dreams in which Namagiri presented him with voluminous scrolls of complex mathematical equations, and afterwards, he remembered them. She was revealing the truth of the Universe to him. My family was connected to her long before then, too. We're so proud of that connection ..." The man paused. "Do you smell something?"

"I'm sorry," Sam whimpered. He may as well jump on this one right away. "I had an accident. Here," he pulled out his wallet. "I can pay to have it detailed." He pulled out three $50 bills, not sure if they were truly damp or if everything now seemed damp in his imagination. Anger—but mostly confusion—slowly registered on the man's face. He pulled over to the side of the road.

"Get out of my car," he said simply.

"I'm so, so, so sorry. Please: take this money." The man made no effort to take the cash from Sam's extended hand.

"Get out of my car," the man repeated in the same flat tone.

Sam dutifully exited the car. As he stepped out he dropped the three fifty dollar bills onto the seat. Once Sam was out, the man rolled down the passenger side window and threw the bills out of the car with a scowl. He drove off. When Sam bent down to the pick up the bills, his knees collapsed under him. Sam enjoyed the sensation of being low to the ground, and he went fully prone, face-down in the dirt on the roadside. Being down low felt good, because it would be harder for someone to see him, and he was a total fucking embarrassment that no one should ever have to see.

"I saved us, Sam. There's nothing to worry about now. I saved us," Manfred's tone was placating. Sam didn't respond.

He lay there for about three minutes before Manfred spoke again. "I don't know if this is safe. Cars may not see us. You don't want to be run over," he said.

Sam thought about it. "Manfred, I would absolutely *love* to be run over by a car." Neither said anything for another couple of minutes.

"You should want to be run over, too," Sam finally continued. He spoke with precision, each syllable enunciated. "Anyone as trite, as uncreative, as predictable, and as mean-spirited as you should simply want to die. You have nothing to live for. Nothing to offer. You are so boring, you should just bore yourself to death. Aside from having erections and releasing urine, you have nothing, absolutely nothing else, in your sad, sad life. Death would be good for us both. It would be mercy." Sam continued to lie on the ground.

He then remembered a cartoon. A man's wife was obviously driving him nuts, nagging and nagging in the background. In desperation, the man was getting ready to shoot himself in the head, positioning a rifle between his knees, pointing the muzzle under his jaw. In the next panel of the cartoon, he imagined himself shooting his wife instead, and he now looked happy. Sexist cliché and advocacy of violence aside, Sam thought there was a valuable parable behind this cartoon. One could wallow and suffer and be the victim of others. Or, one could get up, face the aggressor head-on, and change the circumstances. He didn't need to lie down and die. Someone else—someone very specific—could, for all he cared.

"Manfred: there is a solution," he began.

"What is that?"

"It's simple," Sam replied. "I convince a psychiatrist I'm a woman trapped in a man's body. You get surgically removed. I defy you to explain how this isn't a good plan."

Energized by the idea, he bounced off the ground. Upright again, he adjusted his backpack. This meant there was piss all over his back now, but so be it. He looked down and noticed river patterns down his legs, outlining the flow of urine in dust. Clearly, trying to hitch another ride was no longer a possibility. Walking wasn't going to be fun either, now that his already-uncomfortable shoes were squishing with urine. Fortunately, the Hindu guy got him three miles closer to his destination.

"You've never talked about something like that before," Manfred cried. "It's disgusting! Those transgendered people are vile. Playing God like that. Telling God, 'Oh, you got it wrong when you made me.' What a horrible, horrible sin. You wouldn't dare!"

Transgender. The word registered with Sam, reverberated with him. Transgender. Those are real people. He'd have to pretend to be one of them. Wasn't that sort of like dancing around in blackface? *How offensive,* he thought, *how offensive and disturbing.* The flaws in Sam's plan were becoming apparent. What would he tell his poor mother, who had already suffered so much? He had no solution.

The thought of being run over by a car became alluring again. But that was unfair to the driver—he or she would almost certainly be traumatized by it, possibly hurt, and maybe financially ruined.

He tried to fall back on the comforting thought that he had a deal worked out with Manfred, but how good was the deal? They only got out of *jail*, what, five or six hours ago? Manfred was already pissing in the car of a Good Samaritan; he was already back to ruining Sam's life. There was no way his deal with Manfred would ever bear fruit. Manfred would break it and screw Sam over, yet again.

He remembered some advice to teachers he randomly came across: Don't argue with a bad kid. If you argue, you bestow legitimacy on the argument. Use few words. Entertaining Manfred with an argument was a bad move and simply encouraged more of the same. However, there was something he *could* do to Manfred, something he had never contemplated before, not once in his life. Dignity had prevented him from even conjuring the thought. But he was standing on the side of the road covered in piss. Dignity was nowhere to be found.

"No, Manfred, I won't unload a bunch of bullshit on everyone to get you surgically removed," Sam eventually said. "But I do have something for you. Call it a lesson."

Sam squatted down right there. Everything he was doing was unnatural, and he had to force it hard. He stayed in position, squeezing and grimacing for more than a minute before it finally happened. Then he stood up and started walking, his first steps awkward as he accustomed himself. It took Manfred a few more seconds to realize what Sam had done. Sam broke into a radiant, glowing smile.

"Sam!" Manfred screamed. "You took a shit in your pants! What in the world is wrong with you? Of all the twisted and revolting things to do!"

Sam reached down and adjusted the shit. It was a mushy one, and he pushed it forward in his underwear, smearing it right up there with Manfred. Manfred continued to scream. Sam continued to smile.

They walked along like that for about a mile. At one point, a car full of young people drove past and must have seen the shit outline in Sam's backside, because they honked and screamed/laughed something incoherent out the window. Sam responded with a triumphant fist pump into the air. *Yeah, fuck it*, he thought.

"Deal's off, Sam!" Manfred exclaimed furiously. "You'll never be with a woman. You'll die a virgin! Forget about it."

"Oh, the deal had no worth. You're such a bigoted moron, you couldn't even take a ride from a kind-hearted stranger. You'd get your damned baptism and that would be it: you'd be back to your old ways. At least the baptism is off the table, too. We'll burn in Hell together, my friend."

After another half hour of walking in shitty, pissy pants, the truck stop sign appeared in the distance, on the outskirts of a small town. He had gotten his revenge on Manfred and had no regrets, but with the truck stop right there, he wondered what the hell the plan was. He might get arrested again if he walked in there covered in piss and shit. There had to be a law against that sort of thing, right? He quickly figured he would play it as if he was ill. People *are* allowed to get sick, even in public.

He had stopped at the truck stop enough times to know it included a convenience store with a gift shop. T-shirts would be on sale, and if he was lucky, perhaps shorts and flip-flops. He thought he remembered seeing showers in the back, but he had never gone back there because, well, that area was for truckers.

Before re-entering civilization, Sam decided to clean himself to the best of his earthly possibilities, using whatever resources available, even if those resources consisted of leaves and twigs. He hid behind some trees about 100 yards away from the road, in a little oasis of serenity. He pulled off his jeans and underwear. Most of the stink went with the underwear as it plopped heavily on the ground, but he knew that he had to put the jeans back on, and they were still smelly and discolored. Putting the shoes back on would also be emotionally taxing.

Sam looked to his backpack for ideas. He felt stupid for having left his dirty clothes at home. But as he was holding his backpack, he heard a scrunching sound as he fingered something in the side pocket. He opened the pocket and found an array of ketchup and mustard packets from a fast-food restaurant. It seemed like those packets had always been with him. He couldn't remember where he got them, or his backpack without them.

Sam used a cleaner section of one of his socks, squirting the ketchup and mustard onto the sock, rubbing the concoction into his pants, and then wiping off the excess. Manfred congratulated him on "jewing out" at that fast-food restaurant and hoarding the free stuff; Sam ignored both the insult and the backhanded compliment. By the time he put the jeans back on, the red and yellow combined into a dark orange, covering the brown. The smell of condiments at least partially counteracted the smell of shit, as best he could tell—then again, he had been around the smell long enough that perhaps he was becoming numb to it.

"You're leaving your shitty underwear and socks here?" Manfred asked.

Sam laughed at Manfred for suddenly being concerned about littering. Maybe he had grown close to that particular pair of underwear and couldn't bear the thought of saying goodbye.

"I'll get a bag and come back for them," Sam said, more for his own benefit than Manfred's. But as he turned his back on his discarded, disgusting clothes, he looked around nervously. He experienced a frightening sensation, one of being watched. Being watched and laughed at. It was one of the creepiest feelings he had ever felt. After he applied some critical reasoning, Sam discarded the thought. Hiding behind the trees, away from the road and truck stop, no one could be watching him unless it was through binoculars. Was he really interesting enough to warrant that effort? Probably not.

He stepped out from behind the trees and walked to the truck stop.

CHAPTER 14

Even as he walks along the road, the fool lacks sense and shows everyone how stupid he is. (Ecclesiastes 10:3)

Sam needed to be light on his feet without letting anyone learn the true nature of his state. From a distance, it looked like he had gotten sick and thrown up all over himself—not an ideal thing for people to think, but better than the truth. Close proximity would reveal the vomit to be a fine mélange of ketchup, mustard, urine, and shit. He had to move fluidly, flowing from aisle to aisle quickly to avoid human contact, as if he was Pac Man and the other shoppers were the carnivorous ghosts. He could almost hear the dot-eating sounds from the game—*waka waka waka waka waka.*

After the events of the last few days, Sam wondered if this was how he'd spend the rest of his life.

He tried to go to the T-shirt aisle first, only to have someone else walk over before he had a chance to peruse the inventory. He slipped away and pretended to examine the beef jerky options. He feigned reading the list of ingredients on a package, shaking his head in an exaggerated fashion, as if he found something offensive among the myriad of unpronounceable chemicals. An older woman came over to find some beef jerky. He would have liked to stay and tell her, with a straight face, to avoid one specific brand because it contains monosodium glutamate, which may or may not be a real concern. But that would have to wait until he wasn't covered in shit, so instead he slipped away to the sunglass rack.

The T-shirt aisle cleared up and he glided back there, taking detours as needed to avoid other customers. He knew he didn't have much time because someone might meander over at any moment, so he quickly scanned the options. The first several shirts seemed nice enough, with forgettable images, but all were size small. Sam, being a somewhat smaller-than-average man, always wore extra-large shirts because, for some illogical reason, large was always too tight. He had no idea what biological species the small size was designed to fit.

So he kept looking. The first shirt he found in a reasonable size was an extra-large with an image of Justin Bieber. Then there was a 2X-large shirt with a crass cartoon including a giant chicken, a drunk man, and three women with enormous boobs. There was text on it, in huge font obnoxiously proclaiming ... oh, who gave a shit what it said. Another customer started walking over, forcing Sam to make a snap decision. Was wearing a Justin Bieber shirt designed for adult men really an option? He decided not, so he picked the crass one. Sam figured he was better off looking like a generic college asshole than an adult male with a Justin Bieber fixation.

Some flip flops were available, and he selected a pair appearing close to his size. Pants were harder to find, but he wasn't picky under the circumstances. He settled for a pair of bright blue shorts a few waist sizes too small. He would have liked to search longer for something in his size, but noticed there were no customers at the cash register, so he figured he needed to check out while the window of opportunity was open.

The clerk, a lanky young man with a goatee, gave Sam the same expression Sam would have given if their positions were reversed. Sam flashed an apologetic smile as he put the clothes on the counter.

Obviously trying to avoid looking directly at Sam, the clerk rang up the purchases and said, "That will be $38.47."

Sam pulled out his wallet, hesitated, and said, "Um, as you can see, I got a little sick and couldn't pull over in time. May I rent a shower?"

The guy had the courtesy to look abashed, even if he was probably thinking *I see vomit, but what I smell is piss and shit.* He explained, "I'm sorry, *sir*, but the showers are for members of our trucker network only. I'd like to help you, but I could get in trouble." The clerk did seem sincerely sorry, even if he did twitch while trying to maintain a straight face when saying the word "sir."

Sam didn't bother trying to argue or plead; he had a better plan. He pulled out the money the Hindu man wouldn't accept and placed it on the counter. The clerk stared at the cash for a few seconds, turned around, grabbed a key from a hook below the array of cigarette boxes behind him, and placed it on the counter in front of Sam. He took the cash and put it in the cash register, pulling out change and stuffing it into his own pocket.

Never had a shower felt so good. It was so pleasant and refreshing it almost made the prior suffering worthwhile. Almost.

He felt like a new man until he had to put on those dumb clothes. The shorts were even tighter than they looked in the gift shop; they may as well been spandex. He was grateful for the 2X-large shirt, which was so huge it draped over the shorts. Most importantly, with Sam not wearing any underwear, the shirt did a good job of obscuring Manfred's camel toe equivalent. It was a truly embarrassing shirt, though. He never wore things like this. He felt like the cartoon titties were crawling all over him, yelling *"I'm a stupid asshole! Hey everybody, look at me, I'm a stupid asshole!"*

He went out to the sink area to comb his hair with his fingers in front of the mirror, and he deposited his old clothes and shoes in the trash. Another man was at the sink, shirtless, grooming his full beard. He was tall, thick, and covered in hair and tattoos. He had a long, graying ponytail and deep facial creases that were the result of a life spent outdoors. A bit of a gut hung over his belt, partially covering the belt buckle below a dark "treasure trail" of hairs leading to his pubic area.

"Hey brother, how's it going? Whoa, those shorts are some ballcrushers. That's the only size they had?" the man was far friendlier than he looked, the friendliness belied by his deep, somewhat hoarse voice.

Sam wasn't in the mood to converse, but he didn't have much choice in the matter, so he responded, "Yeah, this is the only pair they had." He didn't say anything further, lest he provide any conversational bait.

"Not a good day, huh?" the man asked.

It was way too open-ended a question, the sort of thing that may trap him in a long discussion. Sam thought for a second, then came up with the response he thought most likely to deter additional conversation. "Well, not the greatest, but it's okay."

"You're managing to crawl off the shitheap?" This was the most sincere bit of sympathy Sam heard in days. But Sam was too slow to realize he needed to say yes and be on his way, and the man understood the answer to be no, saying, "If you're feeling alone, and without options, you just need to know one thing: It's all an illusion."

That was not what Sam expected. "An illusion?" he asked.

"All of it. The boundaries between people. You think your name is whatever your name is, but it's not. You have many names and not one. Boundaries are an illusion. We're all the same. Humanity is One."

"Okay."

"No boundaries?" said Manfred. "There's going to be no boundaries between your mouth and this guy's cock in about five minutes, Sam. This is a truck stop. You know what goes on here! Get out. Get out while you still can!"

"The bad things happening now don't matter in the end," the man was continuing. "None of it is real. I learned all about it when I took some LSD a long time ago, but it all made sense after the trip, too. Learn to accept that it doesn't matter, and everything will be okay for you. But in the meanwhile, if you need anything, I'll help in whatever way I can. Do you need some money or something?"

Sam and Manfred were temporarily of one mind, Manfred screaming something along the lines of, "he's offering you a quick and easy way to earn a little bit of money!" and Sam more-or-less in agreement.

"Thanks a lot, but I need to go!" Sam quickly said. He snatched his backpack and headed straight for the door. He left the truck stop through a side exit. He took one glance back to make sure the man wasn't following him.

After a minute or so, he realized the guy was probably nice. Most likely, he was a cool person to talk to, and may have been sharing an interesting perspective. Their encounter was almost certainly *not* the beginning of a sexual solicitation. But Manfred's warning made sense at the time, whereas what the man was saying didn't make any sense at all. Score one for Manfred.

Sam found himself near a line of parked trucks with varying designs on their trailers. Near the back of the parking lot, away from the main road, stood a trio of scantily clad women. *I guess those would be the lot lizards*, Sam thought, using a term he was pretty sure he had never spoken aloud. Sam laughed to himself, then turned back to the main road and followed it into town. He needed to find someplace with a phone, so that he could call his mom.

CHAPTER 15

*I have given thee cow's dung for man's dung, and thou
shalt prepare thy bread therewith. (Ezekiel 4:15)*

His outfit was embarrassing, but at least he wasn't covered in piss
and shit. That was pretty good, these days.

A couple of small shops and restaurants constituted the town,
if you could call it a town. He stopped for a late lunch, sitting
by the window while he ate a sandwich. He figured he'd ask to
use the phone after he paid for the meal. But as he sat eating, he
noticed something interesting down the road: a used car lot. He
remembered the cash he had withdrawn from the bank. He didn't
have much money, but if he could find something within his price
range, that would somehow be preferable to asking his mom for
help. He finished his lunch and walked over to the lot.

As he perused the rows of available cars, he was disappointed
to see the lowest asking prices were around $5,000, out of his price
range. He would be forced to call his mother, after all.

He was about to admit defeat when a salesman walked out of the office and approached him, a middle-aged black man wearing a cream-colored dress shirt and a royal blue tie.

"Oh, look! That guy has a job," Manfred said.

"Most black people have jobs. What is your point?" Sam silently said to Manfred. To the salesman he said, "Hi. I'm looking for something cheap."

"I was just pointing out he has a job, is all. Like, an actual job where he makes money, instead of waiting around for government handouts. Good for him," Manfred offered.

"Hi, my name is Vince," the salesman said. "Welcome! We have some fantastic cars ready to go at blow-out prices." Vince pointed to the cars Sam had already browsed, well out of his price range.

"Do you point out every gainfully employed white man you see?" Sam silently asked Manfred. He said aloud to Vince, "Yeah, everything is too expensive for me."

"Out of your range? That's too bad. Well, we do have some cheaper stuff in the back. Come with me," Vince said.

"I don't need anything fancy. It just needs to run, honestly. I don't need a radio, I don't need air conditioning. I'd take a Pinto. I mean, if any of those run anymore."

"You don't need to get all riled up about it," Manfred said. "I'm happy for this guy. He's probably not even on food stamps. That's really good for him." Sam decided it would be wise to ignore Manfred's bait from here on out.

Sam followed Vince around to the back, where the variety of cars in the front lot gave way to uniformity. A line of about fifteen PT Cruisers assaulted Sam's eyes. Different colors, but the same car otherwise.

"We get a lot of people trading-in PT Cruisers," Vince explained, "so they're relatively cheap. You know: supply and demand."

Sam walked around and read one of the stickers, revealing a $3,000 asking price. Getting closer, but not there yet. He had taken out $1,500, spent $150 at the truck stop, and bought lunch. Leaving some margin for other short-term expenses, he figured he had about $1,250 to spend.

"Well, Vince, this is certainly closer to my price range, but we're not there yet. I can only afford about a thousand dollars."

Vince clapped and stomped his feet. "Well, that doesn't leave you with too many options, friend! In fact, it leaves you with precisely one option."

"There's something cheaper than a PT Cruiser?" Sam asked.

"No, we don't have anything cheaper than a PT Cruiser," Vince replied. "But there's one turkey, one PT Cruiser that's cheaper than the rest. You can snag it now before it gets shipped to auction. The best thing I can say about it—which I've got to say shocked me—is that apparently no one smoked in it."

Sam followed Vince to a PT Cruiser the likes of which he had never seen. The various dents in the body were jarring, but most distinctive was the paint job: matte black with large flames on the side. Who the hell paints a PT Cruiser with crudely-rendered flames? It was the aesthetic equivalent of a prison tattoo … well, actually, it was devoid of the standard level of artistry you'd find in jail.

"It's all yours for one thousand dollars," Vince said.

"It runs?"

"It runs. And it only has about 120,000 miles on it. Really, that's not so bad. It has an almost full tank of gas, too. Big chunk of your value right there: nice, full gas tank."

"Okay," said Sam.

"You want a test drive?" Vince asked. His tone indicated he was hoping Sam would say no.

"No," Sam replied.

"I don't blame you," Vince said. "Why don't you come with me and see what you can get for $4,000? We have reasonable loan programs. You'll be surprised at how easy it is to get some decent wheels."

"No, you misunderstood. I'll take this one for $1000," Sam said.

"Really? Have you driven a PT Cruiser before?" Vince seemed skeptical.

"Uh, yeah," Sam quickly lied.

"And you liked driving it?" Vince seemed even more skeptical.

"Sure," Sam responded.

"And you like the paint job?" Vince had the look of a man who had just met an alien or Bigfoot.

"Flames never go out of style," Sam kept as straight a face as he could manage.

Vince gave him a considering look. Sam imagined Vince must be wondering if he knew about some stash of drugs or money hidden in the car. It certainly seemed like the kind of car involved in criminal activity. Maybe Vince was trying to figure out how to get a chance to search the car for the stash before selling it, but there was nothing he could do now.

After a few moments of looking back and forth between Sam and the car, Vince finally said, "Well, I just want to make certain you understand what you're getting into. If you change your mind quickly, I can apply your purchase price to a better car. Come to the office, sir!"

The paperwork moved smoothly and quickly—paying in cash made this sort of thing simpler—and Sam ignored the repetitive, offensive comments that Manfred was making, such as, "well, we did our part to keep one family out of public housing for another day." With taxes and other fees, Sam ended up paying all but a hundred dollars of his remaining cash, but at least he had functioning transportation. Vince handed Sam the keys, which came on a keychain with a flame carved in some silvery metal, and Sam walked out to his new, very used car.

It took Sam thirty seconds to figure out why so many used PT Cruisers were for sale. In theory, a retro design was neat, at least to Sam's taste, but intelligent planning still needed to apply. What was up with these enormous blind spots? He was frightened by his lack of visibility. Sam wondered how it was even legal. Why did anyone buy this vehicle? After all, not everyone purchased cars without a test drive the way he just did.

Oh well, he'd simply have to adjust and learn to drive more cautiously.

"It's nice to be on our way again," Manfred said. "And I really like this car," he added without a hint of sarcasm.

"Yeah, I figured you'd like it," Sam said. "The moment I saw it, I thought it had *Manfred* written all over." Sam turned left, back into town.

"Sam, I can see through our shared eye input you just turned the wrong way. We're going back to school, aren't we? School is to the right. But you turned left, no?"

"We're going back to school, but we have one stop to make first," Sam said. "Remember, we need to pick up our shitty underwear."

"Oh come on," Manfred complained. "I was kidding! Let's just get out of here."

"You may have been kidding, but I wasn't. We're going to clean up our mess," Sam said. He pulled into the parking lot of the truck stop.

CHAPTER 16

*Whoever believes and is baptized will be saved, but who-
ever does not believe will be condemned. (Mark 16:16)*

Manfred did not seem happy about returning to the truck stop.
Sam parked far away from the building, at the end of the parking
lot closest to his shit-encrusted underwear.

"Don't worry, Manfred, this will only take a minute," Sam said.
"We'll grab the socks and underwear, bring them to this trashcan"—he pointed to a trashcan at the perimeter of the parking
lot—"and we're back on our way."

Manfred sighed and said, "All right, Sam, but if we see that
fag truck driver who tried to get you to suck his dick, we run and
get out of here."

As he started walking to the bushes where he left his underwear and socks, Sam replied, "Does it ever end with you? First of
all, he didn't strike me as gay, and if he was, I don't think he was
soliciting anything. He was only trying to cheer me up."

"He was trying to get you to suck his cock," Manfred interjected. "Sucking his cock won't make you feel better."

"Second," Sam said, stepping on Manfred's words, "there's nothing wrong with being gay."

"Oh, Sam. I can't believe we're having this conversation yet again," Manfred said. At least they agreed on one thing. "You and I both know homosexuality is a sin. It says so all over the Bible."

"The Bible also says eating shellfish is a sin," Sam said.

"Have you ever seen me eat shellfish?" Manfred asked.

"I concede that point, but I've never heard you go on tirades about how eating shellfish is contrary to God's laws, either."

"Well, anyway," Manfred said, "You need to understand going gay is *not* an option."

"Hey, man, I'm the one who tried to get it on with Anne. I were the one who went batshit and pissed all over her. I think your only complaint about that trucker is you thought he wanted *me* to suck *his* dick and not the other way around."

Manfred seemed stunned. "I did not want that man's mouth on me!"

Sam shrugged and responded, "You couldn't stand the idea of going near a woman, but you didn't have a problem with a guy jerking off next to me. Also, you always want to be rubbed by my man hands." Manfred didn't respond, and Sam continued the attack. Accusing Manfred of being gay was rapidly becoming one of his favorite pastimes. "So my real question is, how do we get you to be okay with being gay? I should take you to a gay conversion camp, only in reverse, where they convince you it's okay to be who you are: a giant flaming homosexual."

They arrived at the patch of trees. He didn't need to remember which tree. He followed his nose. Sam realized he hadn't brought a plastic bag, so he had to improvise. He picked up a stick from the ground and fished it through a leg hole in the underwear and under one of the socks. He picked up a second stick and hooked the other sock. He carefully stood up, holding the sticks far away from his body, and headed back to the truck stop.

Beating the dead horse some more, Manfred said, "Sam, if I was gay, why would I hate gays? Do you think I hate myself? That's stupid."

"Yes. Yes, that's exactly it," Sam replied. "You live in someone's pants, a few inches away from a butthole, and you hate yourself. So you reneged on our deal. Wait, I know! We can take turns. Let's be bisexual."

"It sounds like *you're* the one trying to add men into the mix, Sam," Manfred managed to say through guffaws. "I reneged on the deal because you shit on me. That doesn't mean I'm gay. Let's go find Anne and I'll prove it to you. I'm *All-Man*, the real deal. I'm the one who wants to nail the chicks. You're the one who wants to cultivate relationships and lame-ass shit like that."

Sam wondered where all the Bible stuff was now. Like an inconvenient pile of dust, it seemed to be swept away.

"You're only saying that because you know she'll never have me," Sam said.

A young couple coming out of the truck stop watched curiously as Sam carried the sticks conveying his underwear and socks to the trashcan and dropped them in. They continued to stare at him all the way back to their car, but he didn't care what those people thought. At that moment, his path was clear. He knew exactly what he needed to do. He wasn't looking forward to it, but it had to happen.

Sam climbed in his car and started the engine. But instead of the main road, he drove to the back of the parking lot.

"Sam, tell me we're not looking for that fag truck driver," Manfred said. "Please, please tell me that."

"No, that's not who we're looking for," Sam said simply.

He drove past a line of parked trucks, to the very back of the lot, to where he had seen the lot lizards. They were still there, all three of them, standing under a pavilion apparently built for exactly this purpose. Sam assumed that Sunday afternoons were a slow period, but like Taco Bell, the lot lizard pavilion was probably open just about any time.

Two of the women were white and the third was black. Sam thought he might like to pick the black one, to put Manfred to the maximal test, but one of the white ones reached his car first. She didn't move quickly, given her six- or seven-inch heels, but she was fast enough to win the race with her co-workers.

"Sam, come on, what are you doing?" Manfred said nervously. "We both know you're not picking up a prostitute. What would Anne think? Come on! Let's not waste time. We still have a long drive ahead of us."

It was the combination of the towering stilettos with the tight, short shorts that made her profession obvious. A small bandanna was wrapped around her breasts. Sam had the sex drive of a normal 20 year old, yet he found her presentation to be thoroughly unappealing. Not even on a primal, "go catch the rabbit and eat it" level, did he find her remotely attractive.

Regardless, he had to press on with his plan. This shit with Manfred would go on and on until he took a stand. Being his usual self wasn't working. Doing something so completely out of character was exciting and he anticipated it would bring about progress in his life. He had been stuck in some sort of time loop, repeating the same actions and the same mistakes over and over. Now he was finally breaking the cycle, with *new* mistakes. He had never been so scared in his life.

"You looking to party?" she asked, leaning in.

You looking to party? Sam repeated to himself. Is that really what a prostitute would say? Like, in real life? He adopted his best deadpan tone as he replied. "Yeah. Yeah, I'm looking to party." *Right here at 3:00 on a Sunday afternoon. What a partier I am*, thought Sam. *A wild and crazy partier.*

"Nice car, baby, you've got hot style," she added. He had no idea if she was being sarcastic or sincere. She was leaning halfway into the car, and Sam got a closer look at her frayed, crimped, bleached blond hair—hair that had seen no end to cosmetic abuse and suggested nutritional deficits. He was mildly curious if this woman was good looking or not. It was impossible to know under the layers of sun damage, caked makeup and ridiculous clothes.

This was such a bad idea, such a colossus of a bad idea—and that made it worthwhile, so he could force a change in his pattern.

"Sam, are you sure you want to do this with *her*? Let's go to school, find Anne …"

"You'll do this *now*, Manfred, and you're going to give me peace!" Sam snapped.

"I'll give you a piece, but who's Manfred?" the prostitute asked. Sam had been terrible about speaking to Manfred aloud these last few days. "I don't do no bulk discounts. You're both paying full price. Eighty bucks each." She was peering into the back of the PT Cruiser and looking for the second guy Sam had been talking to.

"Well, ma'am, Manfred is my penis. He's been a really, *really* bad boy." Manfred made a loud, extended noise like he was choking on something.

"He's a bad boy, is he? Well, we better teach him a lesson," she said.

"Oh, we sure will teach him a lesson!" Sam responded.

Sam handed her $80, thinking he probably could have negotiated her down to $45 or less. Manfred would have been even more horrified by a lengthy debate about how much sex should cost; he wished he had haggled.

"What's your name?" Sam asked.

"Cat. I'm Cat," she said. "What's yours?"

"Sam." He immediately regretted not coming up with some alias. "Ok, well, let's do this."

She gave a considering look at the car. Sam assumed she was trying to figure out where they'd do it. Most of her clientele had sleeping cabs in their trucks. She said, "Come on and take me for a drive." With that, she walked around the front of the car and opened the passenger door. The door stuck for a second, because the car was a piece of shit, but she was able to jerk it open.

"I can't believe you're letting that creature in the car!" Manfred wailed.

"Well, next time you see someone like Anne, perhaps you'll have some appreciation," he responded with resolution. Cat plunked down on the passenger seat. An urgent thought entered Sam's mind. "Listen, if I do anything weird, I'll pay extra." (He quickly realized that was somewhat ridiculous, as he possessed about fifteen bucks.)

"Weird like what, baby?"

"Like ... if I can't get it up, or if I pee or something. It wouldn't be much pee, though. But if it's anything, I'll pay extra. It would only be one of those two things."

"I can roll with that," she said as if getting peed on happened more often than not. "So, what exactly do ya wanna do?"

What did he want to do? Get her the hell out of the car: that's what he wanted to do. Go eat pancakes with his mom. How do people have sex with prostitutes, anyway? Sam supposed it probably got easier with experience. But it would require a lot of nerve, alcohol, and/or peer pressure to get over that first wall protecting someone against their own bad judgment. Not to mention, he found her more-or-less revolting. But, he was sticking to it. Hell, he had already paid her.

"Well? What do you say? Whatcha wanna do?"

"Um, I don't know," he answered. She stared at him and in turn, he stared at the ground.

"Never done anything like this before?"

"Nope."

"And you seemed so sophisticated! You've got the flames going and all, looking badass in this car." He couldn't recall ever being referred to as sophisticated or badass, and certainly never both at the same time.

"How about you just drive and I'll take care of you," she finally said. It was a relief to be instructed what to do, because Sam's brain had gotten tired of being ignored and had essentially turned itself off.

He started the car and drove away. Without saying anything, she unsnapped his seat belt to get a better position. Normally he would have objected to this —what if a cop saw or they had an accident—but with his brain off, he was putty. Terrified putty. Manfred hadn't said anything in a while. Sam sensed the raw, speechless terror radiating out of him.

Fortunately, she didn't dally. Her hand started rubbing Sam's too-tight shorts and it didn't take long before Manfred began to respond. She might be hard on the eyes, but at least she knew what she was doing. She used her free hand to turn on the radio and she navigated to an easy listening station, rhythmically stroking him to the strained sounds of Amy Grant.

Things slowed down when she tried to pry off his shorts. She must have expected they'd just slip off, but, as tight as they were, they may as well been fused to his legs. It took a long time, and Manfred was starting to soften up by the time she finally managed to pull them off. Then, after she got Manfred hard again with more rubbing, she bent over. He wasn't quite sure how she was able to contort in that way, but there she was, Manfred deep in her mouth.

It wasn't easy to pay attention to the road, but traffic was light. He was trying to find a place to pull over, because this was getting pretty intense. Was it this good because she was a professional, or despite that? For all he knew, a blow-up doll or a Japanese robot might feel equally good. Maybe.

It didn't stop. She had an ability his hand didn't, to keep him on the brink of orgasm without getting there. Manfred seemed to agree. After his initial terror, he seemed to be enjoying it. Sam imagined a new, entirely different future, one with an obnoxious-as-all-hell Manfred with a *brand new* set of constant, asinine demands and only sporadic religion.

Sam became aware of the new song playing on the radio—the Starland Vocal Band doing *Afternoon Delight*. On a normal day, he'd risk a car accident to get it off the radio. But now, of all the freaking times for that song to come on, he absolutely *had* to get rid of it. The incredible newness of everything going on—and now this awful song—was overwhelming.

His brain wasn't connecting to his arm in the normal way, and he flailed out in a blind, zombie-like manner toward the radio, hitting the power button with the backside of his hand. Mission awkwardly accomplished. She apparently interpreted his motion as an ecstatic one and, without missing a beat, squeezed and pulled with her lips to play into it. He reeled, involuntarily closing his eyes, jerking the steering wheel, and jamming his foot into the gas pedal as the PT Cruiser rounded a curve on an embankment. The car plowed straight through the guard rail and over the edge. It must have done several flips as it rolled down a steep hill. In the midst of terror he felt a sharp pain like nothing he experienced before, reaching peak intensity when the car crashed into the ground.

Everything was pain. The scene in front of him was blurry, but then came into focus. They had apparently been partially thrown from the car. Or, part of the car had disintegrated around them. Sam wasn't sure.

Sam couldn't move, but saw the prostitute in front of him. She had a large quantity of blood dripping down her chin and neck, and she seemed to half-vomit something bloody out of her mouth. She stared at whatever it was in horror, and then she looked at Sam. She returned her eyes to whatever she spat up. "That's the most fucked up thing I ever saw," she cried. With that, she left and started crawling up the embankment, a long gash dripping blood along the side of her arm but otherwise apparently unscathed.

Reality hit home. The pain was too all-consuming to assign it to a specific body part, but the bloody object she had spat up was

Manfred. Her teeth must have cut right through him when they crashed. The pain multiplied as he tried to turn his head to look down. There, instead of Manfred, was a fountain of blood. He used his hand to try to staunch the flow of blood, but it bubbled up through his fingers.

He had no idea how long he lay there, bleeding and suffering intense pain. All sense of time was lost. He feebly tried to call for help, but it came out as a soft, pitiful cry. No one was anywhere nearby. He started feeling cold. Freezing cold. The only thought he could assemble in his mind was, *I should have just called my mother ...*

Sam was fading in and out of consciousness. He couldn't be sure if what he saw was real or not. Two creatures of some sort were standing near him. They were between seven and eight feet tall. They had red, bumpy skin, with large horns coming out of their foreheads. When one opened its mouth he saw long, sharp fangs. *What the hell ...?*

Sam didn't know what to call them except demons ... they were *demons.*

One of the demons stayed at a distance. It seemed to be dancing around, holding a pitchfork, its pointed tail whipping around as it leaped about happily and skipped in a circle.

The other demon stepped up to Sam, towering over him, and it said in a menacing, deep voice, "Welcome to Hell, Sam." It cackled and added, "Now you roast in the Lake of Fire forever with the Dark One!" It poked him lightly with its pitchfork, just a little prod. "*You* should have accepted Jesus Christ. You *should* have been baptized."

It took all Sam's energy to roll his head away from the demon, and he saw Manfred suspended in the air in a column of bright golden light. As he watched, Manfred ascended into the sky, following the light up to a scene of pure white clouds against a blue sky, and a beautiful, ornate gate in front of a city of light. Harp music was playing and Sam heard a booming voice say, "Manfred, come to me, my son. You were baptized … in your heart. Sit beside me in Heaven." Sam watched as Manfred continued to glide into the heavenly scene above.

But in front of Sam was darkness. Darkness and demons.

Sam moaned, "Manfred … going to … Heaven?" He couldn't believe it. Was there no justice? "Manfred … is … bad. He has … no morals …"

Sam didn't know if any sound was actually coming out of his mouth, but the demons seemed to hear. "Why … me?"

"What can't you understand?" one of the demons thundered, extending his arm with incredulity. "Manfred accepted Our Lord Jesus Christ. *That* is what matters. That is *all* that matters. Salvation is given. It is not earned. You wretched fool! All you needed to do was to accept, and you didn't. Now: you burn." The other demon was doubled-over, laughing.

Sam couldn't make sound. He was numb now, and the demons kept poking him with their pitchforks. He was vaguely aware of one demon pointing at Manfred, absurd as he approached the bejeweled golden gate, severed and alone. The demons looked at each other, and then back at Manfred. They seemed surprised by something.

The last thing Sam saw was Manfred reaching the pearly gates and disappearing in a flash of light. When the light was gone, there was nothing but darkness.

Sam and Manfred were dead.

CHAPTER 17

Beloved, do not believe every spirit, but test the spirits to see whether they are from God, for many false prophets have gone out into the world. (First John 4:1)

What a beautiful wedding. Everything had been perfect.

Mary rolled over on her side to look at Bob, sleeping next to her. It had been an amazing night. She fell asleep happy and content.

At some point in the night, she woke up with a start. It was in the room. That evil spirit-demon-thing had returned. Like a terrified small child, she pulled her head under the covers. *As long as it can't see my face, I won't provoke it. It will go away, it will go away, it will go away*, she thought. It was only inches away from her face. She could feel its rage.

This wasn't the first time the evil spirit-demon-thing had harassed her. It came the first night she was with Bob, and again on the day she picked out her wedding dress. Both times, it lingered there, seemingly hanging over her. She couldn't see it, but she could *feel* it. All she could do was cower, and hope it would go away on its own. She didn't understand what it wanted.

It seemed to take forever to go away this time. Finally, she realized the presence was gone. She pulled her head out from under the covers. Everything looked perfectly normal.

Was she crazy? If she was just scared in the dark, wouldn't that tall lamp in the corner look like an alien? Wouldn't the tree branches outside the window, and the strange shadows they made against the walls, look like a looming monster? No. None of those things were the source of her fear and she wasn't crazy.

The next morning, she was tempted to ask Bob if he had also felt the demonic presence in the room. But she didn't want her new husband to think she was nuts. He already knew about her near-death experience. No need to pile it on; she better keep this one a secret.

PART TWO

CHAPTER 18

Love is patient, love is kind. It does not envy, it does not boast, it is not proud. It is not rude, it is not self-seeking, it is not easily angered, it keeps no record of wrongs. Love does not delight in evil but rejoices in the truth. It always protects, always trusts, always hopes, always perseveres. (First Corinthians, 13:4-7)

He was one of the petals. The petals were lighter than air. He was twirling and dancing, folding and unfolding, and glistening with velvety soft dew. Everything was peaceful, calm, warm, and devoid of worry. A gentle breeze lifted him into the air. He was flying without sound or effort, taking in the beach, the water, the forest below, in dazzling color.

Some of the flowers were still with him, and now he could hear laughter, clear and bright—pure, happy laughter. The flower petals danced together in a circle, twirling along, not touching each other but somehow feeling closer than any physical touch, bright and cheerful in the sky, hundreds of yards in the air, unafraid. Below, the sand on the beach played tricks with his eyes. Sometimes pink, sometimes golden, always lovely. He and the other petals glided downwards. At one point he said, "Wheeeee!" and the other petals responded, some echoing, some laughing, all radiating happiness.

He landed on the beach with a gentle bounce. He inspected the colors of the grains more closely, each with hundreds of glistening facets as if through a microscope, making the scene even more spectacular.

Viewed from above, the beach had been breathtaking. Viewed intimately, the grains of sand boasted individuality, no two the same. He wanted to look at each one, learn each one's name, suddenly certain that each one indeed had a name. There must have been billions of them on the beach, all precious and special. *Meet them all, meet them all*, he thought. Time was not of consequence. It would be perfect forever.

He was absorbed in exploring the sand when a voice asked, "Do you want to know the truth?" It was a matter-of-fact voice but not unkind. It was simply a voice asking a question. He didn't answer. He didn't want anything to interrupt this moment.

His silence was apparently answer enough, because he was allowed to continue to explore the sand. One of the petals morphed into a bubble before his eyes. He laughed happily, and he became a bubble, too, and where he had been dancing with petals, he was now dancing with bubbles, bouncing up and down on the ground. The bubbles would bump into each other harmlessly and affectionately, laugh, and then land on the ground where the individual grains of sand awaited them.

He had no idea how much time had elapsed, but the voice repeated, "Do you want to know the truth now?" Then it added, "There's nothing to fear."

This may be paradise, but Sam knew it was time. "Yes," he said, and the beach and bubbles faded from sight.

CHAPTER 19

Listen, I tell you a mystery: we will not all sleep, but we will all be changed—in a flash, in the twinkling of an eye, at the last trumpet. For the trumpet will sound, the dead will be raised imperishable, and we will be changed. (First Corinthians 15:51-52)

Sam woke in a bright room. He was lying on a soft bed, propped on a giant pillow. Opening his eyes was hard. Everything was blurry, but slowly came into focus. He didn't see any furniture and the walls were stark white.

I must be in a hospital, he thought. He struggled in vain to remember why he would be in a hospital.

He saw a figure across the room. Sam knew he couldn't yet trust his eyes, but the figure appeared to be floating in the air. He stared at the floating man, squinting, trying to dissect what had to be an optical illusion. A voice said his name from the other direction.

"Welcome, Sam," the voice said. "It's wonderful to see you, young man."

His creaky body struggled to roll over. After flipping around he saw a man, probably in his mid-20s. He was decades younger than Sam was accustomed to seeing him in the framed portrait in his room, but Sam recognized him instantly. He was George Washington Carver.

Obviously it was a hallucination because George Washington Carver was long dead, but here he was, 20-something and shaking Sam's hand. Sam's confusion at the sheer impossibility of the situation was pushed aside by his feeling of inadequacy. How could he have a conversation with George Washington Carver? What could he possibly say that this genius would find interesting? He stared dumbly.

Fortunately, Carver broke the silence. "I wanted to thank you for your admiration. I'm flattered someone of your generation took such an interest in the story of my life."

Again, Sam didn't know what to say. Maybe he should say *thank you*, or perhaps *you're welcome*. He was painfully aware of his inability to form words.

Carver's smile washed away the awkwardness and make Sam comfortable. "You will do very well here," he said. "Happiness and personal satisfaction will be yours. You will realize all your deepest, longest-held dreams. I wanted to be here for you now because your mother isn't here yet, nor is your friend Andy. For now, it is my pleasure to introduce you to Julio." Carver pointed behind Sam, in the direction of the figure that may or may not have been floating in the air.

"Julio has been assigned as your mentor and transfer agent," Carver explained. "Please request to see me if you need anything, anytime." He shook Sam's hand again and turned to walk away.

Before closing the door behind him, Carver turned back and said, "You're a good peanut, Sam." With that, he left the room and closed the door behind him.

Sam rolled back over to see the figure called Julio. Julio wore a cropped, neon-green shirt made of some kind of mesh, his midriff exposed. His black vinyl pants were tight, low-cut, and stopped mid-calf. He wasn't bothering with shoes. Sam almost laughed at the outfit, the most ridiculous he could remember, but this whole situation was too strange for him to laugh.

Julio walked over. *Walked over.* Sam must have been imagining things when he saw him floating. Maybe it was simply because the man was so tall. With his head seven feet above the ground, he might appear to be floating from a distance.

"Sam! Buddy! Here you are!" Julio said with a level of excitement no one had ever held for Sam before. Julio bent over for an awkward hug, his long arms wrapping around Sam, who was still lying in bed. Julio made a sound like "rahhhh" as he grasped Sam. It was an oddly welcoming sound. Julio seemed to know Sam, even if Sam sure as hell didn't know him.

Not knowing what else to do, Sam put his arm around Julio to return a cursory hug. As the hug ended and Julio pulled away, Sam found his head positioned right next to Julio's exposed belly.

"As your friend George mentioned, my name is Julio, and I'm your transfer agent!" Julio seemed excited about every word coming out of his mouth. Sam had never witnessed such enthusiasm. "You can think of me like a social worker, sort of employed by the State, if you will. I'm assigned to help you out and get you all set up here."

Julio plunked himself down on the foot of Sam's bed. "I'll just tell you straight-up what's going on, no riddles; I know you don't like riddles. Are you ready?" Julio grabbed Sam's feet and squeezed them. "It's the year 3542."

George Washington Carver? Funny dressed man? The year 3542?

"May 17, 3542. Yep, that is today's date. You are on Earth," Julio said, answering a question Sam *hadn't* been pondering. "Again, today is May 17, 3542. You're here because we kicked ass, Sam! We beat the shit out of the natural order of things, and humanity created its own afterlife and addressed all the wrongs of history. High-five!"

Julio held his hand palm-out for the high-five, but it was a bit too high for Sam to reach and he wasn't altogether prepared to reciprocate, anyway. Julio was frozen with a smile on his face for about ten seconds, his hand still extended for the unrequited gesture. Eventually he put his hand down, but his smile remained unchanged.

Sam finally formulated a reasonable question to ask. "I died?"

"Boy, did you ever!" Julio laughed. "We had so much fun with it, too."

All at once, images began flooding back into Sam's memory: the lot lizard, the car crash, the intense pain. He remembered seeing Manfred on the ground, followed by that pig bastard rising to the pearly gates in a pillar of light. Then he remembered the demons.

Sam stared at his hands. Covered in blood the last time he saw them, they were clean now. "Oh my God … I'm in Hell," he mumbled. He looked up at Julio, who was still smiling with a hint of laughter in his eyes. "I'm in Hell, aren't I?" he said louder. Then words failed him. He screamed and screamed.

And suddenly he was back on that beach, exploring the sand and bouncing and twirling with the friends he made there, his troubles forgotten. At some point, it started to rain ... happy rain. Each drop was an individual, tiny flower. When they landed near him, the rain-flowers would say "Hi" in the sweetest voices. He played with the rain-flowers until the rain stopped. After the rain, it was safe for a Pegasus—wait, make that a whole herd of flying horses and their adorable babies—to come out and dance and sing with Sam and the flowers. Sam became convinced he was in Heaven.

He was gliding next to a baby Pegasus who was just learning to fly, when the same voice that had asked him if he wanted to know the truth—the voice he now recognized as belonging to Julio— spoke. "Okay, so, this is our calming beach simulation, if you haven't guessed yet," the voice said patiently. "As awesome as it is, none of this is real. We're going to try again, and bring you back to what *is* real. Please don't freak out this time. You're not in Hell. Repeat: You are not in Hell. Everything is cool."

He was back in the bed and Julio was there.

The simulation worked. Sam was calm as he asked, "So, you said I'm not in Hell?"

"No, no, no. You're not in Hell," Julio said, waving his hand. "You'd be amazed how often I get asked that question. It's much more often than people ask if they're in Heaven. Like I said, it's the year 3542. Yes, you died. Yes, there's an afterlife. Yes, it's like Heaven. But no, it's not supernatural or spiritual or religious or anything along those lines. It's just straight-up science. Immediately before the moment of your death, we grabbed you, medically restored you, and brought you here."

"But, the demons ..."

"Yes, well, about that," Julio said, his smile somehow becoming even broader than it already was. "Well, we do love our practical jokes. You died, and there were no witnesses. Once the lot lizard, as you thought of her, crawled away, we were free to make the retrieval process, you know ... fun."

What the hell was he talking about? His death was a practical joke? Sam stared at Julio. There were no words for this scenario.

"It was perfect, wasn't it?" Julio effused. "Manfred was riding your ass about getting baptized, and you never did. Then you managed to die in a way that separated you from each other. It's not often a transfer agent gets this lucky. When I told Hans about it, he said we just *had* to have some fun. So we got some demon suits and pitchforks, and Hans created the overhead light with that sensational model of the mythical pearly gates. You saw the rest. Wasn't it impressive?"

Sam's brain slowly processed. "Repeat this for me again," he said. "What day is it?"

"It's May 17, 3542," Julio said, patiently.

"So, I've been dead for over 1500 years?"

"You always were so good at math," Julio said.

"I died in that accident with the prostitute? In that PT Cruiser?" For the first time, Sam realized how humiliating his death was. Partly because of a prostitute biting off his penis. Partly because of that idiotic T-shirt. Mostly because of that car.

"Oh, yeah," Julio said. "And I gotta say, if I had watched your life up until that day, I would've figured I'd be cleaning up some ugly suicide. I have to hand it to you, kid. You really managed to go out with style. Did I mention how much I loved the flames?"

As he listened to Julio speak, Sam had difficulty putting his finger on exactly what made Julio seem ... *off*. Of course, the cropped neon green mesh shirt and tight plastic pants were partially at fault, but it was more than that. It was several little things in the way Julio spoke. He didn't have any accent to speak of, but he stressed certain syllables in odd and unexpected ways. He would speak quickly and at length, but he never seemed to stop and take a breath. Whatever it was, Julio's speech seemed unnatural.

Sam studied the room. It was about as nondescript as a room could be, white and sterile, with nothing futuristic about it. It was empty, except for a bed, and the bed looked like an ordinary hospital bed.

"I still don't understand how I got here. How did I meet George Washington Carver? Was I frozen somehow? This is my real body, right? This is my hand, the hand I've always had? This is my arm? This is …" Sam trailed off. He had a penis, a normal penis with no teeth marks, but it wasn't Manfred. It was just a penis. "Where's Manfred?"

Julio had a gleam in his eye as he replied, "Don't worry. We're taking care of Manfred. He's on a different development path. You can meet with him later. He's fine, or as fine as usual. He's a piece of work!" Julio laughed again. "I admit: I didn't think Manfred was real; I thought you were crazy. We didn't understand until Manfred ascended to Heaven, and we saw the secondary set of brain waves. What a shocker! You know, it's fortunate we played that trick on you guys. If we hadn't, we probably would have missed him altogether."

Well, having a normal, non-talking penis was all he had ever wanted. But the whole situation wasn't computing.

"So how did I get here, to the year 3542?" Sam asked.

"Think about a photocopier. It makes a copy of an image on piece of paper. We have that on a sub-atomic level. Normally, we travel back to one trillionth-of-a-second *before* someone dies, and in that trillionth-of-a-second, we swap out the body with an atom-by-atom copy." Julio was making hand gestures as if they would help illustrate the concept.

"The copy has the exact DNA—every hair is in the right place—and no one would ever, ever detect a difference. Then we bring the real bodies to our medical unit and make them healthy and young. We usually de-age them to about 20 years old. You were easy, since you're already 20. Saved the de-aging machine some work. That stress-related zit was, like, your biggest issue. Well, and getting you a new dick. Oh, and new blood. You pretty much lost all your blood. But, yeah, you were easy."

Julio spoke so fast and it was hard to keep up. "There's life after death, because in a trillionth-of-a-second, people from the distant future swapped out my body with an identical copy, and brought me to their version of Heaven?" Sam summarized uncertainly.

"Yep. That's exactly how it works."

"You do that to everyone?"

"I don't know about *everyone*," Julio responded, "but most people, yes. At least, we're planning on getting most people. Someday, we'll work on animals, too."

"Where are you putting them all?" Sam asked. "I thought Earth was already getting tapped out on space and resources, and that didn't include everyone who had ever died."

"Duh, Sam. There are more planets in the universe than granules of sand on all the beaches of Earth," Julio said. He apparently felt the need to clarify, as if it were a grave point, "But the Earth has a few more grains of sand if you count the deserts."

Sam felt dumb, and limited in his perspective, to not immediately think of outer space and its trillions of empty planets.

"Would you like to hear the basic story?" Julio asked.

Sam nodded. He wanted to hear the story, even if there was no way he could keep up. Julio needed a throttle somewhere between his brain and his mouth.

"OK. Let's see, let's see, so much to tell!" Julio began. "Well, The Rapture started in the year 3539—that's what we call it, because we're funny like that—and since then we've been ..."

"The Rapture? Like, from the Bible, when Jesus resurrects the dead and brings them to Heaven? That Rapture?"

"Yes, that Rapture," Julio said rather dryly. "Things have been wild since the Rapture started. I specialize in people who died in your area of the planet between the years 2005 and 2015. One of my friends specializes in Ancient Egyptians. Another friend is focusing on the French Revolution, and I have another friend who only deals with people who died in November 2086: no one from any other year, no one from any other month, *only* people who died in November 2086. All these people, from all periods of history, are going plop, plop, plop, plop right here in 3542. We have soldiers who fought with Genghis Khan alongside flappers from the 1920s. So much vibrancy and diversity!"

"What the hell are you wearing?" Sam knew other questions had greater importance but he couldn't stop himself. The shirt in particular just didn't make any damned sense. Going shirtless or wearing a shirt that covered your torso: both of those concepts made sense. But why wear a shirt that only covered half a torso? The inexplicability of the shirt was a question Sam could wrap his mind around. All the deeper questions were beyond him.

"You like?" Julio responded, putting one hand on his hip while swishing at his attire from head to toe with the other hand.

"Um, it's funny. It's laugh-out-loud funny, if that's what you were going for."

Sam immediately regretted his response. He didn't want to offend Julio, after all. But the man didn't seem remotely offended. "Yeah! I like funny!" was his sole response.

"How old are you?" Sam continued in the vein of low-level, all-my-little-brain-can-process questioning.

"I was born 281 years ago." Sam took a good, close look at Julio. He couldn't place the guy's ethnicity whatsoever. Maybe … Brazilian? He had green eyes, but with skin and hair much darker than usual for green eyes. Perhaps he had some Asian in him, too? Sam had no idea. One thing was clear, though: He did not look 281 years old. He looked 25 at best.

"You stay young?" Sam asked. "You're immortal?"

"Sure. Why not?" Julio replied simply.

Sam started feeling comfortable around Julio. Normally, he needed to know someone for a long time before he could be this blunt and direct, but he asked, "Why do you sound weird? Like, your cadence, or something? I'm not a linguist, but you sound weird."

"I don't know. Maybe because I had to learn to speak for this job," Julio answered.

"Really?" Sam asked. Of all the unexpected things that had come out of Julio's mouth, for some reason this one caught him off guard the most.

"Really. Think of it as telepathy. We all have tiny—chips, as you would call them—inside our brains. This is why I'm glad I'm working with your era and not the French Revolution. Try explaining this stuff to them! You at least come from an age with the Internet and instant messaging. I can send a message to anyone, as fast as I can think it. That's how we all talk. My ancestors haven't spoken for about 1,200 years now. Apart from laughing. We do love to laugh." He laughed some more, as if to illustrate the point. "When I decided I wanted to work as a transfer agent in a speaking era, well, I needed to learn how to speak aloud. It's hard!"

"They drill into the skull and implant a chip into the brain? Do I get one of those?" Sam asked.

"That's more or less what we do, and yes, you'll get one at some point. But, Sam, well … you're having a hard enough time keeping up with one conversation at talking speed, never mind lots of simultaneous conversations at the speed of thought." Julio stared at Sam silently for a few seconds, the longest Julio had gone without speaking since they had met. "So let's just wait until you're ready, okay?"

Sam was in no hurry to have anyone drill into his skull, so he accepted that answer without complaint. Something else occurred to him, something he had dismissed as crazy. Given everything else he'd heard, it didn't seem so silly anymore.

"Were you … *floating* … when I first saw you?"

"Oh, you saw me then? Sorry about that. Yes: We all fly now. Someday, when you're ready, you'll also get your skeletal replacement so you can fly wherever you want to go."

Flying sounded more appealing than having a million voices in his head, but he still wasn't about to sign up for a *skeletal replacement.* Anyway, that didn't matter now. Sam realized he was still missing the key component here.

"So you didn't answer my earlier question. Did you freeze my body or something?" Sam thought he knew the answer, but wanted to hear it from Julio's mouth.

"No, no. We didn't put you into a cryogenic freezer or any-thing along those lines," Julio replied with a smile. "It's flat-out time travel. We cannot change history. We cannot prevent any suffering or death. But we *can* swoop in at the last trillionth-of-a-second, right before a life ends, and make the transport. History stays the same, at least to the nearest trillionth-of-a-second. That's close enough."

Sam was already tired, despite having just woken up. But there were so many questions.

"Wasn't it altering history when you appeared as demons to play your little practical joke?" Sam's voice bordered on anger.

Julio had enough courtesy to put on a guilty expression. He pursed his lips as if choosing his words carefully, and replied, "Well ... we might have interfered with the air flow a little, maybe diverted some airborne bacteria or something, but probably noth-ing that would have a lasting effect. More importantly, we waited for your, um, lady friend to vacate the scene. We couldn't risk her seeing any of this, but once it was only you, we were free to put on our little show without altering anyone's life. People often see weird stuff right before they die, courtesy of their transfer agents. They're exiting the stage, so to speak. At that point, it doesn't mat-ter what they see. They can't act on anything. When Steve Jobs died, his last words were, 'oh wow, oh wow, oh wow' because ..."

"Steve Jobs died?" Sam exclaimed with shock.

"Yeah, Sam. Steve Jobs died." Sam instantly felt stupid. "He had terminal cancer and it really put a damper on his prospects of living to be 1,587 years old. He died and was retrieved, like you. Anyway, transfer agents have to have fun sometimes. It's not exactly by the book, but I hope you'll agree that ultimately, it worked out very well."

Julio seemed to be looking for Sam to show some sign of agreement, as if Sam were in a position to absolve him of guilt. All Sam said was, "You couldn't have stopped the pain? Not in any tiny way? That hurt!"

Julio sat down on the edge of Sam's bed and said, "No, I couldn't. Sorry. Truly, I am sorry about that. That would be breaking all the rules. You had to die precisely the way you died."

For the first time, he looked sad. "It's the one bad part of this job. You see someone who's dying in a terrible way, and there's nothing you can do to help. All you can do is swoop in and do the body swap thing, in the imperceptible moment before they die. We can provide a wonderful afterlife in 3542, but nothing can be done about their horrible past. It's not easy. When you work with the past, you're constantly bathing in wonderment at the incredible cruelty people have engaged in throughout history … seeing it all the time … trying to keep your head on right afterwards …" Julio trailed off in an odd way.

Then Julio hopped up from the bed and added, with new focus and vibrancy, "I wish I could have spared you the incident where your dick got bitten off. But, in the long run, I think you'll be much better off with your new dick. It doesn't talk."

With that, Julio laughed and turned away. As he glided toward the door, he said, "Get some sleep, Sam. We have all eternity to talk and get your questions answered."

CHAPTER 20

And God shall wipe away all tears from their eyes, and there shall be no more death, neither sorrow, nor crying, neither shall there be any more pain, for the former things have passed away. (Revelation 21:4)

When Jim woke up in the morning, he was more excited than he had been in weeks. *Oh boy*, he thought, *today is the day Julio will reunite me with Mary.*

About two months ago, he had awoken in a sterile, white room and met Julio. He thought he was meeting God or Saint Peter, even if his attire and manner of speaking weren't exactly ... *biblical.* Once he learned he was in the year 3542, he had been excited about his new lease on life. The last few months had been a blur, as he slipped in and out of lucidity as cancer ate away at him. Now, in 3542, he felt invigorated and feisty.

As the weeks went by, his excitement at the endless possibilities faded. He didn't know anybody and he couldn't imagine how he'd fit in to this futuristic society. He kept himself occupied, though. He tried to dream up his ideal house, but after struggling for a while, he realized he only wanted his old apartment, the one he had shared with Mary. The one he had died in.

He also met some of his ancestors. His great-grandparents on his father's side had been among the first to be brought forward, for some reason. He became jealous of them; they were together, and he was alone. He missed Mary so much.

Jim tried experiencing a few historical lives. He had been Abraham Lincoln and Napoleon, two of the more popular choices. Julio suggested he try the lives of people he knew, such as his parents or even Mary, but Jim said no. The last thing he wanted was to witness his parents having sex. He was even more emphatic about not wanting to live Mary's life, despite Julio's repeated, rather forceful urging. It seemed gross and strange to eavesdrop on a life wherein he had sex with himself. But perhaps the thing that scared him away even more was the thought of having to watch himself die from cancer, from a different perspective.

All of this loneliness was about to end, though: today, Mary would be retrieved and they'd be together once more, in perfect health in a place like Heaven, for eternity. They'd have the children they always wanted, and what a world they would be born into! He had the computer make him a fine suit and transport him to the retrieval facility. In an instant, he appeared in the building he knew all too well, where he had first met Julio. He was early. Leaving ten minutes before it was time to arrive always made him late before, but in a world where you could get wherever you wanted in the blink of an eye, he always found himself arriving early. He sat down, anxiously awaiting Julio.

The room was identical to the one Jim originally awoke in, except for a structure erected on the far wall, a sort of tunnel, all in white. The tunnel led to an elevated bed in the middle of the room.

A couple of minutes later, the door opened. Excited to get started, Jim said, "Julio, I'm so glad you're early. I can't wait to get going!"

But it wasn't Julio who walked in: it was a different man, also dressed in a suit. He was about the same height as Jim, so between the clothes and the non-statuesque figure, Jim figured he was another transplant from the past.

The man also seemed excited. "Good morning! Are you here to help with the Mary Reynolds retrieval?"

Wrong Mary, Jim thought. *He must have gotten mixed up and gone to the wrong room.*

"No, I'm sorry," Jim replied. "I'm here for a different retrieval. I'm waiting for Julio Carter-Nguyen to get here."

Scheduling errors weren't too unusual. Speaking in terms of the technology alone, sure, everything should run error-free. However, the human element factored in heavily, particularly with all the new arrivals who didn't have communication chips inside their brains yet.

The year 3542 had such a motley assortment of people. There were brand new babies, people from the distant past who had been adjusting for years, and people from the past who arrived yesterday and were still freaking out. Sure, Jim figured: Bring someone here from Ancient Rome or the Qing Dynasty, and what chance do they have to navigate the rooms and understand the retrieval schedule without a glitch?

So, this man was just lost. He was there for a Mary Reynolds. Jim tried picturing a Mary Reynolds; he thought she sounded a bit Colonial. He would look very natural in a Puritan hat. Maybe he was a Salem witch trial type, but all friendly and well-adjusted now.

"Julio is your transfer agent?" the probable American Colonist asked.

"Yeah. He should be here any minute. Are you sure your retrieval was set for 9:30 in Building 419, Room 45?"

"Definitely: Building 419, Room 45. Julio's friend, Hans McCoy-Ortega-Li, told me to make sure I was here at 9:30 sharp. You know, I've met Julio a few times," said the other man.

Dead giveaway, Jim thought. He was wrong. This man was not from the 1600s or 1700s. People from that era would never say "you know" in that context. The word choice suggested this guy was roughly his chronological peer.

The man continued, "I couldn't sleep all night, I was so excited." He paused and then said, "Wait, I've been rude. I didn't introduce myself. I'm Bob Reynolds."

"Nice to meet you, Bob," Jim said, reaching out to shake his hand. "I'm Jim Franklin."

As Jim grasped Bob's hand firmly, Bob froze, a look of shock on his face. Bob stared at Jim for a few seconds, still in mid-handshake, and asked in a soft voice, "Were you a home inspector from Toledo?"

Well, how in hell did he know that? Jim wondered. He stared at Bob, trying to place him. Finally, he replied, "Why, as a matter of fact, yes."

They stood there, hands still clasped, staring at each other with curiosity. They were interrupted by a voice saying, "Whoa, whoa, whoa. Bob, what are you doing here?" Jim and Bob finally released hands as Julio glided into the room. That constant smile was missing from his lips.

"Hi, Julio," Bob said. "I'm here for the Mary Reynolds retrieval. Hans told me to be here at 9:30."

The smile started to return to Julio's face, but he also shook his head ruefully. Jim imagined Julio was having a conversation with Hans right now to discuss this mix-up.

"Sorry, Bob, change in plans," Julio said. "Hans was confused. Will you please wait in the hall? Thank you." There was no pause between Julio's question and his *thank you*. Bob made a docile, polite exit. Before closing the door behind him, he said, "It was nice to meet you, Jim."

Jim didn't reply. Once Bob was out of the room, he turned to watch Julio. "Never mind what just happened with that man ... whatever his name was ... that Bob guy," said Julio.

There was no way Julio didn't know who Bob was. He had known Bob by name, and even if he hadn't been sure, he was able to look it up without missing a beat. Julio was trying to make it seem like Bob wasn't important, and the only conclusion Jim could draw was that Bob *was* important. Julio must be hoping to throw Jim off the trail.

"You know," Jim said, "he seemed to know me. I didn't recognize him. I'm terrible with names and faces. Was he one of my old customers or something?"

"Nah, you didn't know him. Don't worry about it." Julio wasn't paying any attention at all. "Okay, Jim, it's time to get Mary! Are you excited?"

At the mention of Mary, Jim forgot all about Bob. "I couldn't sleep all night!" Jim exclaimed.

"Well, step into the tunnel like we practiced yesterday," Julio said. "You remember what to do?"

Jim had been rehearsing this moment all last night. He was shaking with a mix of excitement and fear. He stepped to the far end of the tunnel and Julio said, "All right, here we go!" The lights went bright and white mist billowed from the floor all around him. Julio sure had a flair for the dramatic. None of these effects were technically necessary.

Mary appeared on the bed, empty only a moment before. She was dead, horribly mangled. Without thinking, Jim ran toward her. Something must have gone terribly wrong with the machines!

"Jim! That's the copy, remember?"

Jim stopped himself mid-sprint. "Oh, yeah, sorry," he murmured. How could he have forgotten? They just practiced yesterday. But seeing Mary covered in blood, with a compound fracture, terrified him. He had to consciously remind himself he was merely looking at a clump of molecules, the atom-for-atom replication that would be deposited in the distant past, swapped in a trillionth-of-a-second thus enabling the retrieval to take place without altering history.

Jim walked to the end of the tunnel, back into the fancy mist. He could hear Julio saying, "All right, get ready, Jim. The nanomedics are working." Julio was intent on some computer screen that must be displaying directly in his brain, monitoring Mary's progress. "Okay ... no more car accident ... no more punctured lung ... we've fixed that compound fracture. She's physically 22 again. We're a go. On the count of five ... are you ready? 1 ... 2 ... 3 ... 4 ... 5 ..."

And there she was. Mary! As beautiful as the day they met, the years wiped away. Her bed tilted forward to Jim as he walked out of the mist, bathed in the glowing light. It had all seemed so overdone during rehearsal—for some reason he had not gotten this light show when *he* was brought forward—but the lights and mist somehow seemed appropriate now, even if it was too bright. Mary looked at him with bewilderment, then wonder, and then radiant joy.

"Mary! Mary! We're back together in Heaven, my love!" he called to her. This wondrous future world *was* Heaven … now that she was here. Jim couldn't wait to show Mary all the wonderful new developments and to experience the universe with her.

"Wait, Jim! Stop!" Julio suddenly yelled.

Jim turned to see Julio through a small window in the tunnel wall. Jim couldn't believe Julio was interrupting this moment, but Julio's face made it clear something must be very wrong. "What is it, Julio?"

"Jim, I fucked up big time!" Julio said. "Don't take a step closer. Look at me! She doesn't die in the accident with the *blue* PT Cruiser. She dies 12 years later in the accident with the *green* PT Cruiser. I can't believe I did this! Hans flustered me, I'm all disorganized. Quickly: Tell her she has more work to do on Earth or some bullshit like that. It'll be fine. Just tell her you'll see her soon."

Jim didn't want to send Mary away now that she was finally here. He stared at Julio, silently fuming, until he realized this was easy to fix. He calmed down and said, "Okay, so you'll get the right PT Cruiser next time? It's no big deal?"

"Well, other than the fact I just altered the past and need to fix this, it's no big deal," Julio said with exasperation. "But for your purposes, yeah, we'll be able to do this again, with the right version of Mary, in a couple of hours. But you need to tell her she has more work to do on Earth *right now*!"

Mary's joy had faded and now she just looked confused and scared. He wanted to tell her everything, but he knew he couldn't. He struggled to find the right words.

"Mary, Julio fucked up." The words escaped his mouth before he realized what he was saying.

"Jim!" Julio hissed in annoyance through the window.

Jim glanced at Julio, who was shaking his head. He turned back to Mary, determined to come up with something better, for her sake. "Mary," he tried again. "This isn't your time. You have more work to do on Earth." He threw out a few lines of widely-accepted spiritual mumbo jumbo, stuff he heard in a TV show or movie at some point. "Return to Earth now, and when your time comes, we'll be together for eternity." That sounded good. He thought he saved it pretty well.

Mary gave him one last look, a mixture of mystification and joy, and disappeared. Jim sighed, but realized it was a temporary setback. Julio would reset everything somehow and in another couple of hours they'd do it again and Mary would be here. He had waited months; a few more hours were not an issue.

Jim stepped out of the tunnel to stand next to Julio, who seemed flustered but managed to smile when he looked at Jim.

"Good lord, those PT Cruisers have terrible blind spots, don't they? You may as well have an elephant running alongside your car," Jim said.

"Tell me about it. That's my second fatal PT Cruiser accident this week," Julio said absently, likely having conversations with a whole clean-up crew. Somehow, they'd have to knock Mary out, re-age her, break her bones, and drain her of blood. Then they'd have to return her to the car and swap out the replacement Mary with the real Mary. Jim shuddered at the thought, but she would never know the difference. She'd just wake up broken in her car or maybe a hospital, and proceed with her life.

"So, I should come back in a couple of hours?" Jim asked.

"Yeah, come back at 11:30," Julio replied.

"That works out great. I wanted to get a haircut before seeing Mary. I don't have those hair-grooming micro-computers that float around in your bloodstream yet," Jim said.

"What?" It took a distracted Julio a few moments to catch up to Jim. "Oh. Yeah. You need to get those sometime soon. Real time-saver. See you later."

Jim wondered why Julio felt the need to economize his usage of time, given his immortality. But it didn't matter. In a few hours, he'd begin eternity with Mary.

CHAPTER 21

*In My Father's house there are many mansions ... I
go to prepare a place for you. (John 14:2-3)*

Julio hated Hans. OK, he loved Hans. Hans was his best friend,
his partner in crime, the ying to his yang, the creamy filling to his
chocolate wafers, the chocolate chips to his...

I could really go for a cookie, Julio thought. A cookie appeared in
his outstretched hand and he ate it hungrily.

He still hated Hans. Of all the inventive practical jokes they
had played on each other, Hans had taken things to new level of
irresponsibility by sending Bob to the Mary Reynolds retrieval.
Consequentially, Julio would now be stuck in many extra sessions
with Jim and Mary. The mistake with the PT Cruisers didn't help;
he decided no matter what JESUS said, he would absolutely refuse
to retrieve the person who designed the PT Cruiser.

I'll get you for that one, he thought to Hans.

I'm sure you will, Hans returned.

Julio glided through the bright white corridors of his retrieval facility, lamenting the lack of color for the seven millionth time. Granted, the all-white scheme had been his decision. No one would have stopped him from using pastels or neons. Some transfer agents went with weight-bearing clouds. Other transfer agents picked outdoor motifs including actual trees and grass. That would be a peaceful way to wake up to the future, but Julio decided it wouldn't work well for the people in his retrieval time period. People who died in the early 21st century often thought of the future as looking like *2001: A Space Odyssey*, so they expected a bright and sterile backdrop to their futuristic new home. Plus, the retrieval process wasn't about *the setting*; it was about *the person* being brought forward. So Julio had reluctantly chosen the all-white motif, but that didn't mean he personally liked it.

It had been a rough couple of weeks. A real parade of losers and dregs had graced his transfer portal. There was a peeping tom, a stalker obsessed with a banal reality TV star, a nuisance litigant, a politician with a diaper fetish, and a man with more than 150 drunk-in-public (DIP) violations. One of his recent retrievals died by cutting himself with a chainsaw; he was high on PCP when he determined he was a tree, and *wanted* to be cut down. Julio had not one, but *two* "cat lady" recluses. He tried introducing them, thinking they'd hit it off. However, they were just as repulsed by their own kind as they were repulsed by every other non-feline.

Mary Reynolds was a bit of an exception: not specifically immoral nor a misfit, though she was a touch boring. Julio had retrieved her first husband, Jim, several months ago, and he was progressing very slowly. Thanks to Hans, the problem would only get worse now that Bob was in the picture. But Mary herself had reacted fairly well to her retrieval (her second retrieval, counting the mishap) and appeared to be on the fast track to integration into modern society.

Mary proved to be no harbinger of normalcy, though, as his next transfer case eclipsed it all: Sam freakshow Meyers, a boy who spent his entire life, short as it was, fighting with his penis until he was killed while receiving vehicular oral sex. Last week, after finishing the preparatory work on Sam, Julio threw his arms up in the air. He announced to Hans: *That's it, I'm out of here. I'm joining you in Tudor England.*

Oh, does adding an Elizabethan accent make your spoken voice more tolerable? Hans asked.

I don't have an Elizabethan accent on command right at this moment, but I can learn, Julio replied.

I'm not sure you can. Your spoken word is atrocious.

Is not.

It IS atrocious, and you're only longing for Tudor England because you're jealous of all the fancy tights I get to wear, Hans replied.

No, I'm NOT jealous of your fancy tights! I have good, idiotic clothing of my own! I need to get away from these weirdos, Julio thought to Hans in exasperation. *I thought I picked a good time period, but lately it seems like every one of these people is completely fucking unhinged.*

Oh, poor thing, what have they done to you now? Hans asked cheerfully.

It's been a farce, and the frosting on the cake is this *guy.* Julio sent Hans the information on Sam Meyers.

A few minutes later, Hans came back. *What the hell are you complaining about?* Hans asked. *You have a sensational time period. I love that Sam Meyers creature. I'll help you with him. We're going to laugh about it for years*

Hans planned the whole thing. It was way over the top, demon costumes and all, but Julio admitted it was fun. It had gone beautifully, at least until Manfred had shown up as real. Now, Sam was revealed as *reasonably* normal (given the circumstances), and Julio was actually looking forward to integrating him. The post-joke process got off to a smooth start, assisted by George Washington Carver's cameo. "Certainly, I'll help. I've never been asked to do one of these retrieval introductions for a white man before," was Carver's immediate response to Julio's request.

Manfred, on the other hand … well, Julio was stuck with Manfred. Manfred was alive, and life mattered, so he couldn't just chuck Manfred in the trash. He had to come up with some way to turn Manfred into a halfway worthwhile life form. The first task was to alter Manfred so he could speak aloud and not just in Sam's mind. Then Julio planned out several therapy sessions.

With both Sam and Mary asleep after their retrievals, Julio popped into the room where Manfred was staying. Not knowing what else to do, Julio had made the room simple, placing Manfred on a small table next to a pair of inanimate testicles closed up in a hairy scrotum, so he'd feel "at home." Classy.

"Hello, Manfred. It's good to see you again," Julio lied.

"Where have you been?" Manfred demanded. "Do you know how boring it is here?"

"You were supposed to sleep. Sam has been sleeping for half a day," Julio said.

"Well, I wasn't tired," Manfred replied. "You left me a lot to think about. I've mostly been plotting since you left."

Plotting, Julio repeated to himself. That didn't sound good. "So, Manfred, today I'm here to talk about something very important here in the year 3542. Something called *empathy*."

"Oh, no," Manfred responded. "Is this going to be more bullshit about morals? You've already tried to convince me there's no God. Not that I believe you—that's the same shit Sam tried to sell me and I watched him get sucked down by demons. But if you *are* right and there's no God, then I see no reason to bother trying to be some goody goody shithead." Manfred was unequivocally okay with profanity now.

Julio remembered how Sam had suffered with Manfred. "You might have professed Christianity, but when did you ever try to be good?"

"What do you mean?" Manfred seemed to take offense at the suggestion. "I was always good. I was the only thing good in a sea of sin."

Julio swallowed back a sigh and said, "Alright, let's take a hypothetical situation. Suppose someone tells a lie about you. They say, 'Manfred's a socialist.' They say that, but they don't have any idea what the word *socialism* means. They just say it because it sounds bad. How does that make you feel?"

"How do you think, dipshit?" Manfred snapped. "The bastard's lying about me. When I find him, I'll kill him."

Julio came up empty as he tried to imagine how a disembodied penis with no particular capacity for locomotion could kill anybody. He posed the question to Hans, who sent back some images of a penis hurling itself off a skyscraper and crushing the skull of someone thousands of feet below.

"OK, so now imagine there's another word," Julio continued with Manfred. "I'll just make something up. *Lopamoo*. You figure, if you call someone else a lopamoo, it will hurt their feelings. So should you call that person a lopamoo? Or should you learn what lopamoo means and whether or not it truly applies?"

"Will it help me if I call them lopamoo?"

Will it help you? Julio thought. *Why would you think calling someone else a lopamoo would help you?*

"Yes," Julio responded after considering the question, "in the short term, suppose it helps you."

"Then fuck it," Manfred replied. "Lopamoo! Lopamoo!"

"But how would you feel if someone else called you a lopamoo and you weren't?"

"Asshole. I'd kill them!"

"Then should you call someone else a lopamoo for no good reason?"

"Sure, why not? Lopamoo."

Exasperated, Julio tried one more time. "But if you wouldn't like being called a lopamoo when you weren't, does it seem fair to call someone else a lopamoo when they're not?"

"Huh?" Manfred squeaked.

"Do you remember the Golden Rule? Do unto others as you'd have done to you?" Julio asked.

"What does that have to do with anything? I find it pretty offensive an Atheist like you is trying to preach religion to me. I *live* my religion, you queermo lopamoo."

The session was going absolutely nowhere and making Julio feel stupider by the second, and now the system informed him Sam was waking up. Julio decided it was time to leave. He needed new and creative ways to get through to Manfred. "Think about what we talked about," Julio said absently. "I'll be back later." Without waiting for Manfred's response, Julio transported himself to Sam's room.

When he arrived, Sam was in the bathroom Julio added to Sam's room. Julio had spent a few minutes earlier in the day setting up the bathroom like the one in Sam's mother's house. He had the razor, shaving gel, electric toothbrush and toothpaste, and Sam's personal favorite, the flushable wipes. Julio was in no hurry to show Sam how unnecessary and primitive every single one of these hygiene products was. For example, it wasn't time to explain oral colonies of specialized bacteria to keep your teeth and gums clean and healthy.

Sam was putting on a change of clothes Julio had laid out for him—clothes from Sam's era—when Julio announced his presence.

"How's it going, Sam?"

Sam quickly recovered from any initial shock at seeing Julio outside his bathroom door and said, "It's nice to see all my favorite personal care products are still being manufactured in 3542."

"I can manufacture anything you want, any time," Julio said.

"Like a nanofabricator or whatever they called it, from *Star Trek*?"

"Yeah, pretty much like that," Julio replied. It was a halfway decent comparison. Julio stored away the word *nanofabricator* as the word to use to describe the technology to Sam. "We can re-arrange the atoms in the shape of whatever you want them to be."

"Good, because I'm hungry," Sam said. "How long have I been sleeping or dead?"

Sam seemed relaxed and unfazed so far. That was a good sign. "Long enough for you to be hungry," Julio replied. "Let's see," he said, looking up Sam's activity log in his head. "We retrieved you yesterday afternoon. We took a few hours to fix you up, get the blood back in you, that sort of thing. It takes a surprisingly long time to fill someone with blood. You'd be amazed."

Julio stared at Sam, looking for some sign of amazement. When Sam didn't react, Julio continued, "Anyway, you met George

Washington Carver last night, and we talked, and then you slept for another thirteen hours."

Sam appeared to be considering the implications of how long he had slept, as if he didn't have all eternity before him. Finally, Sam said, "Do you have one of those atom re-arrangers here? Like I said, I'm starving."

Julio knew Sam was looking for some kind of device like the one from *Star Trek*, so Julio led him over to a table and said, "Sure, right over here," as if one couldn't fabricate anything without that magic table. "Tell the computer what you want."

Sam looked around uncertainly. "What computer?"

Julio already dumbed things down by using the 21st century term *computer*. He couldn't think of any easy way to explain the system, so he simply replied, "Just say what you want."

"I want a Chipotle burrito," Sam said with a half-smile. He must have been kidding—he couldn't possibly expect the restaurant to still be around, no matter how good their business model was—because a clear look of shock emerged on his face when the foil-wrapped cylinder appeared on the table. Sam looked at Julio, an unasked question in his eyes, and reached greedily for the burrito. While Sam ate, Julio related his encounter with Manfred to Hans, who for once couldn't come up with anything to say. Hans just called Julio a lopamoo and signed off.

Shoving the last piece of burrito into his mouth, Sam didn't wait to finish chewing before asking, "So if I can get a burrito at the drop of a hat, can't evil people get a nuclear weapon?"

Julio suppressed a laugh. People from the 21st century were always so damned obsessed with nuclear weapons. Ooooo, nuclear weapons. "We're not worried about evil," Julio replied simply.

"But who's the leader? Is there a president or a congress or anything?"

Julio got that question from everyone he retrieved and had a ready evasion. "Sort-of, but it would be hard to explain. You don't have any direct parallels. I'll say this: Our leadership bench is deep. There are tens of millions of people who could do it about equally as well. Our politicians don't suck. We have perspective your era didn't, and none of the secrets and lies and envy your society did."

"Perspective, secrets, lies, and envy?" Sam summarized Julio's words. Julio always found the people he retrieved seemed to repeat what he said as if it was their idea.

"Perspective is something I'll discuss with you when you're ready," Julio said. "Secrets: Well, one big adjustment you'll have to make is that privacy is pretty much gone. Think about it. We know everything about the past. Thomas Jefferson and his slave mistress and his betrayed children: Cat's out of the bag, buddy. You, Sam: Did you ever wipe your nose and put a booger under a restaurant table when you were a kid? I know you did. Gandhi or Queen Elizabeth could have seen you do it, too. In regards to envy, you'll notice the nanofabricator makes anything you want. Do you think anyone will be jealous of your shoes? They could instantly make the exact same shoes. Secrets, lies, envy... gone. Functional, decent behavior: high."

After eating, Sam said he wanted to see what it was like outside the facility, so Julio led him down the hallway and through the door. As happened every time Julio took someone outside for the first time, Sam's face showed that strange mix of awe and disappointment as they stepped outside. Instead of a Jetsons-like array of futuristic skyscrapers and flying vehicles whizzing by in all directions, it was a picturesque, naturalistic countryside. There were no weeds or dead plants; everything was healthy and vibrant. For someone from Sam's time, this scene would look like the Garden of Eden.

"I guess we're out in the country?" Sam asked.

"Nah, not really," Julio responded.

"But I don't see any roads. Not even walking paths."

"Well, we can all fly, can't we?" Julio said. "So why would we need roads or even walking paths?"

"I can't fly," Sam said. "What about newbies like me? There must be lots of us who don't have their skeletal implants or whatever they're called."

"So go ahead and walk," Julio replied. "The grass can handle it. Anyway, even if you can't fly, you don't need to walk."

"Do you have some sort of matter transporter device to teleport people from one place to another?" Sam asked.

Julio laughed. "My job is so much easier when I get people who have watched *Star Trek*." It was true. "That's exactly what we have, more or less. The chip in my brain interacts with the forces around us to move objects where I want them to go." He snapped his fingers. "Just like that."

They wandered around for a few minutes while Sam peppered Julio with questions. Sam asked about his funeral, so Julio had to tell him there were only three actual mourners there, plus a small group of tragedy gawkers. Julio thought Sam would be amused by his nomination for a "Darwin Award," but he wasn't. It would take a little time, Julio supposed. But he'd get there.

Julio kept answering Sam's questions. Did Sam's father embezzle money from his job? Was JFK killed by a lone gunman? Did the Kansas City Royals ever win another World Series? Julio accessed answers to Sam's questions easily. The only question Julio couldn't immediately answer was whether or not Kelly Ducas had liked him in the eighth grade. Julio offered to find out if he really wanted to know, and was relieved when Sam said to not bother.

For every important or at least intellectually interesting question Sam asked, he tended to follow with something petty and self-absorbed. After asking the true fate of the lost Roanoke Colony, Sam's next question was if the philosophical trucker in the rest stop really wanted to have sex with him. Julio laughed aloud. He had wondered the exact same thing and took some time while Sam was asleep to learn the answer. It turned out that while the man wasn't specifically looking to have sex with Sam, he would have been open-minded had Sam asked.

"How do you know all this stuff? Do you watch people from the past with little invisible floating cameras? Do you read their minds? You seem aware of a lot of private thoughts."

It was too soon to give Sam an answer to that question, so he used a firm tone of voice to say, "No. We have a better option than little cameras or mind reading, but I'll explain it later." Julio quickly changed topics before Sam could follow up. "Reflecting on your past is fine and good, but we'll need to start thinking about your future. Where would you like to live?"

Sam looked around, undoubtedly searching for an apartment building in the wilderness. "Am I already supposed to have an answer to that?" Sam asked. "I mean, what are my options?"

With a broad smile, Julio replied, "Well, you're basically in Heaven, right? You can live in any type of house you like, on a virtually unlimited range of planets. Let me give you an idea."

With that, Julio transported them to a big empty warehouse, something no one would consider home-like.

"Using the same nanofabricator technology I used to create your burrito, I can create whatever type of house you'd like," Julio explained. "Do you want to live in the Sistine Chapel? That's a popular choice." Julio executed the transition and the warehouse transformed into the Sistine Chapel.

After doing this enough times with enough transfers, Julio didn't need to wait for Sam to ask the question, so he said, "This isn't an optical illusion. You can touch it. It's not a trick. You can take an axe to it, if you want, and hack parts away to use as firewood, and those parts will burn. Or, you can rearrange the atoms and make, I don't know, a room based on a scene you might find in Shakespeare's *A Midsummer Night's Dream*."

Julio opted to be somewhat ostentatious—recent retrievals liked visual shows—and had the Sistine Chapel evaporate into shiny dust. Then the dust re-formed into a fairylike scene, with a velvety moss floor, trees and flowers that sparkled, and a purplish sky. A hammock bed was suspended between two trees with a stump as a nightstand next to it. "Whatever your idea of a castle is, you can have it."

Sam looked around and finally said, "This is a beautiful room, but I can't help but think it's for a ten-year-old girl." Still, Sam walked around the room, admiring the exquisite touches and clever ways to incorporate fairy and forest motifs into furniture. Julio decided to let Sam process in silence.

Julio didn't know where Sam's thoughts were leading him until he asked, "What happened to my mother?" He paused, and then added, "Or Andy?"

Ah, here was a topic Julio had been waiting to get into. "JESUS hasn't scheduled their resurrections yet, but that will probably happen soon." *Let him chew on that one for a minute*, Julio thought, laughing to himself.

"Jesus hasn't scheduled their resurrections?" Sam repeated, confused.

"No, not yet," Julio replied with as straight a face as he could muster, enjoying Sam's expression.

"Jesus?" Sam asked.

"Yeah, JESUS."

"Jesus?" Sam repeated.

"Yes, already. JESUS. JESUS is the only pathway to Heaven." Julio said with mock impatience.

Julio let Sam's confused expression stew for just a little longer, and then decided it was time to put him at ease. "That's an acronym. J-E-S-U-S. The Judicious Extraction System Utilizing Science. Specifically it's—well, something you would call software—that computes all the variables and calculates who to bring forward when, in what order. We can't bring people forward willy-nilly. We need a plan, so JESUS provides one."

Sam surprised Julio. Instead of standing there stupidly, he asked, "Do transfer agents who work with, say, Hindus or Buddhists have different names for it?"

"Interesting question! Let me find out," Julio replied, excited to have a question to research. He quickly found a fellow transfer agent who knew another transfer agent, who knew yet another transfer agent who specialized in 20th century Nepalese transfers. Julio posed the question to her. Once he got his answer, he told Sam, "Yes, they do have different words for it. But, they're not as funny. I think they're boring names."

Are you the one who found a talking penis? the Nepalese specialist asked. Julio didn't know how she knew, but he assumed Hans was somehow involved.

Unfortunately, I am, Julio replied.

Several other transfer agents tuned in to hear the story, and the Nepalese specialist asked, *why is that unfortunate? It sounds like an amazing discovery.*

That's because you haven't been forced to spend any time with him.

While Julio silently debriefed his fellow transfer agents on the Manfred situation, Sam asked, "Why did JESUS schedule my resurrection before my mom's and Andy's?"

"I don't specifically know, but I have a pretty good guess," Julio replied to Sam. Simultaneously, he described Manfred's new favorite insult, *lopamoo*, to the other transfer agents. That should paint the picture of the non-enviable position he was in.

"What?" Sam asked.

"What what?" Julio asked back. He wasn't sure what Sam was asking.

Exasperated for some reason, Sam said, "What is your pretty good guess as to why JESUS scheduled my resurrection first?"

"Oh, that," Julio responded with a smile. "Like I mentioned when we first met, we all thought you were fucking nuts, man. You were completely deranged, fighting with your dick all the time. You were going to take a lot of extra time and work. Andy and your mom seemed further along and easier, insofar as mental health is concerned. It wasn't until during our joke, when we saw Manfred separated, that we realized you're more-or-less sane and Manfred is real."

CHAPTER 22

A fool shows his annoyance at once, but a prudent
man overlooks an insult. (Proverbs 12:16)

They all sat around a table, staring at their hands. The only one willing to talk was Julio.

"Guys, I'm sorry about what happened," Julio said. "The thing you have to understand is that my friend Hans is an ass-clown. He had no business reaching out to you like that, Bob. Things were never supposed to go down this way."

Julio looked uncharacteristically uncomfortable, his standard smile nowhere to be found. He surveyed each of them in turn, but no one was looking up to meet his eyes.

On Jim's left was his beloved wife, Mary, with whom he had been so excited to be reunited. But after the first aborted attempt at retrieval and the odd Bob situation, Jim did a little research before returning for the second try.

Once he had discovered who this Bob joker was, the actual retrieval became an unpleasant experience. Jim had insisted they forego the tunnel and the light/mist show and just bring her back. When she appeared in the tunnel, Jim hardly wanted to look at her.

Yet, as he showed her around the wonders of the year 3542, Jim had started to feel better. It was just him and her again. They were good friends, even if the romance hadn't yet returned. Then Bob joined them and everything was wrong again.

Bob, sitting to Jim's right, said, "Jim, I'm sorry about what happened. If I had known you didn't know about me, I never would have shown up. But what happened has happened, so I think we need to try to make the best of the situation." Jim glared at Bob, who was obviously trying to make himself look good in front of Mary and Julio. And, in doing so, make Jim look bad.

Mary was quiet and kept her head down. Everything here was still so new to her. Jim wanted to help her through her transition. The last thing she needed was this tension, but Bob was too damned selfish to step aside for Mary's good.

"If you were so interested in making the best of the situation," Jim muttered, "you wouldn't have injected yourself back into it in the first place."

Bob seemed like he was about to respond, probably with some passive-aggressive attack to make Jim look like the villain, but Julio spoke first. "Mary was supposed to wake up to find Jim—someone she knew to be dead—to ease her in. Meanwhile, Jim, we planned to help you understand that Mary discovered a wonderful new man named Bob, with whom she built a new life. Until, of course, the accident with the second PT Cruiser took it all away."

"Yeah, and you waited only a couple of years until you remarried!" Jim snapped. "You didn't even wait for my pretend corpse to get cold, did you?" He regretted saying it immediately. She wasn't the problem. Bob was.

Julio continued, "Jim, I know you're thinking Mary moved on too soon, but if you saw things from her perspective, you'd find out it wasn't simple. That's why I wanted you to experience her life before the retrieval and I think it's even more important you do so now."

It suddenly became all so clear to Jim, and he was having none of it. "So that's your plan?" he shouted. "You want me to experience Mary's life so I can get used to fucking Bob, so we can have a little ménage-à-trois polygamist eternity together? Well: I'm sure as shit not going back in time and fucking Bob."

Julio looked exasperated. "Come on, Jim," he said, "it's not like *that*. If our intention was to get you to fuck Bob, then I'd just hold him down on the table right now and let you go to town."

Bob made a little grunt but otherwise stayed quiet. Mary's mouth fell open; she must have been incredulous at not only Jim's sentiments, but by his newfound profanity, as well.

Julio cleared his throat and continued, "The point is you need to see life through Mary's perspective. Once you do that, you'll understand the decisions she made were not necessarily easy, but they made sense given her circumstances."

Mary, who had been sitting there quietly through all of this, finally spoke up. "Oh, Jim, I really am so sorry," she said, tears welling up in her eyes. "I felt your spirit with me, watching me. I was so torn up about what to do."

"That must be why it took you two and a half seconds to say yes when Bob proposed," Jim groused. He hadn't meant to say it so loud; he wasn't controlling himself. Tears filled Mary's eyes as she covered her mouth with her hand. Bob looked angry, as if he wanted to attack Jim. Well, Bob could go fuck himself right in his self-righteous ass.

"And that's another thing, Jim," Julio said. "You cannot go visit the past without my permission. Consider the viewing chambers to be absolutely forbidden until further notice. Absolutely forbidden. Do you understand?"

Jim realized he probably shouldn't have tried to operate the machine on his own. He certainly had no idea how it worked, but the computer was able to guide him through the process. Still, Jim wasn't going to sit here and be lectured by Julio, a man who couldn't even tell two PT Cruisers apart and who completely failed to mention Mary's betrayal.

"What's the big deal, Julio?" Jim protested. "All I did was go back and watch her say yes to Bob as if there was nothing at all to think about, and sleep with him in my bed—*my* actual bed *I* bought with *my* money *I* earned from *my* job."

"She sensed you there!" Julio exclaimed. "That's a huge problem! She thought a demon was in the room. She didn't have any interest in ghost story pseudo-documentaries the first time through. But after you went back and terrorized her, she started watching them all the time. Her interests changed, her actions changed, her statements changed, it all changed because she was so terrified by what you did!"

"Good, glad to hear it. I hope she crapped her pants," Jim said. Again, Jim realized too late he never should have said that. He couldn't bring himself to look at Mary to see how she reacted.

"Julio, I think ..." Bob began.

"All right, everyone, I think it's time to take a break for today," Julio interrupted, apparently not wanting to hear what Bob had to say any more than Jim did. Julio stood up, towering over them. "The three of you need to stay away from each other for a while.

I'll be working with each of you independently. I promise: we'll make this work."

Jim and Bob stood up. Bob didn't appear any happier than Jim with the lack of resolution. They both walked toward the door. Mary remained seated and Julio walked over to her.

Jim overheard Mary say to Julio, "I just wish I could have been there to see my daughter grow up. Bob said that she ..."

He didn't stick around to listen to the rest. Why had no one mentioned Mary and Bob had a daughter? She and Jim hadn't been able to have a child in time, but Bob had apparently stepped in and knocked her up right away. Now that daughter would be an anchor keeping Bob tied to Mary, and Jim on the outside.

"Assholes! They're all assholes," Jim mumbled as he stormed away.

CHAPTER 23

The wolf and the lamb shall feed together, and the lion shall eat straw, and dust shall be the serpent's meat. They shall not hurt nor destroy in my holy mountain, sayeth the Lord. (Isaiah 65:25)

Sam moved out of Julio's transfer facility into a house of his own. He didn't want to, but Julio had pretty much kicked him out, telling him he needed to start his new life in his own home. The nano-fabricator could create Versailles or the Taj Mahal or whatever he wanted, but Sam was too guarded, too uncomfortable, to display much personality. So he recreated his dorm room, which he had kept anonymous and plain. There was nothing for anyone to make fun of, because there was nothing at all.

Julio came by each day, to introduce him to interesting people. One day, he met Andy's future wife (that is, *future* relative to when Sam knew Andy), who had been brought forward before Andy. "Hey, it's Mr. Cream-Filled!" she said with enthusiasm upon meeting him.

Sam never knew this was Andy's secret nickname for him. Andy's wife explained that when they were 11 years old, Sam used the term "cream-filled" exactly 69 times in a donut shop. He had done it on Manfred's order, back in those days when sexuality wasn't at all understood, but was still overpoweringly funny. Sam had all but forgotten the incident. Yet, for Andy it was—secretly—a definitive nickname-creating event. He knew that Andy wouldn't have wanted him to know about the name, and he felt bad knowing it. Sam gave this whole erosion of privacy, everyone-knows-everything deal a mixed review.

On another day he met some distant ancestors. Sam had never heard of any of these people. The only family member whose direct relationship he could figure out was his three-time great-grandfather, who had been killed in the Civil War.

Sam also got to meet some of the people he had tangentially known during his lifetime. He was able to apologize to the Hindu man who picked him up while hitchhiking. The man had come to believe many things he found unbelievable while alive, but Sam wasn't entirely sure he was able to convince the man about his talking penis. Either way, he forgave Sam for urinating in his car. Then he met a girl named Katelyn, who he didn't recognize until she told him she was the lot lizard who had bitten Manfred off. She was pretty now. He had the distinct feeling this meeting was more for her benefit than it was for his.

But then one day Julio made an announcement: These visits would need to pause, and Sam would have a week of alone time. Julio said it was important to digest everything he was experiencing and to think about what he wanted to do with his future, and he had to do that without distractions.

The only company Sam would have was his computer, from which he decided to learn about history, beginning with the time of his death. Julio seemed unsurprised by Sam's selection of a computer design. It was a combination of a television and a computer with a verbal interface. It was outlandishly primitive by the standards of 3542—something like this probably came into existence not too long after Sam's death—but it fit Sam's vision of the future perfectly. Speaking to an invisible computer, no matter how effective, was a bit scary. His TV-Computer had a gorgeous 90" high definition plasma screen. It was an antique to be treasured as far as Sam was concerned.

TV-Computer played whatever he wanted, showing him footage of history where available, answering his questions immediately. He could pick an actor or actress, and view their full catalog of work starting with the last thing he saw while alive, up until they were veteran performers in the twilight of their careers. By the time he got to the mid-2040s, the history lessons began to lose their personal connection. He realized many of the people he knew, either personally or in the culture at large, had died off.

Being alone and not having the interesting visits was dour, but he didn't realize how nerve-wracking it would prove. Sam had never been *alone* before. There was always Manfred. By the end of the night, he was trying to banter with TV-Computer, but attempting to converse with it was like trying to party with an internet search engine. It had no personality and provided no emotional concord; it simply provided information.

By bedtime on his first night alone, Sam was wallowing in self-pity. It was the longest he had ever been without interaction. He tried to talk to his new penis a couple of times, fruitlessly, and didn't even want to jerk off. He was fixated on his lame funeral, and how maybe three people were truly sad. One of the sad people was Andy, but when Sam thought more about Andy, he was only jealous. It was difficult yet liberating to admit it: he was jealous. Andy went on to a rewarding life with lots of interests, a warm family, and a reasonably enjoyable career. There was nothing strange or dramatic in Andy's life. That would have been nice.

By the second night, his brooding was fixated on his current situation. How would he ever contribute anything to this civilization? All the problems had been solved, all the mysteries unraveled. He wouldn't have anything to worry about, but he also wouldn't have the opportunity to make his mark on anything. The world of 3542 was the fantastical result of humans learning more and more science, while simultaneously embracing more goodness, and he had contributed *zilch* to it. He was a freeloader on the accomplishments of others. Was he destined to have a meaningless life, where having fun was his only purpose? Hey ... that wouldn't be *such* a bad thing! One could do worse. Yet he still ached for something more.

The sentiment opened a new can of worms. Was he a pompous ass, thinking he needed to make a mark on something? If everything was perfect, then any mark he'd make would be ugly graffiti. Or the virtue of "helping others" ... if no one needed help, he should be happy, not sad. Yet, here he was. Empty.

It was during the third night alone when Sam's depression led him to ask TV-Computer, "Can I get a sad song?"

"Yes," came the robotic answer. No sad song was volunteered. TV-Computer was simply saying, yes, it is indeed possible to get a sad song. So damn helpful.

Sam picked the saddest song he remembered, an old one in his perspective, one released before he was born. "How about that

Don't Know What You Got (Till It's Gone) song by Cinderella?" It was a request straight from his heart.

"I am sorry. That song was not brought forward," the robotic voice answered.

"What do you mean? It wasn't brought forward?"

"It was not deemed to have the musical merit necessary to be added to the musical archives. It was left behind in the past."

It didn't have the musical merit to be archived? After all the random historical material he had seen on his TV-Computer, it didn't make sense Cinderella wouldn't be there. What would the band members think when they got brought forward? If TV-Computer hadn't been so completely devoid of personality, Sam would have thought it was playing a joke on him.

"Come on! What do you mean? If I want a song by Cinderella, I should be able to get a song by Cinderella," Sam insisted.

Sam must have imagined TV-Computer sighing before it said, "Oh, very well. Retrieval in process." The music started with its slow opening piano. TV-Computer played the music video, with its sweeping landscape views. The video focused on the lead singer—Sam didn't know his name—sitting at the piano and singing in a high-pitched, screeching voice Sam remembered sounding much less obnoxious back in the day.

Now that TV-Computer had expressed the apparent future opinion of the song, Sam couldn't help but agree, noting how many generic, maudlin references to "baby" there were. Regardless, it was working for him, especially the first time the singer belted out the title line.

As he watched the band play their unplugged electric instruments and lip sync with a passion normally reserved for weddings, it hit Sam all at once. This song was about him and

Manfred. He didn't know how Cinderella had known, but the song had clearly been written with Sam and Manfred in mind. Not that he had ever called Manfred "baby" or talked about his "heartache" or even used the word "ain't." Sam and Manfred were enemies for 59 minutes of an average hour, and friends for one minute. But he missed Manfred. There. He said it. He missed Manfred, the horror of his life. He was alone and broken without that shithead.

It wasn't as if Sam wanted to tell Manfred he loved him; those words would never escape Sam's mouth. Part of him just missed having Manfred to kick around. When there was Manfred, an even bigger screw-up was right there on display. He always knew the bottom hadn't fallen out, because Manfred was still alive on a lower level, literally and figuratively.

Sam couldn't believe how critical he was being of the song— including noting every time the singer couldn't be bothered to pronounce the last "g" in words ending with "ing"—while simultaneously enjoying the hell out of it. The song filled a void for Sam emotionally. But when he really broke it apart and analyzed it ... well ...

Anyway, the song was the closest TV-Computer had come to interacting with Sam, so he chased after further interaction once it was over. "So, it was objectively considered to be a bad song by the future people?"

"Apparently." TV-Computer didn't offer any further opinion.

"Did it get bad reviews here that stopped it from being resurrected or whatever?"

"No," was TV-Computer's succinct response.

TV-Computer wasn't much for conversation, but Sam continued to try. "I thought the song was a hit back in my day."

"It made a significant amount of money for the band and received a fair amount of airplay," TV-Computer admitted.

Sam became curious, for reasons he couldn't explain, about what his contemporaries had thought of the song. Was he the only one who felt moved by it? "Do you have access to user reviews?" he asked. Before TV-Computer would give another yes/no answer, he added, "If so, please read some user reviews for me."

TV-Computer seemed almost annoyed at having to answer this question. It said, "I am querying," and was silent for a few moments. Sam didn't buy for a second that computers in 3542, no matter how much data they were sifting through, needed as long as this one took to provide an answer. He was about to cajole it into speaking again.

"One noteworthy review states, 'This is cock rock at its most exquisite,'" TV-Computer finally said. "I do not know what 'cock rock' means. I can query that next, if you would like. Another review states, 'Retard alert, calling all retards: this is a *POWER BALLAD*, and that is why it has Power.'" TV-Computer paused to let the gravity of the review sink in, and continued, "Here is another review, 'Pussies sang this song and they can eat each other's assholes like champions. When they're done with their ass chomping, they pick up guitars and... "

"Okay, I get the point!" Sam interrupted. Truth be told, he didn't get a single point out of that. He was sorry he asked.

Things did not get better for Sam the remainder of the week. The next night he asked TV-Computer to give him a list of potential professions in 3542. It was an overwhelming list, with nothing jumping out at him, though he was somewhat intrigued by the jobs associated with the resurrection plan for animals. As the list continued, Sam began looking for one of the professions he was already aware of: transfer agent. Once transfer agent was named, Sam asked for more information.

"Becoming a transfer agent is a common choice for people newly brought forward," TV-Computer told him. "You may enter an apprenticeship after living a minimum of one thousand lifetimes, with at least one hundred in the era of specialty."

Well, piss on that parade. How in hell was Sam supposed to live a thousand lifetimes? The depression came pouring back in.

CHAPTER 24

As a dog returns to its vomit, so a fool
repeats his folly. (Proverbs 31:6)

It was his sixth day alone and Sam was in his room watching the news feeds from the year 2069. Julio had instructed him to allocate some of his time to thinking about his situation with TV-Computer off, but it was too depressing. So he kept watching TV-Computer, and when he did turn it off he lay down in his bed and fell asleep.

He woke a couple of hours later and immediately reached for Manfred, but his new penis was limp and uncommunicative. If Manfred were still down there, he would be demanding a handjob right about now. He'd request either some religious programming or something with lots of explosions, and then he'd complain and complain and complain until Sam complied.

This new penis didn't say anything at all. Sam sat in the dark, his body not tired enough to go to sleep, his mind too tired to do anything productive.

He requested some pencils and paper from the nanofabricator, thinking he might write something. After sitting there for several minutes without thinking of anything to write, he wadded the paper and threw it on the ground. He looked hard at the pencils and requested a sharpener. For the next hour or so, he sat in a chair sharpening the pencils down to the nub, with a glazed expression on his face, until his wrist hurt. He maintained enough presence of mind to keep drool from dribbling down his shirt, but that was about his limit. Was he really this useless and pathetic without Manfred?

TV-Computer wasn't initially judgmental when Sam asked for a nanofabricated replica of Manfred, but it drew the exchange out in excruciating detail. There was no way Manfred's exact dimensions weren't "on file," yet TV-Computer asked Sam humiliating clarifying question after humiliating clarifying question. No doubt, TV-Computer thought Sam was a loser and a pervert and it enjoyed taunting him, though it was just a machine. TV-Computer even told him that most people who want dildos request larger ones. Anyway, Sam eventually found himself holding a goofy Manfred replication. It was familiar, but it wasn't Manfred.

Sam began feeling self-conscious fondling a dildo in front of TV-Computer, which had been his only companion for the last six days. So he threw the dildo in the corner and asked TV-Computer for a Manfred sock puppet, as if that would be less weird. Sam put his hand into the puppet and giggled, and a pulse of energy surged through him.

"Eeee, Sam, you're a sinner," Sam said in a high, squeaky, incredibly annoying voice, a slightly exaggerated imitation of Manfred. He giggled again. He asked TV-Computer for one more thing, something he didn't think it would be able to provide. But to his delight, the screen came alive with The True Christian Channel, an apparent re-run direct to him from the early 2000s, with the older gentleman sitting next to his blonde co-host. A giant grin split Sam's face.

The coiffed blonde said, "Daniel from Indiana writes to ask how people from distant lands, who have never heard of Jesus Christ, can find salvation."

The older gentleman regarded his co-host patiently, waiting for her to speak. "Well, Daniel, a lot of people like to believe God will find a place in Heaven for those who have never heard the Word of Jesus, but have otherwise lived by His tenets," she offered meekly.

"No, no, Shelley. You're incorrect," the man said softly in his smooth Southern accent. "If someone hasn't accepted Jesus Christ as his Lord and Savior, the door to Heaven is closed, even if that person is an Aborigine living in the Australian Outback who has never heard the name of Jesus Christ. Jesus is the only path to paradise, no exceptions. That is why babies need to be baptized right away. Everyone who understands the Scripture knows this, Shelley. People with Jesus in their hearts—truly in their hearts— *will* find Jesus Christ. The hardships of the Outback aren't enough to keep them away."

"But can't we make it easier for them? Can't we tell people about Christ?" the co-host asked.

"Why, yes. Yes we can. But to do that, we must find the resources to help us spread the Word to every corner of the globe. God will multiply what you release to Him," the man said. "Make a donation to God, and He will multiply it boundlessly, making the harvest come. But if you spend your money on a vacation, or a new wardrobe, or new furniture, or on some other selfish indulgence, you won't witness the miracles of God. You'll only witness the miracles when you open your resources—your hearts *and* your wallets—to Christ."

"They need all the donations they can get, Sam," Sam squeaked, waving Sock Puppet Manfred in front of him, "so they can rid the world of immoral behaviors." Then he spoke normally, "Uh, Manfred, these televangelists are bigger Atheists than I am. They don't believe in one damn thing. They just want to trick gullible, scared people out of their money."

"How dare you!" replied Sock Puppet Manfred. "They're the true believers. They're the moral standard-bearers. You could learn a few things from them."

The coiffed blonde televangelist was speaking in a comforting tone. "Your donation helps us spread the word of Christ to Jews, Muslims, and Atheists. Planting your seed lets us reveal Christ's love to The Children while they are still innocent and tender-hearted, while they are still willing ..."

"What Shelley is trying to say," the male televangelist interrupted, "is the Earth is a moist land on which you release your seed. Moist and fertile, the harvest grows. But there is no lesson more difficult to learn than how to first mount the generosity required to release the seed."

Ah, that was the vintage sleaze Sam longed for. "Yeah, I'm sure it was *real hard* for you to learn to release your seed." Then he imitated Manfred in his squeaky voice, "I'll release my seed in your face if you don't shut up!"

"Release your seed in my face and I'll shut it off, Manfred. I'll shut off the TV and give you no hand. Just you watch," Sam threatened.

Sam went back to his squeaky voice, and Sock Puppet Manfred responded, "You think I'm kidding, you godless Jew? Shut up and let me watch my show. Start rubbing me, too, or else I'll splooge all over this place."

"Oh, really? Maybe you need to smell my butt. You want to smell my butt? Here, go ahead, get on down there, check it out." Sam thrust his puppeted hand down the back of his pants, squealing, "Nooooo! I'll be good!"

Sam pulled the sock puppet out of his pants. "Good, 'cause I don't want you in my ass."

"I bet you secretly do, you old queen," Sock Puppet Manfred squeaked, and Sam wrestled his puppeted hand to the floor, pinning the sock puppet to the ground.

"Here, let me show you a *real* penis." With his non-puppeted hand he whipped out his new penis. "Oh, yeah, Manfred, here's my new friend. You see this? Yeah, take it all in. This is what a real penis looks like."

"Ewwwwwww, that's queer shit! Get away from me!" Sock Puppet Manfred cried.

"You're all jealous and intimidated," Sam replied. "Should be, too. You damned well should be."

Sam was focused on introducing his pretend, old penis to his real, new penis when the male televangelist said something he didn't expect.

"Shelley, I'm sorry to interrupt you. I'm sorry I treated you like a piece of furniture all these years. I honestly never even knew if Shelley was your real name. It just popped in my head the first day you were on the show, and so you were 'Shelley' from then on.

"And I'm sorry to you, the viewer, for harassing you into sending me money," the voice continued. "Your emotions shouldn't be a violin for me to play. I'm done manipulating people with promises of salvation and threats of damnation."

Sam couldn't believe his ears. Not only were the words unbelievable, but the voice sounded somehow different. It was fundamentally the same voice, devoid of the Southern accent, and it sounded ... *closer*. Sam looked up cautiously and found the image on TV-Computer was frozen.

He fell back in sudden terror as he noticed a man standing a few feet to the side of the screen.

There, standing in Sam's room, was a young man who looked quite familiar. Sam looked at the man, and then at the frozen screen, and then back at the man. There could be no doubt this man was a younger version of the one on the screen.

Sam then realized he was lying on the ground with a penis sock puppet covering one hand, his other hand grabbing his new penis. Why did this sort of shit always happen to him?

He rolled so his back was to the man and he pulled up his pants, and then turned to face the young televangelist.

"Hello, Sam. My name is Jonathan Parsons," the man said. It didn't sound familiar to Sam, who had never paid close enough attention to learn the name of the host. "I've come to meet my biggest fan!"

Sam stared. His anger at having someone walk in on him without knocking was canceled out by his embarrassment at being caught rolling on the ground with his dick in his hand. The end result was he didn't know what to feel, or what to say.

"You're embarrassed because you were naked with a sock puppet of ... oh, I see, a penis?" Jonathan asked. Sam quickly pulled off the Manfred sock puppet, which he had forgotten was still on his arm. "Don't worry, I've seen much worse. I've *done* much worse. I've even abused socks worse! True story: When I was in high school, I masturbated into my father's socks sometimes. I'd leave the cum right there in the sock, and I'd put the sock back into his clean drawer. It always got blamed on my twin brother. Everyone knew it had to be him, because he was the black sheep who refused to go to church. But, I'm not here to tell you stories from high school."

"I don't mean to be rude," Sam said. *Rude like people who just show up inside your house unannounced*, he added silently. "But what are you doing here?"

"Well," Jonathan began, "I'm here to tell you something you've probably already pieced together: I was a raging piece of shit. I was a thousand times more rotten and worthless than you ever were. Yet, I still got a second chance when I was brought forward to the year 3540. Humanity is that loving and compassionate. They brought me forward and fixed me, and they can do the same for you."

"I've already been told how lucky I am to be here," Sam said coolly. "But the problem is, the future isn't lucky to have *me*. I'm not useful to humanity in 3542."

"As you are right now, at this instant? You're right, you're not useful," Jonathan said.

That direct honesty wasn't what Sam expected to hear. What did he mean, *as you are right now*? "Are you saying I need Manfred to take the next step forward?"

Jonathan looked confused. "You mean your little sock puppet?"

"No, not the puppet …" Sam mumbled in response.

Before Sam could say any more about Manfred, Jonathan cut in as if Sam was Shelley. "No, this isn't about your little sock puppet or anything like that. This is about *you*, just like it was about me when I arrived two years ago. We're deeply flawed individuals—you, me, and everyone else who gets brought forward. We all seek perfection. When I used to talk about angels in Heaven, I was more or less right but didn't know it. We're all on the path of perfection."

Sam had no idea what Jonathan was talking about, if he wasn't talking about Manfred.

"Can you guess why JESUS brought me forward before you?" Jonathan asked. Sam had heard this man talk about Jesus so many times, it was odd to hear him refer to Jesus as the acronym Julio had revealed.

"I have no idea."

"It's because I needed a lot more work than you did," Jonathan explained. "You can consider me a test case. If they could fix me—a truly awful person in my first life—then normal people would be easy. When you arrived here, like most people, you were first brought to the transfer room. But I was treated very differently. I wasn't fit to enter this world in the same way you did. I was thrown into a Lake of Fire."

"Yeah, well, they do have a sense of humor, don't they? I was treated to a demon show when I died," Sam replied.

"Believe me," Jonathan said, shaking his head, "this wasn't a joke. I was thrust into a Lake of Fire again and again until I learned."

Sam decided not to ask about the logistics of throwing someone into a Lake of Fire—he assumed they had Lake of Fire technology—and focused on the part most likely to be relevant to him. "How did you learn?"

"I had to go back and live the lives of all my victims. That was my Lake of Fire."

This was the second time someone had mentioned living other people's lives, Sam realized. The first had been TV-Computer reading the qualifications required to become a transfer agent.

"Have you ever heard the quote by the poet Robert Burns, 'oh, what a gift God would give us, to see ourselves as others see us?'" Jonathan asked. Sam looked at him blankly; he had never heard the expression. Jonathan continued, "Well, I did more than *see*. I experienced it. More than a hundred lives, from start to end. So many times, I had to be a poor soul already hurt, already vulnerable, and then tricked into believing salvation was through God, and the path to God went directly through Jonathan Parsons. Well, empathy only comes from experience. In experiencing those lives, I learned what I did to those people."

"I'm sorry," Sam said, "but I don't know what you're talking about when you say you lived other people's lives. I've heard it mentioned before, but what does it actually mean?"

"I'm talking about reincarnation, Sam," Jonathan said.

"Reincarnation?"

"Reincarnation," Jonathan said. "That's the next phase of your journey. Think about whose perspective on life you would like to understand, and Julio will set it up. On that note, I'll take my leave. I've probably said too much already."

Without another word, Jonathan walked to the door and left, apparently deciding it was more important to exit using the door than to arrive that way.

Jonathan was gone before Sam had a chance to ask the question burning in his mind: what happened to the Southern accent? Did it fade away in the environment of the future, or had it been fake all along? Sam really wanted to know. Oh well. It sounded like there were more important mysteries.

CHAPTER 25

Two are better than one, because they have a good return
for their work. If one falls down, his friend can help him
up. But pity the man who falls and has no one to help him.
Also, if two lie down together, they will keep warm. But
how can one keep warm alone? (Ecclesiastes 4:9-11)

This had been the most challenging period in Julio's transfer agent career. First, there was the Jim/Mary/Bob debacle. Then there was Sam Meyers, who was almost done with his solo week—and the week hadn't been a success. Sam had chosen his old dorm room as his home, which was disappointing though not terribly unusual. Julio monitored Sam constantly and considered it the most pathetic response to being brought forward in memory.

It was normal for someone to get depressed for a day or two during a solo week, but in Sam's case, things spiraled downward. The sock puppet stuff was entertaining, but not necessarily beneficial, so he recruited the televangelist to try and give Sam a boost. But it didn't make any sense. How could a sci-fi fan like Sam be so despondent in the future? He hadn't even asked once about getting the chance to explore the cosmos in his own personal *Enterprise*. What was that malfunction?

Yet the biggest frustration for Julio wasn't Jim/Mary/Bob or Sam. Both situations were difficult, but neither took the cake. No. Julio's greatest headache was Manfred. He was as bad as Julio remembered from his time living Sam's life during his preparatory work, making Julio at least a little more sympathetic to Sam's failure to adapt.

After all he witnessed Sam endure over the years, Julio wasn't sure why he expected to get through to Manfred. But Julio had tried, with two or three daily sessions. He was in constant communication with the small army of other transfer agents who wanted to be part of the action.

They suggested techniques, but nothing worked. Julio's hands were somewhat tied. A truly bad person could go through a series of reincarnations of the people they had wronged, forcing them to learn about the suffering they caused. But no one knew what would happen if a sentient penis brain went into a human brain for a reincarnation, and Julio wasn't willing to take the risk.

Besides, there was only one person whose life it would make any sense for Manfred to live, and that was Sam. What if sending Manfred back into Sam's consciousness was what created Sam's talking penis in the first place? The paradox was overwhelming. No, they would have to deal with Manfred themselves, without any of the normal tricks of the trade.

Thus, it came to pass that thirty-six transfer agents had joined Julio *in person*. It was strange, having all those transfer agents physically in the same room. They had come from far and wide, wherever they had their personal transfer facilities, to be here to learn about this horrifying penis. What was it? How did it come to be? Why was it so fucking awful? Julio figured this was one of those things you needed to see for yourself. They all observed Manfred together, and caucused—again, *in person*—to develop a plan of action.

A rather goofy plan—though no one offered a better idea— took shape. Like an art project in a summer camp, all the transfer agents used the nanofabricator to design their own fake penises. By the end, they each had a single penis under control in voice and motion. They created unique personalities. Julio's was named Goober and was a class clown. He created an awesome backstory for Goober, in case Manfred ever asked.

They put all the penises in a playpen-like cage in one of Julio's viewing chambers. The penises looked like a writhing pit of worms. Some had high, squeaky voices like Manfred, while others were baritones. A couple of the transfer agents who specialized in other cultures went with accents from their specialty regions. One penis had an exaggerated French accent, another one Chinese. Two penises were being played as flamingly gay, and were intensely, immediately attracted to each other.

They developed a storyline of a magical world populated solely by penises. Once there, Manfred would hear whispered rumors of a *second* magical world populated by vaginas. Manfred could advance or impair the group's progress, or change its goals altogether, depending on his own development.

Julio transported Manfred to the pen and introduced him to his new world of peers, telling him, "I've been working hard, Manfred, and I've found a special home for you. You are not alone. You have a place in the world."

Manfred was delighted. It seemed as if he was feeling a sense of belonging and community, for the first time in his life. There was no way to be certain how Manfred ticked, with reincarnation options off the table, but Manfred *seemed* exuberant.

The other penises focused on Manfred as might be expected when a new arrival appeared. Some of the penises were friendly, while some were rude. All were designed to be only one or two levels above Manfred in terms of social evolution. This way, they'd still be realistic, believable peers. They would guide Manfred, slowly but surely, into decency.

A few hours after getting started, the other transfer agents had returned to their respective locations. Each was still involved, manning their penises from afar while going back to their normal lives. Julio also kept his distance, permitting the scene to unfold naturally.

Julio's optimism was short-lived. The smallest penis, Waffles, started getting picked on by the others and Manfred was quick to join in the bullying. "You'd be taller if you were fully erect—oh, wait, you are."

Over the next several days things only got worse. Manfred organized his own clique that ostracized the "bad penises." The gay ones, Flash and Pussycat, were quarantined and given "counseling" to stop being gay. One of the penises mentioned using a condom, and in response Manfred declared condoms were a crime against nature. Then he accused that penis of being a sick degenerate.

Manfred seemed to quickly forget about everything outside of his little group of peers. The next evening, when Julio stopped by in person, Manfred acted as if the visit was something novel.

"Oh, hey, lopamoo," Manfred said cheerfully. "Long time, no see. I'm glad you came to visit."

"Well, that makes one of us," Julio replied. Manfred didn't seem to notice the insult. "How are things going?"

"It's so nice to be free, not stuck in some douchebag's smelly underwear," Manfred said. "I can finally create the society I've always wanted, without a faggy loser whining. But let's not talk about that turd. Forget I mentioned him. You're lucky you caught us in time. We're all setting out to find the land of vaginas. We're going to suppress them. They've been allowed to run around doing whatever they want for far too long ..."

CHAPTER 26

What has been will be again, what has been done will be done again; there is nothing new under the sun. (Ecclesiastes 1:4-9)

"So, yeah, Julio, this guy named Jonathan came by. He's the asshole who used to steal money from well-meaning suckers in the name of Christ ..."

"Your alone time is at an end, Sam. Aren't you happy?" Julio interrupted, ignoring Sam's comments about Jonathan.

"I guess I'm happy. Anyway, Jonathan said ..."

"I'll admit it didn't go as well as I had hoped," said Julio. "Most people experience a bout of depression, but it passes. They usually start doing a lot of research on the possibilities available and they get excited. You, on the other hand, wallowed in depression for the whole week. Then there was that business with the sock puppet." Julio's voice was as bubbly as ever, even if he was talking about how disappointed he was in Sam.

The more Sam thought about it, the more humiliated he was that people—he had no idea which people or how many people, but at least Julio and Jonathan—had been watching him.

"After sending in Jonathan to help," Julio continued, "it occurred to me the problem really is just the penis. I thought you would have adjusted better to having a normal penis by now. But, I was wrong. I lost five dollars now, because I thought you'd make it." Julio's voice was as happy as ever, until he got to the part about losing five dollars, which seemed to make him genuinely sad. It didn't make any sense to Sam, given if Julio wanted five dollars, the nanofabricator could make it for him.

Sam said nothing, and Julio kept talking. "I'll repeat this again: Manfred is okay. Manfred is learning the elementals of critical thinking and decent behavior. For example, we have him close to agreeing it's immoral to beat your wife. At first, he insisted a man should get a pass at it, because it's his wife and all. But we've discussed it a lot and well, he has accepted it's bad. But his understanding is still textbookish and I don't have confidence his heart is in it."

Julio seemed lost in thought as he discussed his dealings with Manfred, and then snapped back into the moment. "Oh, Sam, can't you tell how draining it is to deal with him? Don't you know better than anybody? You need to pull your head out of your ass and stop pining for him. There's no nice way to say it."

Sam knew everything Julio was saying was accurate. His problem wasn't an intellectual or logical one.

"I know I'd succeed by having you spend an hour or two with Manfred every day; maybe bring you in as a teacher. At least you would remember what life was like with him, and you'd stop your current silliness. But that would keep you both in the same dependent relationship you've been in all your lives, and we need to break that forever. So, I'm doing something else. I'm going to move you on to the next phase, even if you're not technically ready. First, let me ask a question, unrelated to anything we're talking about," said Julio, pausing. "Why was Dick Cheney okay with gay marriage?"

If Sam made a list of questions he thought Julio might ask at that moment, why Dick Cheney was okay with gay marriage would be pretty low on the list. He knew Julio was very familiar with America in that era, but to hear him casually discussing details associated with circa-2000 American politics was, well, unexpected.

"There's nothing in his resume to suggest it," Julio continued. "He was a conservative Republican. The ballot drives against gay marriage helped deliver the Republican base to the polls and got him re-elected. Yet, there he was—vice president under a president trying to get a constitutional amendment against gay marriage—and he was fine with gay marriage. Why?"

"Well, because he had a lesbian daughter," answered Sam.

"Is it safe to say the big difference between Dick Cheney and George Bush on gay marriage was solely personal experience, and not abstract knowledge?" Julio asked.

"Yeah, that seems pretty safe to me."

"You're right, it is a safe assumption. Experience is the best teacher. Books can help, but books only go so far. Until you apply your hand at something, you don't really *know* it."

Julio paused and waited for some subtle sign of agreement from Sam, and continued. "Let's circle back. You know we've already given you the afterlife in a non-mystical, non-superstitious framework. But wait, there's more ..." Julio said in his best infomercial pitchman voice. "As a bonus, you also get *reincarnation* in a non-mystical, non-superstitious framework!"

"Yeah, what I was trying to say earlier is Jonathan mentioned reincarnation to me," Sam said, glad to be on a topic of his choosing.

"I know you think reincarnation is a joke," Julio said, continuing to ignore Sam's references to Jonathan. "You once heard a woman on a talk show claiming she used to be Cleopatra, and you thought it was yet another outlet for narcissism—and in that case you were correct, by the way. You associated it with Hollywood flakes and New Agers and that's about it. But would it surprise you to learn General George Patton believed in it?"

Sam felt like he was accessing one of the brain implant computers everyone had in 3542 as he pulled everything he knew about George Patton from his mind: strong World War II general, "blood and guts Patton," forcing merciless marches through Europe yet loved by almost all his soldiers, possibly assassinated at the end of the war, wanted to fight the Soviets next ... that was about all Sam knew, that was the full download. And, no, Patton didn't seem like a prime candidate for New Age crackpottery.

"He was a bit of a poet, too. Let me recite some excerpts of a poem he wrote, called *Through a Glass Darkly*, addressing his belief in reincarnation," and Julio began to recite the poem slowly and precisely, each syllable fully enunciated in Julio's odd just-learned-to-speak-aloud intonation.

The poem detailed Patton's first recollections as a caveman fighting to kill a mammoth, his experiences in ancient armies, as a mariner and as a soldier in Napoleon's army. He claimed to have fought, and died, as innumerable different people throughout time.

After the poem, Julio continued, "During the European campaigns Patton often possessed information he couldn't have known. He had detailed knowledge of historical battlefields he had, in fact, never stepped foot upon. He explained this mystery as being the result of his having personally participated in these ancient battles."

Sam had forgotten where this conversation had started. He still wasn't quite sure where it was going—Dick Cheney, General Patton, reincarnation—but he had an idea. He felt like he had the concept, but was missing the mechanism by which it might happen.

"Now I'm going to tell you the most important thing I'll ever tell you," Julio intoned gravely. "There are lots of professions and hobbies out there. You can be a transfer agent. You can explore the Universe. You can be a theoretical physicist. You can babysit children. Those are all fine things, but they're not the point of existence. We're an eternal people now, Sam. We can do almost anything we want. In the long term, the most important goal is to seek perfection. We're always learning and improving ourselves, both individually and as a species, and the best way to improve ourselves is through empathy."

Sam waited patiently as Julio spoke. He was about to ask a question when Julio spoke again.

"Let me ask you something else," Julio said. Sam returned to his mental list of questions Julio might ask. "Do you remember the first time you saw something pornographic?"

Again, not a question on Sam's expected list. Of course, he had no idea when he first encountered something pornographic. Sometime when he was a prepubescent kid, no doubt, but apparently Julio was better versed in Sam's life than Sam was himself.

"It was the puzzle of a naked woman Jerry had up the street," Julio said, answering his own question when it was clear Sam could not. "You knew what the 'bad parts' were, as you called them, and you wondered why people bothered with showing the hands and the feet and the face, when the bad parts were what they wanted. You figured, in your seven-year-old mind, that perfect porn would consist of naked boobies lined up all together, with all the other body parts cropped out of the picture. As an adult, you came to understand how largely ineffective that would be, as far as porn goes."

"Uh, okay," Sam mumbled. He was not really following this tangent.

"So my point is, looking at boobies out of context doesn't do much. You may get *something* out of it, but only at a juvenile level. Without an entire body, your mind doesn't have much to work with."

Julio paused, as if waiting for Sam to respond in some way. Sam had no idea what kind of response Julio was looking for, but he decided he needed to say *something* during this rare opportunity to speak. Unfortunately, the only thing Sam thought to say was, "Julio, I don't have the faintest idea what you're talking about."

"All right, let me put this puzzle together for you," Julio said with a grin. "Just reading about other people's perspectives is not enough to gain real empathy. As naked boobs without the context of a whole body merely gives a cursory thrill, reading someone's memoirs provides limited benefit. Sure, you might say, Christopher Columbus had some exciting days, but most of the days on a boat in the middle of the ocean were pretty dull. But if you skip those boring days, you don't really understand who the people are or why they made the choices they made. You need to experience every single minute in every single hour in every single day, and then you *understand*. With understanding comes empathy. With every life we live, we come closer to attaining perfect understanding of the big picture."

There must have been an easier way to make that point than talking about pornographic puzzles, Sam thought.

"So, if you could live the life of anyone in history, whose life would it be?"

CHAPTER 27

*The serpent was craftier than any of the wild animals
God had made. He said to the woman, "Did God really
say, 'You must not eat from any tree in the garden?'"*

*The woman said to the serpent, "We may eat fruit from the trees in the
garden, but God did say, 'You must not eat fruit from the tree that is in
the middle of the garden, and you must not touch it, or you will die.'"*

*"You will not surely die," the serpent said to the woman. "For God
knows that when you eat of it your eyes will be opened, and you
will be like God, knowing good and evil." (Genesis 3.1-5)*

Amorphous objects filled the room. He could only see a foot or
so in front of him and he had no idea where he was. He was
overwhelmed by fear and tried to call out for help, but his throat
and mouth felt weird. He couldn't form any words, only strangled
cries. He had a moment of panic as a large object moved toward

him, engulfing him in shadow. He was surrounded and the vast object lifted him in the air.

He tried to raise his head to see what was going on, but he couldn't hold it up. The object that held him grabbed him by the back of his neck, pushing him toward something circular and as big as his head. As he got closer, he was able to make out more detail, and realized with shock he was approaching a giant boob. The nipple appeared the size of a golf ball. As much as Sam enjoyed boobies, none of this felt right. He tried to squirm away but his muscles seemed powerless. There was nothing he could do to stop the nipple from being pressed into his mouth.

He bit down, not knowing what else to do. It felt natural, for some reason. A warm liquid filled his mouth, and he realized he was hungry. Or maybe thirsty. He couldn't tell, but he bit down and sucked hard on the nipple, and somehow he felt calm.

The reality of the situation became clear to Sam. He was a baby, being held and breastfed by his mother. As he thought about what was happening, he felt an intrinsic revulsion at drinking breast milk, triggering his gag reflex. He coughed and spat out what he could on the breast being pressed into his mouth. But then hunger overcame him, and he sucked greedily. When he felt full, he lost interest and fell asleep.

A loud noise woke Sam, and his first impulse was to cry. A black woman, much larger than he was, picked him up with ease. She held him tightly, pressing him to her bosom. He felt comforted and dozed off again. He may as well get used to this routine; he was a baby, and now he was stuck like this for the long haul.

He heard voices and realized the large blobs in the room were other people, talking with the giant who must be his mother. Sam listened to their conversation. The voices were faint, but he could make out parts of what was being said. One of them even commented, "Sometimes, I think he knows everything we're saying."

Well, of course he understood. He spoke English. But he wondered if he was doing something wrong. Was he supposed to pretend like he didn't know what was going on? He didn't want Julio to be mad at him when he got back.

—ɯ—

Jim didn't know what compelled him to return to Julio's facility. He supposed he simply needed someone to talk to, and he couldn't talk to Mary, not after the scene a couple of days ago. He understood this was paradise, with unlimited opportunity and eternal life. So why couldn't he just enjoy it? He needed Mary; that's all there was to it.

There were several rooms in Julio's facility. The transfer rooms were all white, like the hallways. The plain white stood in stark contrast to Julio's bizarre wardrobe and bright personal color scheme. If this was a facility Julio had made for himself, why the lack of color? Maybe he liked to stand out against the white background.

As Jim walked around, looking for Julio, he heard some noises from one of the rooms. It was one of the viewing chambers, and there were lots of squeaking noises. Jim walked in.

—ɯ—

Every day, Sam felt dumber and dumber, as if all his knowledge was slowly slipping away. He had a vague recollection of some former life, but it was fleeting. He remembered having a name, but didn't remember what it was. He couldn't remember what had seemed strange to him about his skin.

Life was simple. He slept a lot, and sucked on the big round thing—he couldn't remember what it was called—whenever he was hungry. For a while, he found himself disgusted by the things that came out of his body. Sometimes it was liquid and sometimes it was smelly brown slime. The big person would clean him and everything would be okay again. Why did he think that was so gross before? He couldn't remember.

One night he was awakened from his sleep by loud noises, and he cried in terror. The big person was screaming and so were the other two small people in his family. The big person picked him up and they started running. Someone else grabbed one of the little ones and ran in a different direction. Scary people were coming after them all. He didn't understand why.

It was all happening so fast. All he could do was scream and scream.

—⁂—

With Sam safely downloaded into his reincarnation, Julio turned his attention to his bigger problem.

He did pretty well today, his co-worker Cecilia informed him. *Relatively speaking, at least. After his late-night talk with Waffles, I think Manfred decided to publicly embrace their friendship.* Julio had a hard time swallowing that, and Cecilia said, *I didn't believe it either, but when Harley and Zeus started ganging up on Waffles, Manfred interceded.*

Interesting. *How did he intercede?* Julio asked.

Cecilia seemed a little more uncertain as she responded, *Well, he told Harley and Zeus he'd "pump eighty rounds" into each of them if they didn't "back the fuck off." However, it's possible Manfred was simply being territorial and not protective; maybe* he's *the only one allowed to torment Waffles. In either case, Harley and Zeus are making their way over to Waffles now, if you want to head over there to take a look.*

I'll visit later, Julio answered. *How far away are they?*

Oh, you have plenty of time, Cecilia responded. *They're at least seven inches away from Waffles.*

The penises had left the playpen and begun their trek to the mythical Land of the Vaginas, and lots of these little dramas were playing out along the road. But they played out slowly. The penises could scarcely move; their motions consisted of flopping around and rolling. Taunts of, "I'm going to get you, I'm going to get you," might take hours.

Julio decided to go talk with Mary first, to check in on her. Afterwards, he'd circle back to the Manfred showdown.

—⁂—

"I'm Carver's George," he said, the way his Aunt Susan taught him. "I'm looking to rent a room so I can go to school here."

He had walked a long way to reach Neosho, only to find the school closed for the day when he arrived. The long walk was hard for him, as sickly as he was, but Neosho had a school willing to accept Negroes like him.

"Well, first things first, we have to teach you how to tell someone your name," the woman, whose name was Mariah, told him. "The proper way to say your name is, 'George Carver.'"

He and his brother James were the only Negroes on the Carver farm; he had no idea what became of his mother following that scary night when he was a baby. Seeing another Negro, such as Mariah, was almost surprising. Until today, he had scarcely left the farm. James had done well working the fields, but George had been too sick for heavy labor, so he spent more time indoors with Aunt Susan. She taught him how to read and write.

"My name is George Carver," he said at the school, the way Mariah taught him, "and I'm here to get an education."

—∞—

Julio was full of surprises, but nothing prepared Jim for this scene. There, on the floor, spread out across the room, was an array of dildos.

Well, I guess I know how Julio rolls, Jim thought.

But the dildos weren't lying still on the floor. They were moving around, albeit slowly. It was like he had fallen into a pit of snakes, only less scary and more ridiculous. His curiosity got the better of him and he moved in to get a closer look. He was surprised the dildos appeared relatively small and flaccid. What was the point of a small, flaccid dildo?

Suddenly, there was a high-pitched cry as Jim's foot accidentally landed on one of them.

Without thinking, Jim said, "I'm sorry." It was the first time he had ever apologized to a dildo. He heard laughter coming from some of the others. He wasn't sure why, but the laughter bothered him. If a giant stepped on him, would Bob and Mary laugh at him like this? "Why are you laughing? I stepped on your friend," he said.

"That's not our friend," one of the dildos responded. "That's just Waffles."

—⁂—

There had been several schools along the way. For the most part, they had been useless. What was the point, when you knew more than your teacher? There had been Neosho, followed by Fort Scott, where a productive and relatively happy period of his life had come to an abrupt end one afternoon. He witnessed a black man being beaten and dragged through the street by an angry white mob. The man's skull was cracked open on the sidewalk, pieces of his brain literally landing on the ground, with a quantity of blood that didn't seem physically possible. There was nothing he could do to help, and he would never stop thinking about that day. He couldn't stay there. He needed to move again.

The next place would be different. This was a college. Highland College. This is what he had been dreaming of, a chance to learn more and pursue his art.

When he arrived, everyone stared at him. They were all white and looked at him as if he was the first Negro they had ever seen Well, he had been accepted, so they'd have to get used to him.

"You can't come in here!" said a stern white man wearing a suit.

He pulled out his letter of acceptance and showed it to the man.

"Nothing in your application said you were a nigger," the thoroughly unpleasant man said. "We don't accept niggers here at Highland. You need to leave. Now."

—⁂—

Jim reached down to examine the dildo who had spoken to him. He gingerly reached for it and when his fingertip made contact, he recoiled in revulsion as he realized he was touching real skin. These weren't strange non-erect dildos; they were actual penises! He stumbled back a few steps, careful not to step on another one, re-assessing the scene.

Curiosity brought him back. "What *are* you?"

"What does it look like we are? We're dicks. My name is Manfred, and I'm the King of the Dicks."

"Excuse me?" another of the penises said with a cough. "King? King? You're our King now? Uh, yeah, right."

"Shut up, Zeus, you're damned right I'm the King," the penis called Manfred hissed. Then it said to Jim, "I'm leading my people to the Land of the Vaginas, which we will subjugate. What are you doing here?"

Jim couldn't help but chuckle. If Mary's faithless behavior was any indication, the Land of the Vaginas was definitely in need of subjugation.

"My name is Jim," he said after a moment of hesitation during which he reflected on the fact he was having a conversation with a penis. "I'm here to see Julio. I've got woman problems, too."

—⁂—

It was certainly unexpected, the day Booker Washington came to visit him.

"I want you to come to Alabama and head our agricultural department at Tuskegee," Washington said.

George considered it. He was doing well for himself at Iowa State. He had been the first black student and was now the first black faculty member. He had been prolifically productive in the laboratory, and must have been well-regarded, if someone like Booker Washington had personally come from Alabama to recruit him.

"What kind of offer can you make?" George asked.

"I cannot offer you money, position or fame," Washington replied. "The first two you sufficiently have. Fame you will no doubt achieve on your own. These things I now ask you to give up. I offer you in their place: work—hard, hard work, the task of bringing a people from exploitation and poverty to full potential. Your department exists only on paper and your laboratory will have to be in your head."

George loved what he was doing, but ever since that day so many years ago when he had seen a black man beaten to death, he had known that, even after spending so much of his life among whites, he needed to do something to help his fellow Negroes get out of poverty and despair. Slavery was long gone—he had been too young to remember when it had been abolished—but its lasting imprint on the nation was evident. It was time for him to give back, to contribute as much as possible to elevate his society and realize the promise of America's ideals.

—⁂—

"Your wife sounds like a whore," the self-proclaimed King of the Dicks told him. Jim was glad for the validation, no matter what the source. Everyone else he met in 3542 seemed to be on Mary and Bob's side.

"I admit I've come into these viewing chambers a few times already," Jim confided. "To witness how she cast me aside. Now, Julio has forbidden me to use the portal."

"That doesn't make any sense," Manfred said. "Why would he stop you from gaining knowledge?"

This penis made a good case. All Jim wanted was knowledge, right? But Julio's warning was still there in his mind. "He did forbid me. There must be a good reason."

"Julio is always trying to control everybody! I say go ahead and do it. Maybe you should step through and 'take care' of Bob, if you get what I'm saying."

He realized he shouldn't listen, but Manfred's words were enough to tempt him. Nervously, Jim spoke up. "Hey, machine," he said to the viewing chamber, "can you show me Mary Franklin's and Bob Reynolds' first date?" The machinery apparently knew which people in history he was referring to and when and where their first date had taken place. The inside of the viewing chamber glowed and he saw the two of them sitting in a fancy restaurant.

"Hey, Jim," came Manfred's voice. Jim had forgotten about the King of the Dicks. "You've got some important work to do now, but may I ask a favor first? I'm trying to lead my subjects to the Land of the Vaginas, but it takes forever to move around. Can you give us a lift? Just to help us on our way? I'm not certain, but I think it's on the other side of the room."

He didn't want to pick up even one of those penises, and an armload was more than any man should have. Still, they didn't seem threatening, and certainly seemed to support his cause. Jim knelt down and started picking up penises.

"Don't forget about Waffles," one of them said.

"Waffles is tiny and worthless," Manfred said. "He'll slip through this guy's fingers, and he'll never satisfy a vagina. Jim, please step on that shrimp again and again, and put him out of his misery."

—⁓—

"What will Bob do?" Mary asked.

Julio gave her a reassuring smile. "He's putting together a great life. He's learning about modern medical science. He'll be fine."

It was a brief conversation. He had explained how it would be best if Bob were out of the picture for a while—per the original plan—and she and Jim would spend time together, at least long enough to get Jim stabilized. Hans' practical joke had really screwed things up. He had to hand it to Hans on this one. Oh, he would have his revenge. He was plotting that right now.

Suddenly, other transfer agents started pinging him with alarm.

Did you step on Waffles?

Something's going on in the Manfred simulation.

Are you carrying Bruno around?

Did you pull Moose into the air?

Someone just squeezed Skor. Was that you, Julio?

Not me, Julio returned.

Then you'd better get over there right now.

Lots of other simultaneous conversations like that one occurred, all in a twenty-second span. Something was up.

"Mary, I'm sorry," Julio said, interrupting a question Mary had begun asking. He sometimes forgot she had only been here for less than a week. The Mary-Jim-Bob fiasco seemed like it had been going on for months. "Something's happening, and I need to go right now." He didn't wait for her to respond. He pictured his destination and disappeared.

—⁂—

As he sat there, all those eyes staring at him, all those important people in their fine suits sitting behind the dais, he became self-conscious for the first time. He was wearing his old suit, the same one he had worn twenty-five years earlier for his first lecture at Tuskegee. Everyone told him he needed to get a new suit before testifying in front of Congress, but he had insisted, over and over again, they wanted to hear what he had to *say* and were not interested in how he *looked*. After all, this wasn't about him; it was about a piece of proposed legislation overlapping his area of expertise.

That had been easy to say when he was at school, wearing his regular clothes. Now he was sitting in front of the House Ways and Means Committee, and he felt woefully underdressed. He knew at least half of the people on that dais, despite all his accomplishments, still considered him part of a lesser species. His old, faded suit would only support their prejudices.

Well, he couldn't change his clothes now.

After all the formalities were completed, George had his opportunity to make an opening statement before they asked questions. He was given only ten minutes, so he didn't have much time to make a lasting impression.

"Honored gentlemen," he began, "I am here representing the American peanut farmer. As you probably know, I have spent my life devoted to helping the American farmer and diversifying crop production in the South, with a focus on uses for the peanut ..."

—⁓—

It was surreal to Jim. He stood there, with roughly fifteen separate, writhing penises squeezed between his arm and his belly. He'd need to come back for the rest, as he didn't want to overload and risk dropping one, given they were apparently alive and could feel pain. All he was doing was walking to the other side of the room. He'd be done soon, and then he'd get back to Mary and Bob. He'd mess up their first date, so they'd never have a second one.

"Jim!"

Jim turned his head and Julio was standing right there, where he hadn't been an instant before. In a blind panic, Jim thought of nothing but the fact he was carrying a bundle of penises, like some kind of weirdo. His mind paralyzed by embarrassment, his instant reaction was to toss the evidence. So he turned and flung the bundle.

Once they left his hand, his brain began to work again. Julio was probably much more concerned that Jim had Mary's past showing in the viewing chamber, even after Julio had forbidden him. Jim watched in horror as the bundle of penises flew through the air ... and headed straight for the viewing chamber. But when the penises entered the chamber, they *didn't* land on the dinner table in the restaurant, as one might expect based on their flight trajectory. They simply vanished into thin air.

Uh oh, Jim thought, *that's not good*. The look on Julio's face confirmed something extraordinarily bad happened.

—⁓—

Julio desperately ran the calculations. He counted twenty-one penises still in the middle of the floor, and three penises had missed the chamber and landed on the side. Thirteen, including Manfred, went through the machine. He cross-referenced the specifications for the missing penises to get their masses.

The penises obviously hadn't stepped on the scale at the entrance to the chamber, so it would be calibrated to the last person who had entered. He checked that against the total mass he estimated for the penises. He then did the time calculation, providing a historical time range to which the penises may have traveled. For each possible time within that range, there was also a range of possible locations. The system was fixed to ensure travelers would land somewhere on the surface of Earth. As the Earth moved through the universe, this calculation became complex even by 3542 standards.

Julio put together a file containing the possible array of space-time locations where the penises might have arrived and sent the info for wide distribution. It would take a while, but they'd find Manfred.

As for Jim ... well, Julio hated to do this sort of thing. He didn't have much choice at this point, not after Jim had betrayed his trust again, only a couple of days after he had specifically told the man he couldn't touch the observation chamber. Jim would be cast out of Eden, so to speak, and sent away to some developing culture on another planet.

—∞—

Everything in George's body was sore. It was like when he was a child, always so sick and frail. Well, he was seventy-eight years old, as best he knew—he was never certain of his date of birth—so that sort of thing was to be expected.

It was almost bedtime and he was tired. He would just go downstairs and get a drink before retiring to bed. When he reached the stairs, he abruptly felt his right leg give out. He lost his balance and tumbled down. The pain was immense as he first landed, and got worse with every step he hit on the way down.

His head hit the hard floor at the bottom of the stairs.

CHAPTER 28

I returned, and saw under the sun, that the race is not to the swift, nor the battle to the strong, neither bread to the wise, nor riches to men of understanding, nor favor to men of skill; but time and chance happeneth to them all. (Ecclesiastes 9:11)

George opened his eyes. Wait, no, not George. Sam. He was definitely Sam again.

Well, that was an experience. It was the longest dream he ever had, except it wasn't a dream. It was real and it lasted 78 years. If it was the year 3620 now, little had changed. Certainly, modern fashion remained fixed, as Julio was wearing his customary neon mesh shirt and vinyl pants combination.

"Good morning, Sam," Julio said brightly, though his eyes seemed to be looking right past Sam.

"So *that* was reincarnation?" Sam asked. Julio nodded and Sam continued, "You have access to all existence, and can put me right into a dream recreating anyone's life, and make the dream so convincing I honestly think I was that person, living his or her life."

Julio was starting to open his mouth and Sam had a sense he was going to make a clarifying comment, but Sam was on a roll. "And that's what Jonathan was talking about—that was his own personal Lake of Fire. His transfer agent made him experience a bunch of dreams in which he lived the lives of his victims. That's basically what he told me. But I didn't completely get it until right now."

"Sam, I'm so proud of you," Julio said. "You're almost half right! It *wasn't* a dream. You did live the life of George Washington Carver. To put it in the terms of your era, *you* are software—or, at least, your mind is software. You went back in time to when Carver was born and your *software* began running on the *hardware* that was Carver's brain. You really did experience his lifetime, right as it was happening."

It was a strange thought, but he was getting used to strange thoughts. He asked, "If it was me living his life, wouldn't I be changing the past?"

"Have I mentioned how much I enjoy working with your era in history? If I had pulled you from fifty years earlier you wouldn't have the foggiest clue what I was talking about," Julio began. "Even better, you died young, so you grew up with computers. Think about it like this: your software had *read only* rights, not *write rights*. You couldn't make any changes because you had no input. You were going along for the ride as a passive observer. But since it was the same circumstances and the same hardware, you *believed* you were making all the decisions he was making."

"Well, yeah, except for right at the beginning. I remember knowing who I was, as a baby. That part was weird. I was stuck inside a baby and powerless," Sam recalled.

"Yeah, that's how it happens," Julio replied. "At first, you're still yourself. But the knowledge fades pretty fast, right?"

Sam nodded. He remembered his own sense of self fading and him *becoming* George.

"So, does George mind?" Sam asked. Sam had always called him by his full name, but now, after living his life, he would always just be *George* from now on. "It seems like a huge personal invasion. Does he have to sign a permission form or something?"

"No," Julio answered. "Everyone who knows about it, gets it. Anyone who doesn't get it, doesn't know. Except of course, you're sort of in limbo right now. Would it bug you to learn I lived your life, as a routine preliminary task for my job?"

It seemed obvious now. Julio knew all sorts of things about Sam, things he had never verbalized to anyone. Sam figured they had some sort of thought-reading process. In a sense, he supposed, they did, and they even took it a step further by connecting everyone's thoughts to everyone else's. But Sam wasn't emotionally ready to connect to the wireless router or whatever it was these future people had in their brains.

"So you went back and—just like I did with George—you lived my life in the blink of an eye, so you'd know me well enough to transfer me out," Sam said, thinking aloud.

"As to the second part," Julio said, "I apparently still didn't know you well enough to anticipate how you'd react to having Manfred replaced by a non-jerkwad penis. As to the first part, it's an overstatement to say 'in the blink of an eye.' It took you nearly two hours to live the almost 79 years of Carver's life."

"Why couldn't it be instantaneous? Why couldn't I live a thousand lifetimes before a bowl of ice cream melts? Just pop me back there and pop me back here." It was a nitpicky question, Sam realized. As if two hours—the time it took him to watch a single movie in his old life—was a ridiculously long time to spend experiencing someone's entire life.

"There's still a concept of real time," Julio answered. "A program still has to run, and there are limitations to the processing speed."

Sam continued asking questions. "If I wanted to become a transfer agent, I'd have to live all the lives of my patients or clients or whatever you call them?"

"Yes," Julio answered. "I'm in the lives of random, non-famous people all the time. Like I mentioned before, that's how I gain perspective and empathy. Of course, it was also job training. I had to live a hundred lives from your era and your part of the world before becoming a transfer agent, so I'd understand the historical context of the world people are coming from."

Sam remembered TV-Computer telling him he'd need to live a minimum of a thousand lifetimes, a hundred of them in his area of specialty. It seemed insurmountable at the time, but Sam now realized it could be accomplished rather quickly. It would be like going to grad school.

Something else occurred to Sam. He realized he was now qualified to be a botanist, particularly in the area of peanuts. People who lived in the centuries after his death undoubtedly did much more in the field, and Sam could live their lives, as well. He could become an expert. Sure, maybe there were lots of people who had lived the lives of Carver and others in his field, but with so much out there to be learned, and so much of the universe left to discover, the possibilities seemed endless.

Sam flushed with hope and cheer. He felt silly for having missed Manfred so much. He didn't need Manfred at all. The whole universe was waiting for him.

"Hey, can I go back and live *your* life?" Sam asked. That seemed like a good way to cheat, learning everything at once.

"Not until I'm dead, thank you very much," Julio replied. "You need a death or 'hard stop' before someone's life is available. I've never died before."

Sam waited for the extended explanation, but it never came. It occurred to him Julio was being somewhat quiet today. Usually, it was hard for Sam to get a word in edgewise, but today he managed to wedge in dozens of words. Julio seemed preoccupied, like talking with Sam was an afterthought.

"Is something wrong?"

"What?" Julio's head snapped in place looking at Sam. After staring at Sam for a few seconds, Julio said, "Yes, something happened while you were living George Carver's life."

Sam tried to give Julio a visual cue to continue. Why didn't he provide a real answer right away for questions like that? Obviously, Sam wasn't asking if Julio simply knew if something was wrong. Julio had to know Sam wouldn't say, *Oh, I'm so glad you know. That's all I wanted to know, whether or not you knew if something was wrong. I can move along now.*

As Julio sat there silently, Sam finally relented and asked, "What happened?"

"Manfred's gone," Julio replied.

"Well, that's not exactly a tragedy," Sam said, even though he had missed Manfred enough to make a sock puppet of him very recently.

"No, but it is a problem. Someone put him in the chamber and sent him into the past. Now he's who-knows-where, doing who-knows-what damage to human history."

"So why are you talking to me instead of finding him?" Sam asked, but as soon as the question came out of his mouth he knew the answer.

"What do you think I've been doing?" Julio answered. "While we've been talking, I've been working with a large team of people trying to locate Manfred in time and space. Don't worry. It might take a little while, but we'll find him. And when we do, I might need your help to safely extract him."

"Is there any way I can help you now?" Sam asked.

"No. For now, I suggest you worry about yourself," Julio said. "Go back, live some more lives, and try your hand at being alone again. I'll check on you from time to time, and I'll let you know as soon as we find Manfred."

It looked like Sam couldn't close the door on Manfred just yet, after all.

CHAPTER 29

*Women received back their dead by resurrection. Some
were tortured, refusing to accept release, so that they
might rise again to a better life. (Hebrews 11:35)*

"It's *Your Life in 3542!*" the announcer bombastically announced,
rolling each syllable. "With your host, Jonathan Parsons!" The
crowd erupted in applause.

This was a rather comical aspect of the future, from Sam's
perspective, but he was sympathetic to it. Newly retrieved people
from his era were often retirees accustomed to being home to
watch afternoon TV, which, Sam recalled from his summer back
at home after his first year of college, consisted of about 90% talk
shows. Who better to host the show than the former piece-of-shit
televangelist, Jonathan?

Julio recommended the show to Sam during one of their
brief daily conversations, saying the familiar format from the past
helped people get accustomed to the future. Sure, the show had a
limited target audience—only English-speaking people retrieved

from a very specific era—but it was still a large number overall. However, the presence of a studio audience baffled Sam. Who were these people filling the seats every show?

"Thank you, thank you," Jonathan said as he walked onto the stage and bowed. He extended his arms to the cheering crowd. He was wearing a designer suit, like most other TV hosts from Sam's era. "It's wonderful to see you this afternoon. Simply fantastic! A warm welcome to all my fellow transfers from the late 20th or early 21st century. And if you died in a different time, go away!" He laughed at that line, which he opened every show with, and strolled over to a nearby desk.

"What a great show we have for you today," Jonathan began. "We're going to be talking about what worries us, what makes us laugh, and our unanswered questions. It's a wonderful time to be alive, but it can also be overwhelming." Sam nodded along with about half of the live studio audience.

"We're all struggling with different issues. The Atheists in the audience were surprised to find salvation is real. The religious people in the audience were even more shocked to learn salvation has nothing to do with God, but is thanks to those MIT nerds slaving away in the basement of the science building every Friday night. Hey—we were all sort of right and sort of wrong!"

Jonathan picked up some papers and bounced them on his desk to get them flush with each other. The stack of papers and notes was one of the charming anachronisms of the show, clearly designed to give people a sense of continuity with the past, down to the tiny details.

"Our first topic is something many of us worry about: When will our loved ones join us?" Jonathan said, still with no hint of a Southern accent. "We have two mothers with us today who are hoping to see their children again soon, and are worried they may never be reunited. First up, we have Nancy. Please welcome Nancy to the show."

Jonathan extended his arm to the side of the stage, where a woman with sandy blonde hair walked onto the set. She smiled nervously. Jonathan led her out to a section of the stage with two chairs angled towards the audience.

After they sat down and the audience quieted, Jonathan said, "Nancy, thank you for being with us today. Will you share your concerns with us?" He gave her a reassuring smile.

"Thank you, Jonathan," she said timidly. "I'm worried about my son, Harold. I love him so much, and he has good qualities. But he was also a rapist." She paused, fighting back tears, and elaborated, "He raped strangers ... he violently raped strangers. I've learned all the horrible details of his life."

As she sniffled, Jonathan went to the soft, understated voice that had worked so well for him in his preaching days (minus the accent). "Oh, what a painful thing for a parent to go through. How have you coped?"

Between sniffles, Nancy answered, "I no longer blame myself. Learning the details of what he did ... it was crushing. I denied it for the longest time. I actually uttered the words—verbatim— 'my Harold is a sweet boy, he wouldn't hurt a fly.' I thought the first woman was a liar. I'm ashamed to say I called the second victim a slut. By the third victim, I finally started to realize something was wrong." Her sniffles turned to sobs as she continued, "Harold wound up in jail, and I found out he was suspected in four other cases, and now I know those suspicions were true. There was even an eighth woman who never told a soul about it. But I still can't stop replaying all the normal and happy memories of his childhood. He wasn't *all* bad."

"I know. I know," Jonathan nodded understandingly.

"I still love him and I hope he can be saved somehow," Nancy said. "I'm so sorry to the people he hurt, but I can't help the fact I love him. He'll always be my son."

They talked for a while longer, Jonathan asking questions and trying to console Nancy. Jonathan reminded the audience of what a terrible person he was, even admitting to a rape of his own, arguing if JESUS had a place for him, surely there must be a place for Harold. As Sam watched, he wasn't so sure. It seemed obvious JESUS had a purpose for Jonathan, and that purpose was for him to do exactly what he was doing right now. Sam doubted Harold had any such skills that would make JESUS decide to bring him forward. Sam just couldn't imagine what use the future had for some random, lowlife, serial rapist. But what did he know?

So he asked TV-Computer. Not about Harold the Rapist, but about what he figured must be the litmus test for this sort of thing. "TV-Computer, what about Hitler? Is he being brought forward, or was he … left behind?"

TV-Computer must have answered this question so many times, given the way it replied, "Ah, the Hitler question." Sam was pretty sure he heard TV-Computer audibly sigh. TV-Computer explained that Hitler had not been retrieved to date and there were no known plans to do so.

If Hitler were to be retrieved, TV-Computer explained, they would try to fix him and use him to help Aryan Youths and related troubled cases with their transitions. The thinking would be along the lines of, "Here is your idol. Look: *he*'s no longer evil. Perhaps *you* want to consider evolving, too." While that idea made sense, if Hitler could be saved through empathy like Jonathan, Sam had the suspicion it would have happened by now, if it were going to happen. If Hitler had indeed been left behind permanently, Sam could hardly blame JESUS.

After Nancy came a mother from Michigan named Hasna, whose son Ahmed had fallen in with the wrong crowd. Ahmed moved to Yemen and joined a militant group, and died in a failed suicide bombing. Unlike Nancy, who couldn't explain what went wrong with her son, Hasna saw it coming. Ahmed always had trouble fitting in, was bullied ruthlessly, and failed at all efforts to win friends. She assured the audience Ahmed didn't have any true hatred in his heart, only pain and confusion.

After talking with her for a few minutes, Jonathan said, "Well, Hasna, I have a surprise for you." He paused for dramatic effect, then added, "I've been given word JESUS has scheduled Ahmed's retrieval for August 2nd. So it looks like you'll be reunited sooner rather than later!"

Hasna gave a shriek of joy and hugged Jonathan, who hugged her back. *He may not be a scumbag con artist anymore, but he hasn't given up on emotional manipulation,* Sam thought. While reasonably engaging, this section of the show was too reminiscent of the talk shows he was never interested in watching back in the 2000s. It was like the show was being overly dramatic to fight for ratings, even though there was no such competition.

But it ended on a positive note. Jonathan switched to his Southern accent. "As I used to say when I was a televangelist: JESUS saves!" Jonathan and the audience laughed and continued to radiate the happiness they expressed for Hasna. Sam found it interesting to realize that, back in his day, almost no one would have the slightest bit of sympathy for a youth turned murderous terrorist, and who could blame them? Now the audience members of Jonathan's show all seemed to be rooting for Ahmed to be brought forward and cured of the defects that led him to evil. It seemed to be a ringing endorsement of human redemption and evolution.

Sam found the next segment of the show quite entertaining. "It's time for *How Embarrassed Are You?*" Jonathan announced to claps and cheers from the audience.

This was a segment during which people told stories of the most embarrassing things they did during their "first lives." It made for fun viewing, but Sam understood it was also an important segment for transitioning people. For all the wonders of the future, it was strange getting used to the destruction of privacy. When anyone can live your life and thoughts get transmitted like spoken word, there isn't any use for privacy. So, Sam realized, this segment was designed to get people accustomed to their lives being an open book.

First, Jonathan introduced a man named Ian who described his time playing hockey in high school. He looked like someone Sam's age describing an event that happened a year or two ago, but of course this incident in high school may well have occurred the better part of a century ago in Ian's life.

"I must have had some sort of chemical imbalance, because I was psychotic out there. Other than taking some penalties, I played the best game of my life. I scored three goals, but the other team also scored three while I was in the penalty box. There were 15 seconds left and the score was tied. I got the puck and took the hardest slap shot of my life. It went top shelf, and I ripped off my helmet and went down onto the ice in this pose."

The shot cut away from Ian and Jonathan to what was apparently a photo of the incident. He was down on one knee, flexing both biceps, with an ugly snarl on his face that managed to expose all his teeth. The screen cut back to the stage, and Ian demonstrated the pose to Jonathan, which included nodding his head up and down vigorously.

"I screamed, 'Fuck you in the ass! Fuck you in the ass!' to the other team's players near me. The refs had to wrestle me to the penalty box. I told them I didn't care because I just showed everyone 'whose cock they could suck.' After the game, I went to the locker room for my hero's welcome. No one wanted to talk to me, though. The only person who even looked me in the eye was the Captain, and all he said, 'Screw you, Ian.' Turns out, not thinking straight, I had scored on my own net and won the game for the other team!"

Ian went on to describe how his pose had become legendary in school. Whenever people saw him they'd do the pose and laugh. It became a symbol of embracing total failure. Ian recalled seeing a girl breaking up with a guy in the hallway one day. She slapped the guy in the face and kneed him in the balls.

"I'm sure his junk hurt like hell," Ian said, "but as she was walking away, before collapsing in a heap, the guy got down on one knee and made the pose. At some point I had to embrace it and take pride in this thing I had created through my own stupidity."

"Well, that's a valuable lesson, Ian," Jonathan said. "Thanks for sharing with us."

After Ian, Jonathan introduced a dark-haired girl named Jackie. She told her story about the time she had gone to a drug store with the worst diarrhea of her life and exploded in the aisle. She wiped her ass with her underwear, and then kicked the filthy underwear under a display case. Sam felt a kinship with Jackie, at least until that point. He at least cleaned up his shitty underwear scenes.

Jackie then shoplifted whatever it was she had come to steal. "I don't remember, but probably nachos," she admitted. She went home and forgot all about it until she got a call from her friend Larissa a few months later. Larissa wanted to know if Jackie still had the tattoo on her butt of a penguin with the words "Trevon 4-Ever." (Jackie broke up with Trevon about a week after getting the tattoo.) It turned out there was a viral video of the diarrhea incident, taken on a cell phone camera by someone she didn't notice at the time.

The scene switched to a grainy cell phone video of Jackie bending over, pulling off her underwear, and wiping herself with them. The video zoomed in to clearly reveal the penguin tattoo on her ass. It received over eighteen million views. Jackie had to assume Larissa wasn't the only person who saw the tattoo and knew Jackie's identity. Jonathan smiled and shook his head. "Let's leave 2010 in the past, brothers and sisters, let's leave it in the past!" he laughed. The show ended shortly afterwards.

Later that night, Sam tried living the life of Harold the Rapist. Harold died young, and it only took about an hour for the reincarnation "software" to complete. It was disturbing, indulging insatiable desires and listening to people scream. While he was living the life, it was pure elation. After waking up as Sam, he felt guilty and grotesque at having felt that way, despite the fact it was by no means *Sam* who did any of those actions or had any of those feelings.

Over the next couple of weeks, Sam did many more reincarnations in rapid succession. He lived in ancient Greece and Rome. He tried his hand at being a knight in medieval England, a life of little glory and excitement relative to the amount of time spent sleeping on the ground Even after waking up as Sam, he felt very sore.

Sam only went to the future once (well, the past now, but the future relative to his previous life). He lived the life of a prominent deep space explorer, who also happened to be one of the last people to naturally die. He thought it would be exciting and, in some ways, it was. However, for the most part, traveling across vast expanses of nothingness proved to be boring.

He coordinated with TV-Computer to help him play Reincarnation Roulette, in which a random, almost certainly non-famous life is picked by chance. He played twice, once living the life of a starving mother of six, three of whom died as children, in Kazakhstan during the fall of the Soviet Union and once as a well-to-do Portuguese slave trader living in Angola. Then he spiced up his knowledge of American history by living the lives of the U.S. Presidents, starting with Washington. It would take a while to complete the whole set, though.

When he wasn't living lives, he was otherwise fishing for knowledge. He was drawn to all the mysteries he remembered. Who was buried in the Tomb of the Unknown Soldier? Did aliens really land in Roswell? Is there anything truly unusual about the Bermuda Triangle? Sam knew all these things now.

Every time Julio came to visit, Sam had more questions. One day, he asked what had become the biggest question on his mind. "Are great people great because they were always great, or are great people great because everyone is living their lives in the future? Is there a different universe in which General Patton is a private, because hardly anyone lived his life in a reincarnation? Maybe another one in which he's a corporal, because he's gotten just a little bit of attention? I mean, do we make great people great? Or … scratch that, I don't necessarily mean 'great.' I think I only mean, 'famous.' Do we somehow *make* them famous?"

"You hit on the mystery," Julio responded with a half-smile. "All I can say is: I sure hope they were always great and/or famous. If not, we've been changing the shit out of the past. We might be creating huge numbers of parallel universes, something I don't want to even think about."

"Does anyone know how Patton remembered being a soldier in Ancient Rome? I bet a lot of soldiers from Rome have been reincarnated as him. Was Patton somehow aware of their presence and able to glean some of their thoughts?"

Julio shook his head and shrugged in a full-body motion. "It seems like once in a while, a mind can pick up glimpses of the other minds co-existing in theirs during reincarnation. I think this is what happened in Patton's case. He is a forbidden reincarnation right now, by the way, since he seemed to clue in on what was going on. We didn't want him to become aware of the Cold War or Vietnam or Iraq or any other upcoming war. But it seems like he had some inkling of future events, since he wanted to fight the Soviets right away."

"Has anyone thought that maybe reincarnation should be forbidden across the board?" Sam asked.

"You're not the first person to ask," Julio replied. He seemed to be slightly disturbed by this line of questioning. "Who knows if parallel universes would really be problematic. The universe is continuing to expand. Maybe it's just expanding with us, making space for our different realities. It's unknown and not comfortable to think about, but we can't stop learning now. Our path is forward."

CHAPTER 30

Therefore keep watch, because you do not know on what day your Lord will come. But understand this: If the owner of the house had known at what time of night the thief was coming, he would have kept watch and would not have let his house be broken into. So you also must be ready, because the Son of Man will come at an hour when you do not expect him. (Matthew 24:42-44)

Sam had more appreciation for the process as he delved deeper. The medical advancements and the nanotechnology were great, the afterlife itself was sensational, but the sharing of perspective through reincarnation and the development of empathy … that offered a whole different level of awe Sam was just beginning to grasp.

The first noticeable difference in undergoing reincarnations was the strange fluidness of memories. Sam could remember his first memories, from his original life, but he also now shared the memories of other people. The sharing was so intense that the memories started to blur together. The trucker's drug-induced comments along the lines of "all humanity is one" and "the boundaries between people are illusions" became more truthful-sounding with each reincarnation.

He must have listened to Sinead O'Connor's *Nothing Compares 2 U* about a hundred times following a break-up from a guy named Dickie. It took him a while to realize he never knew and certainly never dated a guy named Dickie, and he never cared for that song anyway. His memories were from the reincarnation of someone who had. But his mind was playing a trick on him. The opening line of the song mentioned 15 days, and as he thought about it, yes, Manfred had been gone for 15 days.

"Sam, so glad to find you here!" came Julio's voice as the towering man appeared in Sam's house where he hadn't been moments before. "We found him! We found Manfred."

"You have him back?" Sam asked.

"Back here?" Julio replied. "No, not exactly, but we know where and when he is. Come with me. I don't know all the details. We'll learn together."

Julio transported Sam to the transfer facility, and Sam arrived in one of the viewing chambers. It looked like the other viewing chambers, except for a box containing an array of dildos. They were inanimate, lifeless things. It seemed like some creep's collection, if anyone had any use for modestly sized flaccid dildos. Sam suppressed a sudden impulse to play with them, maybe put on a puppet show.

Light filled the room as the chamber came humming to life. A scene arose in front of Sam, a wilderness covered with rocks and unusual plants. Sam scanned the scene like he was searching for Waldo, waiting for Manfred's outline to leap out.

It took a while, but his eyes focused in on what looked like a pile of sausages sitting in the shadow of a gigantic rock. It was a pile of penises similar to the ones in the box. One of the penises was writhing slightly. That must be Manfred. Sam wondered if, absent the writhing, Sam would have been able to pick Manfred out from the pile.

"Can we get him?" Sam asked. Then he added, "Can he hear us?"

"Second question first," Julio replied. "No, he can't hear us unless we enter the chamber. First question, no, we can't just stroll in there and get him. Keep in mind this is right after Manfred arrived. He's been there for 15 days. That's 15 days of the past potentially being changed."

Sam watched lots of science fiction in his day, but he didn't understand how this sort of thing worked. Yet he couldn't determine any flaw as he suggested, "Why don't we pull him out now before he has a chance to do any damage?"

"Unfortunately, we can't charge in there like cowboys and yank him out from wherever and whenever he landed," Julio answered. "There have been 15 days we can't undo. Whatever Manfred has done for these 15 days is already done. We can't change that. The best we can do is minimize any further damage."

"What kind of damage are you expecting?"

"Hopefully, none," Julio said. "It's not as if he moves fast. If we get *super* lucky, he'll be eaten by a large bird soon after he lands on the ground."

"Could we be that lucky?" Sam asked rhetorically.

"We'll see," Julio said.

They stood there watching Manfred writhing around and very slowly pulling away from the other penises in the pile. Sam grew bored, until a flaw occurred to him. "So what's the plan? For every minute we watch Manfred, he may do more damage."

"Quite right you are," Julio said brightly. Sam was sure Julio wasn't as bored as he was, because Julio could play Solitaire (or some game vastly more complicated; who knew how Julio idly amused himself) or surf the web in his head. "Let's move ahead an hour."

With that pronouncement, the scene shifted ever so slightly. No, Sam realized, the scene hadn't shifted, but the lighting changed. It was brighter, the sun higher in the sky. Manfred had squirmed about a foot away from the pile.

"So far, so good," Julio said before using whatever mental interface he used to shift the scene forward again. This time, the sun was lower in the sky and Manfred was about two feet further away, a marathon for him.

"How far along are we?" Sam asked.

"I've moved us forward two hours," Julio replied.

Sam found himself feeling sorry for Manfred, who had to be terrified, shriveled all alone out there, heroically trying to move yet only achieving pitiful results.

Distant rumbling thunder could be heard, even though the sky was nearly cloudless. The sound grew louder, and the view started to get hazy.

Sam realized he was seeing dust being kicked up. Then he saw a herd of elephants. No, not elephants; these creatures were covered in brown fur and had long, curled tusks. Woolly mammoths? The stampede included maybe a dozen adult mammoths and another half dozen calves.

"Oh, here we go!" Julio exclaimed excitedly, pointing at the charging herd. "This may be our lucky break!"

"Hey ... what year is this?" Sam asked.

"Pleistocene epoch, 12,003 years BCE," answered Julio. "Jim has a good throwing arm," he added. Sam wondered who the hell Jim was, and why he was manhandling penises.

Sam heard Manfred scream, "FUUUCCCKK!" Manfred turtled into himself as the giant furry legs thundered by. Most of the herd stampeded about five yards behind where Manfred lay, but a couple of them passed right above him. Somehow, none of those feet managed to hit Manfred, though he must have seen the underbellies of quite a few.

"Shit!" Julio cried. "They missed him!"

Sam stared at Julio. He wasn't quite sure why the idea of Manfred getting squashed bothered him. Manfred was horrible, but that didn't mean Sam wanted him to suffer. At least not anymore, not since they were separated.

Julio seemed to recognize he had offended Sam and offered, "Sorry if that seemed insensitive. The quicker the death, the less chance he has to alter the past. Now, we have to keep watching and waiting."

They returned to watching in real time, but nothing was happening. Occasionally, a bird flew by, and at one point a lizard—a dinosaur by Manfred's perspective—walked along, uninterested. The penis was not of its food chain, so it ignored Manfred. Sam hoped being seen by a lizard did not constitute changing the past.

Sam became impatient, sitting around and waiting for Manfred to get squashed or eaten or die of exposure or something. "There must be something else we can do," he said.

"Why yes, there is!" Julio said. "I'll set the computer up to monitor for anything that constitutes changing history."

"Why didn't you do that in the first place?"

"I don't know," Julio replied. "I thought we'd observe for a while. I figured there was an excellent chance Manfred would die pretty fast." He paused, and continued, "So how have things been going, Sam?"

Sam was caught off-guard by the casual question. They took a few minutes to discuss Sam's latest reincarnations.

For a moment, Sam wondered when Julio would set the computer up, but realized Julio was certainly doing that presently. Sam didn't know if he'd ever learn to multi-task the way Julio could. He planned to get the brain implant soon—the idea was growing on him—but he wondered if he'd ever be able to have many different conversations at the same time. Was this something Sam could learn? Or did it require evolution of the human mind Sam could never match, because Julio was born 12 centuries after Sam?

Sam knew one thing: if his brain had been better at multi-tasking, he never would have steered his car off the embankment during that blowjob. Manfred would still be attached to him, instead of alone and in danger of being squashed by a woolly mammoth.

CHAPTER 31

For our knowledge is imperfect and our prophecy is imperfect; but when the perfect comes, the imperfect will pass away. When I was a child, I spoke like a child, I thought like a child, I reasoned like a child; when I became a man, I gave up childish ways. (First Corinthians 13: 9 – 10)

It had taken over two weeks to search for Manfred. The task was made more difficult by all the fraudulent memories of talking penises made by crazy people over the years. Just as law enforcement processes the contents of a tip hotline, they had to sift through mountains of rubbish in hopes of finding something legitimate. The processing speed of the search slowed to a relative crawl, like an email server gummed up by spam. Making it worse, the amusement value of these memories had long since dissipated to zero by the 1,000[th] entry ... and there were way, way more than 1,000 entries.

Yet once Manfred was found, the computer only took a few minutes to scan those 15 days and assemble a highlight reel for Julio and Sam to view.

The first thing the computer showed happened three days after Manfred's arrival. The wilderness was obscured by a rock formation, and two men were sitting near the base of the rocks. *Uh oh*, Sam thought, *we have human contact.*

In front of the men was a small fire burning inside a circle of rocks. Above the fire was a tree limb from which the carcass of some large, skinned animal was suspended.

"Killed animal," one man said to the other, holding up a rudimentary spear with a red-stained tip.

"Good," the other responded.

"Eat," the first one said, poking at the cooking carcass with his spear.

"Good," the other one responded. He reached over to grab at some meat from the hanging carcass, but he must have learned the lesson that fire is hot because he yanked his hand back and stared at it wonderingly.

The first one didn't appear to notice, or at least offer any condolence. He announced, "Need kill more animals."

"Ya," the second one agreed.

"Ya," the first concurred with his own thought.

The first one must have been undeterred by the heat because he took a sharpened rock and used it to cut off two pieces of the animal, giving one to the other man. They ripped at the meat with their teeth and chewed in silence.

The two men were covered in thick brown hair, punctuated by sores and rashes and various wounds through which the hair couldn't grow. Where skin was visible through the hair, Sam could see the men were sunburned. They wore small loincloths made from matted hides that left little to the imagination, and Sam didn't want to imagine. By any objective standard, these were two of the least attractive humans Sam had ever set eyes on. At least one of the questions Sam had considered asking Julio got answered for him: he now knew the viewing chamber didn't just have video and audio, but also had smell, because, even from this distance, these men smelled like shit.

"Animal taste good," said the second.

"Animal taste good," the first one repeated. "Ha ha." He didn't just laugh. He actually said the words, "ha ha."

When they were done eating they threw the bones on the ground. The first one looked at the sky, then back at his companion and said, "Water God mad. No sky water long time."

"Ya," the second one replied. "No water make plants die. Dead plants make animals mad." Sam could tell this was a man of few words, but his scientific reasoning seemed relatively sound.

"Need kill enemies. Dead enemies make water come back," the first one said, his scientific reasoning not so sound.

"Kill enemies and animals!"

The first one tapped the second's leg and whispered, "Animals *and* enemies taste good."

Both men laughed for a long time. Sam and Julio just stared.

Sam was starting to wonder why he was watching this and where Manfred was when the first man said, "Thing talking again." He pointed at a bundle of animal hides in a basket sitting on the ground a few feet away.

"Thing funny!" the second responded. "Take thing out!"

The first one reached into the basket and fumbled through a pile of hides and bones before pulling out a squirming object. It was Manfred.

Manfred was making noises that were a combination of screaming and spitting. With every scream and sputter coming from Manfred, the two cavemen laughed riotously. When the noises coming from Manfred finally evolved into words, he screamed, "I can't breathe when I'm buried under a pile of freaking animal hides! I almost suffocated down there!"

The men continued their guffawing. One of the cavemen held Manfred up in the air and poked the air in the direction of the other.

"Ha ha! Put thing under own hide again!" the first commanded.

The second man took Manfred and rubbed him up against his crotch, and both men laughed over Manfred's scream. "Don't you rub your inanimate, primitive dick against me, you sick bastard! Faggot! Faggot! Gay monkey!"

"Ha ha, tickle! Tickle! Here, you rub under hide!" the man holding Manfred said, handing him to his companion, who roughly shoved Manfred under his loincloth.

"You trolls!" Manfred continued to protest. "You illiterate heathens! I can't believe this is the way you gaybots actually speak!"

"He's got a point. It is hard to believe this is the way they speak," Sam commented to Julio, who nodded.

Sam heard leaves crunching and caught sight of another person wearing a similar loincloth, trying to sneak by. Something tugged at the back of Sam's brain, and his eyes clued in and focused on the uncovered breasts. Sam had expected the women to be wearing two-piece hides. Yet here she was, exposed boobs, like one of those *National Geographic* magazines. Like the men, she was not pretty—covered with dirt and bruises and with tangled, dirty hair—but Sam *still* couldn't stop staring at the naked boobs. It was like looking at a piece of gold in a pile of poop.

The man holding Manfred noticed her first and dropped Manfred on the ground, screaming, "Woman!" He pointed his finger at the startled woman.

In an impressive display of athleticism, the other man vaulted over a boulder in the direction the first man's pointed finger. Seeing the man leaping toward her, the woman dropped her basket, sending an array of fruits and root vegetables rolling on the ground as she broke into a run. The man was faster than she was, though, and he snatched her and carried her to an open spot of ground closer to the other man while she kicked and screamed.

The other man joined his companion, saying, "Do here! Do here!" The woman was trying to fight them off, but she wasn't strong enough.

Sam leaned forward with a sudden instinct to jump through the chamber and help her, but Julio shook his head. "No, we can't help her. We can't interfere with the past."

Sam nodded. Of course Julio was right, and it's not as if Sam possessed an intelligent plan to help her. Largely unable to watch what was going on, they turned their attention to Manfred. What would he think about this? Sam thought back to his night in jail, when he sensed no one would have helped if that masturbating man had attacked him. Sam figured Manfred would simply be happy he wasn't being bothered any more, that someone else was taking the heat.

Manfred didn't keep them guessing. "Damn, I feel bad for her," he said.

"Well, that's progress, I guess," Julio said to Sam.

"No! No, Cavemen! Come back here!" Manfred was now screaming at the cavepeople. But they had something better and were no longer interested in the screaming novelty item. So Manfred tried something else. "Animal! Animal!" One caveman looked up, but returned to what he was doing.

Manfred tried again, yelling, "More women! More women!" Apparently, two in the bush was better than one in the hand, because both cavemen instantly charged over.

"Where women?" one asked.

"Many women," Manfred said. "That is what you will get, if you listen to me."

"Huh?" one asked with his head cocked to the side.

"Be … nicer … and you will get more fun. More women, and more fun. I can teach you how," said Manfred.

"Awk. Thing. You look like my thing," said one of the cavemen. This was evidentially an endorsement of Manfred's wisdom and expertise, because after a pause, he added, "I believe you."

The other man nodded vigorously. "I believe all," he said cheerfully. "Show us, tell us." Both men plunked themselves down next to Manfred on the ground, awaiting the knowledge that would pour out, forgetting the woman in the background who was now gathering her roots and scurrying away.

The scene faded to gray as the artificial intelligence decided nothing else was important in that exchange.

"What do you think?" Julio asked.

Sam didn't know if the question was some kind of test. He answered, "I don't know what to think. Good for Manfred for standing up against rape, I guess."

"I have to admit," Julio said, "I was proud at that moment."

"But everything considered, this is pretty bad so far, isn't it?" Sam asked.

Julio gave Sam a little smile and said, "Well, I have two goals with Manfred. One is to make him a decent person, or person-ish thing. As you point out, it looks like I'm getting closer to that goal. But the second, vastly more important goal is to get him out of the past without making alterations. To that end, the fact that the computer found anything at all to show us is bad. Now it's only a question of how bad. Let's move on."

CHAPTER 32

*People who worship idols are stupid and foolish. The things
they worship are made of wood! (Jeremiah 10:8)*

The scene in the viewing chamber once again assembled. As it
came into focus, Sam saw what appeared to be the interior of a
cave. A campfire in the center of the scene provided light, and
behind the fire was a large rock on which Manfred was propped
against a tree branch. Several dirty, hairy men in loincloths, including the two from earlier, sat around the fire in a ring. There
were also three bare-chested women Sam's eyes found right away.
Manfred was receiving their undivided attention.

"Here are the rules," Manfred said. "There are ten of them."

Oh, please, please don't let this be what I think it will be, Sam thought.

"You will not kill," Manfred began. "You will not steal. You
will not witness … false … bears … err … yes, Zog?"

Sam thought of the interrupter as *Caveman #1*, but apparently his name was Zog. Zog didn't actually have a question for
Manfred; he was just trying to keep up. "No kill. No steal. No

witness false bears," Zog said slowly, the concepts making their way into his brain. He scratched his head and asked, "It ten?"

"Well … yes, that is ten," replied Manfred.

Sam made an indignant snort, a flashback to his old days of being incredulous at how clueless Manfred was regarding his so-called heartfelt Christianity. "I would have thought he'd at least remember the stuff about not having any other Gods," Sam muttered.

As if hearing Sam—and Sam did worry for a moment—Manfred retracted himself. "No, wait, that's not ten. There's more. Never say my name in vain." The cavepeople looked around in confusion and Manfred clarified, "Don't say my name when you're angry. Also, no other Gods! I'm the only God for you. And I need a special day. Let's call every 7th day Manfred Day."

Zog was flustered with his recital of this new chunk of rules, and Manfred had to guide him through it a couple of times.

The one Sam thought of as *Caveman #2* had a question. "Manfred, what about war with other tribe? If we no kill, we lose war."

"Well, Oxbo," Manfred said, "Of course killing is allowed during war! I mean, what the hell else are you going to do? If you don't kill the enemy, then what's the damn point of a war?"

Oxbo nodded with satisfaction. "Ahhhhh, nice," he said.

One of the women, the same one from the earlier scene, stood up, asking, "Manfred, what happens when break rule?"

"I'm glad you asked, Zogla," Manfred said. Sam knew this was a question Manfred had been waiting for. "If you break one of the rules, tell me you're sorry and say you accept me as your God, and you'll still go to Heaven."

"What is Heaven?" Zog asked.

"Heaven is where you go when you die," Manfred replied, now in more familiar territory. "But you can only go to Heaven if you believe in me as your God. Heaven has lots of naked women and fresh game and you'll be able to do whatever you want."

"Oooooohhhh," the cavepeople seemed to say in unison.

"But remember," Manfred continued, "it's easier to pass through the eye of the beholder than it is to enter the kingdom of Heaven. Those who don't believe in me will go to Hell. Hell is full of fire and you burn all day and there's no game and no naked women. It hurts all the time there."

"No want Hell!" one of the cavemen exclaimed.

"You sure don't want to go to Hell," Manfred said. "That's why you need to believe in me as your God."

"No break Manfred's ten rules and no go to Hell," Oxbo said to the other cavepeople.

"Wrong, Oxbo," Manfred interjected. "Let me make this clear: If someone believes in me, they are guaranteed Heaven and not Hell. End of story. But if they die without believing in me, they will go to Hell. End of story. You were born with sin. You all deserve Hell, from the moment you're born, unless you believe in me. I paid for your sins. Look at me! I don't even have a whole body! That's how much *I* suffered for *your* sins."

"What then point of rules?" Julio said to Sam, mocking the voices and grammar. Sam found it interesting, listening to Julio, whose voice already had that alien quality, mocking the other set of weird voices.

"Oh, thank you, Manfred," said Zogla. How wonderful she must have found it, this kind thing Manfred had done for her.

"You suffer for all us?" Zog asked. "What about other tribes? You suffer for them?"

"I only suffered for those who accept me as their God," answered Manfred. "If they haven't accepted me, they will burn."

The other cavepeople began talking all at once.

"Other tribe no accept Manfred."

"Other tribe evil."

"Make other tribe accept Manfred."

"Attack other tribe!"

"This is really bad," Sam uttered. Julio nodded.

"Ya," Oxbo concluded. "We attack other tribe. Other tribe have good grassland. We kick ass, take grass!"

Okay, as bad as this is, that was kind of funny, Sam thought. Manfred must have said "kick ass" at some point and it caught on. These people were sponges. Absolute sponges.

"Well, I didn't *specifically* say go attack them ..." Manfred said, but no one seemed to hear him because they were too busy cheering and dancing, excited about the upcoming attack.

"I make spears, you make bows!" Zog shouted to Oxbo.

"This is getting out of control," Julio said.

"How many days has it been?" Sam asked.

"We're only on day four. Eleven more to go!" Julio was clearly worried.

"He managed to take all the worst parts of Christianity and none of the good," said Sam.

"Well, do you think he ever understood any of it?" Julio asked.

"Probably not," Sam admitted, "but for all the time I spent attached to him, I still have no idea what he knows or understands."

CHAPTER 33

Woe to you, teachers of the law and Pharisees, you hypocrites!
You give a tenth of your spices - mint, dill and cumin. But you
have neglected the more important matters of the law - justice,
mercy and faithfulness. You should have practiced the latter,
without neglecting the former. You blind guides! You strain
out a gnat but swallow a camel. (Matthew 23:23)

The viewing chamber moved on to what the computer considered the next important scene. The tribe was gathered on a nondescript field outside the cave. All the men carried a bow or spear. Manfred was curled up on top of a boulder in the middle of the tribe—for some reason, there were always boulders just lying around in the past.

"We go war now!" Oxbo yelled, to the sound of screams and cheers from the gathered throng.

"Wait!" Manfred cried. The cheering stopped almost immediately, and everyone stared at the disembodied penis. "We're not ready to attack yet."

"With power of Manfred behind us, we no can lose," Oxbo said, scratching his head.

"True," Manfred replied, "but not yet. We need to build the church first."

"What is *church*?" Zogla asked.

"The church is my home," Manfred answered. He took a long pause before expounding. "It is a place of worship and glory." He paused again, apparently having difficulty explaining the concept of a church. "It is a place where the word of Manfred can be heard by all."

"Ummmmm," Oxbo mumbled.

While Oxbo made a good point, Zogla stepped up to actually communicate: "We can all hear Manfred now. Why need church?"

"We need a church because right now, I'm just lying on some random-ass boulder! Do you really think that's the way it should be? You think that's good enough? You may all know I'm your Lord and Savior, but another tribe won't understand unless a church displays my glory. Once we have a church, we can tell the other tribe they can join the church and accept me as their God, or else we will destroy them."

"That's actually clever," Sam said. "At least, clever for Manfred."

"He might have just saved us, too," Julio added. "If he averted a war, we may have avoided deaths that could have eliminated a lot of DNA from history."

"The church will also need ten percent of all your income," Manfred continued. Julio snorted; Sam rolled his eyes. The cavemen just looked confused. "Well, you don't have money, I guess, but I will need ten percent of your meat and fur and other good stuff." The cavemen still looked confused. "Oh, I guess you don't understand percentages. Well, use your fingers to count the pieces of meat. You take the first nine pieces, and I take the tenth."

Zog and Oxbo and the others continued to stare blankly at Manfred, wearing some of the dumbest expressions Sam had ever seen. Well, what could you expect from cavepeople getting their first math lesson?

Zogla was the exception. She seemed to have some idea what Manfred was talking about. "Zogla understand. Church need small part, not big part, of meat and fur to help outcasts. They keep alive. Zogla happy!"

All of the cavepeople turned their eyes towards a small group in the back of the crowd, apart from everyone else. The adults in this small, quarantined group seemed physically disadvantaged, some having missing or broken limbs and others old and feeble. There were also several children, probably orphans. The outcasts looked on with hopeful anticipation, eyes too large for their emaciated bodies. A small child allowed herself a toothless smile, presumably thinking about decent food coming her way.

Sam recognized the sound of Manfred sighing. He seemed to be choosing his words carefully. "Suffering in this world doesn't matter. As a matter of fact, suffering brings you closer to God, er, me. What matters is eternal salvation. The meat and fur should be used to promote the glory of the church, and save more people *after* they die."

"Fucking Manfred," Sam spat with contempt.

"Disappointing, yes," Julio replied, "but for our immediate goal it's not a bad thing. We don't really want any of those people surviving if it means changing history." Not being able to help in these situations certainly was painful.

Almost in unison, the heads of the outcasts sank in sadness. The rest of the cavepeople either shook their heads or kept looking around with dumb expressions.

But Zogla kept pressing. "Manfred," she insisted, "you no eat. What do with food if not give to outcasts? Why just display?"

"Woman, don't you have a man to cook dinner for or something?" Manfred snapped.

Zogla replied with defiance, stopping her feet in the dirt. "Zogla no understand why no use meat to help poor outcasts."

"Do you want to burn in Hell, Zogla?" Manfred lashed. "That's going to happen if you don't do what I say. I am your God. If you don't believe in me and my words, you will never be allowed into the Kingdom of Heaven."

His tirade seemed to do the trick, as Zogla backed away, chastened, a shocked look on her face. Some of the other cavemen laughed and pointed at her.

"That's better," Manfred said. "Now, the church will need more than meat and fur. You must also make great works of art."

"What be art?" one of the cavemen asked.

"You know," Manfred replied, "pictures and statues and things like that, made to show my glory."

"We draw pictures of Manfred penis on walls of cave," Zog suggested.

"Exactly," Manfred said. "You will build great works of art in my honor." After a pause he added, "And you must make my symbol and display it at the church and everywhere else."

His symbol? Sam thought. He didn't remember Manfred ever having a damned symbol.

"Zog, go pick out a long stick and a short stick," Manfred commanded. "Oxbo, go get some vines."

Zog and Oxbo scrambled away, and the crowd deflated somewhat. When Zog and Oxbo returned, Manfred gave them instructions, getting them to place the sticks perpendicular to each other and use the vines to tie them together. *A cross! He's co-opting the cross for himself. He just has no fucking limits,* Sam thought. It seemed so obvious now.

"Now sharpen the long end to a point, like a spear, so you can stick it in the ground," Manfred commanded. Zog obeyed, pulling out a knife-like object made of stone and scraping away at the wood.

"What Manfred's symbol mean?" asked Oxbo.

"It means ... it means ... you don't cross me," Manfred floundered.

"Oh, okay. We no cross Manfred," Zog replied obediently.

The scene went gray again.

The highlight reel presented the next scene, mercifully on the fifteenth and final day. It was dusk and Oxbo was carrying Manfred around, and Zog and a couple of other males followed behind. A fire burned in the background. They appeared to be showing Manfred a rock carving. Sam couldn't discern many details, but he could see there was more than one carving. In fact, there was a quite a group of Manfred statues, all arranged in a circle, silhouetted by the light of the fire.

The lighting made the scene majestic, but in reality it was a circle of dick statues, something a fourth-grader might have made with clay and considered absolutely hilarious.

He turned to Julio and had to suppress his laughter, as Julio was glowering at the scene, completely unamused. "This is so familiar," he said, mostly to himself. He turned to Sam and explained, "We're at the location of a rock formation called Craig Rhos-y-Felin. Does that mean anything to you?"

"Can't say it does," Sam replied. Julio was going somewhere with this, but he was dragging out the explanation.

"Well, there's nothing particularly special about this site in itself," Julio continued. "But the rocks here are the source of the oldest rocks in Stonehenge."

"So …" Sam began, stopping well short of verbalizing the thought.

Julio finished Sam's thought: "So this bullshit is the ancestor of Stonehenge."

"It's very nice, Oxbo, very nice," Manfred was commenting. "I like the contour you added to this one here. Very good work." Oxbo smiled at the compliment, even if he almost certainly had no idea what *contour* was. After all, how often does your God ever tell you he likes your work?

"Now church done and artwork done," Zog said. "We attack other tribe next morning."

With those words, the scene evaporated and the viewing chamber was just an empty archway, the sterile white walls behind it now visible.

"Well, it could be better, but it could be worse," Sam said. He had meant to only think those words, and he felt silly having said them aloud. It was an applicable statement to nearly any situation, and thus as meaningless as a combination of words could be.

"You're pretty much right, Sam," Julio said, to Sam's surprise. "But here's something to think about: If I researched that location three weeks ago, before Manfred got chucked into the past, would I have gotten the same information about Stonehenge? Did it exist three weeks ago, or did he plant the seeds to create it, adding it to our remembered past?"

"Holy shit," Sam said. The concept wasn't new, it was exactly what Julio had been harping about, but the concrete example made all the warnings about changing the past sink in.

"Anyway," Julio said, changing gears, his voice back to its normal bubbly quality. "At this point, it is what it is. Now we have a few hours to work out the extraction plan before they attack the other tribe and all Hell breaks loose." He was all smiles as he said those dire words.

"Do we steal Manfred away while everyone's asleep?"

"No," Julio replied. "If we burst in there now, Manfred will be leaving behind a legacy of shitty, shitty ideas. We need to get in there and convince Manfred to undo the damage, before his ideas take deeper root. He needs to convince the cavepeople not to worship him. It's something only he can do. If anyone else tries, they won't believe it, and things will only get worse."

"He's swimming in adoration right now," Sam added. "He's living the dream." As best Sam could tell, Manfred was right where he wanted to be. He remembered Manfred's prophetic words from when they were attached: "I'm going to rule in the afterlife without you getting in my way." How would they ever convince him to give it up? What would Manfred care if he was changing the past? Manfred's concerns had never extended beyond himself.

"I thought about using the friends from the pen—Waffles, Bruno, Skor, Zeus, Kierkegaard, Diesel and so on," Julio said. Sam had no idea who any of those people were. "Frankly, that's my best idea, and it kind of sucks. It's a long-term plan, dropping them in there and trying to manipulate Manfred through them. A long-term plan does nothing to prevent the imminent attack in Manfred's name."

An idea tugged at Sam. "Hey Julio," he said, "have you ever been reincarnated into Manfred's life?" Sam knew Julio always lived the lives of the people he was going to retrieve, including Sam. But Julio hadn't expected Manfred to be real, so he wouldn't have known to live Manfred's life in advance.

"No, I didn't," Julio said. "No one should, it's too dangerous. First off, it's uncertain what would happen if a normal brain was introduced into a tiny penis brain. We're already working on a dolphin retrieval plan, but I don't think you can mix up a dolphin and a dick. Second off, we never put a 'hard stop' on his life, so there would be no end to the reincarnation. Truly, there's no way of knowing what will happen."

"We also have no way of knowing what will happen if the tribe attacks their neighbors in a crusade or a jihad or whatever you want to call it," Sam responded. "We need to understand what makes Manfred tick. We need to know the exact combination of words and actions that will convince him. I don't think we have any choice but to give it a try."

For once, Julio didn't say anything. Sam gathered his courage and said, "I'll do it."

Julio finally said, "Sam, remember we don't know what may happen. It might not work at all. Or, worse, it may hurt you. As in, seriously hurt you, beyond anything I can repair."

"It's a risk I have to take," Sam replied. "I'm the only one who can do it." He lifted his head and looked Julio in the eyes. "He's back there changing history, and I think it's for the worse. He won't talk to anyone except me."

They were quiet for a while. Eventually Julio nodded. "There's logic in what you're saying. If you're brave enough to take this risk, I won't stop you."

"Good. Then I need to get started with the reincarnation right away," said Sam. How strange, he thought to himself, this was the scariest, riskiest thing he had ever done—far scarier and riskier than the stupid vandalism crap—and he was taking it head-on with bravery.

Julio led Sam out of the viewing chamber room to another room, similar to the one Sam had woken up in, empty except for a hospital-like bed.

"Lie down," Julio instructed. "While we've been talking about this, I've been discussing it with other transfer agents and experts in reincarnation science. We've studied Manfred's brain-like-thing and now we have our best hypothesis as to what will happen."

In typical Julio fashion, he stopped speaking right before revealing something important, leaving Sam to prompt him to finish the thought. "What did you learn?"

"We think we'll be able to insert you into his brain, for one," Julio said.

"That's good," Sam thought aloud. At least the plan was feasible.

"As far as the hard stop goes, we can't be sure of the playback speed, but we have an educated guess as to how long to leave you in there. We should be able to pull you out right before you died, when Hans and I played our hilarious practical joke on you."

Sam couldn't help but roll his eyes. Apparently, Julio still hadn't moved on from their joke. It must have been the highlight of his entire life.

Julio gave Sam a reassuring smile and said, "Anyway, go ahead and close your eyes and we'll get this started. You don't have to do anything. I'll take care of it myself."

The last thing Sam heard before he lost consciousness was Julio saying, "Don't worry. I'm pretty sure you'll survive."

CHAPTER 34

*Though my father and mother forsake me, the
Lord will receive me. (Psalm 27:10)*

Nothing but darkness surrounded him. It was terrifying. Sam didn't
remember this darkness from his previous reincarnations. Usually
the first thing he saw was light and blurry images through a baby's
undeveloped eyes. This time, he was seeing through Manfred's
eyes, except Manfred didn't have any eyes.

I've never been reincarnated as a blind person, Sam thought. *I wish I
had tried that.* Though, of course Manfred had vision. Somehow he
had always been able to see what Sam saw, right?

Sam started to wonder if something had gone terribly
wrong, as Julio had worried about. Would he be stuck in darkness forever? He remembered from the 300 or so times he had
watched *The Shawshank Redemption* that even a week in solitary
confinement messes with your mind. What the hell would 20
years do to him?

He jolted awake and a blurry scene unfolded. He was pretty sure he was seeing things through Sam's newborn eyes. There was a large, dark shape hovering over him, which he knew was a person, holding what looked like a pair of scissors. Fuck did it hurt.

I just got circumcised, Sam realized. *That must be the very first thing Manfred was ever conscious of. What a way to start your life.*

The large hovering figure grabbed Sam, or, rather, Manfred, and wrapped him up in something. The pain wasn't quite so bad now, but he felt like he couldn't breathe. Sam had no idea where the sensation was coming from. It was like suffocation, but he didn't have a respiratory system. He suspected he'd come to accept the sensation as normal, but he'd always hate it.

She was younger and had her hair done differently than he remembered, but she was definitely Sam's mom. Sam felt dumb for being surprised. Of course it was her.

He saw her frequently. He was usually all covered up, suffocating in darkness, and sometimes he felt a sensation of movement inside him, bringing wet warmth. The first time that happened, Sam realized with disgust he was lying in his own urine. Well, he—Manfred—was lying in Sam's urine. It was all very confusing. And gross.

Sam's mother would show up to pull the diaper off and put on a new one, wrapping him back up again. It was wonderful to get clean, but he hated the dependency. He could do nothing for himself. He was helpless and needed others for everything, and he resented it.

Even worse than lying in his own urine was when Sam—the baby Sam, that is—pooped. He was stuck, writhing in a diaper, sometimes pressed directly against creamy baby shit. He *hated* that.

Sam was becoming less aware of himself every day, as he integrated with Manfred. It was a natural process involved in reincarnation but also disconcerting. One of the last things he remembered being conscious of, as Sam, was when his mother was changing his diaper. She was hovering over him, and he felt the familiar warmth of urine pulsing through him, sending it right into her hands and clothes.

"Oh, God dammit, Sam!" she cried, jumping away.

Sorry, Mom, he thought.

—⁂—

The two of them sat together watching TV. The woman Sam referred to as *Mommy* would put something into a box above the TV and the TV would blink to life. She said it was an old show called *Captain Kangaroo*, which she really liked when she was a kid. Most of the show was lost on him, but he always perked up to watch the part about the boy and his dog.

He sensed a connection to the other mind, the one called Sam, but he didn't understand it. He would try to talk to Sam, but Sam didn't talk back. Yet for some reason, this show made him think of himself and Sam, together fighting against the bad people as a team.

He even liked the names of the characters: Tom Terrific—what a great name that would be for Sam!—and his wonder dog, the Mighty Manfred.

—⁓—

The warmth was building up and knew it would burst soon. Sam was squirming around but was too absorbed in playing with his toys to do anything about it, so Manfred had to squeeze as hard as possible to hold off the flow. He could be doing this forever and Sam would just keep playing. He had a one-track mind when playing with his toys.

Manfred decided he didn't have any choice but to let go for a short moment, allowing a tiny bit of pee through. He didn't want to spend the day pressed against wet underwear, so he hoped Sam would take care of things soon.

Finally, Sam jumped to his feet and ran over to his mommy, declaring, "Mommy, I have to go potty."

She looked at him with annoyance and responded, "So why are you coming to me? The bathroom's over there." She pointed at the bathroom, and Sam turned and walked over there. It was a bumpy ride, as Sam danced and shook his way there. Manfred felt tremendous relief as Sam set him free. He loved escaping from Sam's underwear; he didn't like being closed up. More relief followed once Sam got on the potty and Manfred finally let loose.

Why can't you hold that in while I'm playing?

The thought appeared in Manfred's mind somehow. He was so excited. No coherent thought had ever come from the link before. Manfred tried to make it work in the other direction.

"I tried, but I can't hold it in forever," he tried sending. Now all he could do was wait and see if Sam got the message.

"I *knew* you could talk!" Sam exclaimed, and Manfred felt the same excitement. They were talking! "What's your name?"

"I'm Manfred."

Sam giggled. "Like the dog," he said. It was the happiest day of Manfred's life. Sam started shaking Manfred up and down, trying to get that last bit of pee out. It was fun. He liked being in his friend Sam's hand.

"Mommy," Sam called, "I'm done peeing. Can you wipe Manfred?"

"Who is Manfred?" Sam's mommy asked after she joined them in the bathroom.

"My penis is Manfred," Sam answered. "He's my friend." Manfred didn't know what to think of the expression on Sam's mommy's face. Sam continued, "Manfred, say 'hi' to Mommy."

"Hello," Manfred said. "I'm Manfred." He never felt any rapport with Sam's mommy, who always closed him up in those diapers, but he was excited to make more friends. He was tired of being alone all the time.

"Sam," Sam's mommy said as she dabbed at Manfred's tip with a piece of toilet paper, "I don't want to have a conversation with the imaginary friend inside your penis. That's not appropriate."

Imaginary? Manfred thought glumly.

"I don't think she can hear you," Sam said.

—⁂—

Something must be wrong with me, Manfred thought to himself, not sending the words to Sam. When it was just him and Sam together alone, they would talk and have fun. Sometimes Sam would take him out and play with him. Manfred always enjoyed freedom and being with his friend.

But Sam would always close Manfred up in his underwear whenever anyone else was around. He never said a single word about Manfred.

Sam would still talk to Manfred even when other people were nearby, but every so often he'd accidentally say something aloud he meant only for Manfred, and he'd get embarrassed. After that happened enough times, Sam took to ignoring Manfred altogether when talking to his mommy or playing with Andy or anyone else.

What's wrong with me? Manfred wondered. *Why is he so ashamed of me?*

—⁓—

Sam was excited about Easter. Manfred knew Sam didn't usually do much on Easter, but this time his mom told him it was okay to go with Andy's family to an Easter egg hunt at their church.

While they were in the car, Sam asked, "Are you sure it's okay for me to come along even though I'm Jewish?" Manfred didn't know what the word Jewish meant, but he heard Sam's mom use it enough times.

"Don't worry, Sam. It's fine," Andy's dad told Sam. "You don't need to be a Christian to enjoy the Easter egg hunt."

They spent most of their time outside the church, running through the grass and ferreting for eggs. Sam and Andy were having lots of fun, but Manfred felt left out. He tried to share their excitement about the eggs when they all went inside the church and sat down.

"There's a caramel in this one!" Andy exclaimed as he opened a plastic egg.

"Shhh," Andy's mom hissed, but Sam and Andy kept whispering about the candy inside the eggs.

Manfred didn't care about the candy, so he let his attention wander to his surroundings. The church was probably the most beautiful place he had ever seen. The glass was colorful with pictures of people and places. He didn't see any other penises, but he didn't let that bother him for very long.

Sam's eyes were mostly focused on the eggs and candy, so any glimpses Manfred got were fleeting. He never got a good look at the person in the front of the room, who was telling a story Manfred found fascinating, if only in comparison to Sam and Andy prattling on and on about candy. The story was about someone called "God" who had apparently created all the people and animals on the Earth. The man didn't mention plants or penises, so Manfred wasn't sure about them. Presumably this God guy had created them, too.

Anyway, this God character's son, whose name was Jesus, was sent to Earth to save everyone. It turned out that everyone on Earth was evil and needed to be saved in order to get to a place called Heaven, which sounded super awesome. Jesus tried to tell everyone about his father, God, and their path to something called "salvation." Maybe people who were saved could go to their choice of Heaven *or* Salvation. Manfred wasn't sure.

A lot of people were friends with this Jesus guy, but people were still evil. Finally, bad men captured Jesus and sentenced him to death. Jesus had magic powers and could have escaped, but he decided not to. He'd rather die in order to save everyone else. The idea was, as long as people believed that Jesus was their Lord and Savior—which was weird because God was supposed to be Lord, but maybe there was a whole family of Lords—then his death would save them because he was dying for the sins of humanity and presumably those of plants, animals, *and* penises.

A few days later, Jesus was resurrected, which, Manfred found out, meant brought back to life. He was back in Heaven with his father, God, who was actually the same person, as well as a third person called the Holy Ghost.

It was extremely confusing for Manfred. But it was still a really good story. It made perfect sense everyone was evil. He always knew something was wrong with him, because otherwise Sam wouldn't always be ashamed of him and keep him locked away. It made Manfred sad to think he was evil, but it was a relief to know Jesus had taken care of things. Thanks to Jesus, he didn't need to be embarrassed and worried all the time. This Jesus guy rocked.

Later, after they got home, Manfred asked Sam about Jesus and the rest of the story. Sam didn't know much about it. Sam didn't seem particularly interested but Manfred was able to convince him to start asking some questions.

Over the next few weeks, Sam asked his mother as well as Andy and Andy's parents about it and got lots of background information for Manfred, who soaked up whatever he could. After all he heard, Manfred decided he was a Christian.

"Are you a Christian?" he asked Sam.

"No," Sam told him. "I'm Jewish."

—⁂—

As he and Sam got older, Manfred started getting some feelings he didn't understand. He had always liked the way it felt when Sam touched him, but things entered a whole new level. It was weird enough when tiny little hairs started growing around his base. He didn't know what to make of that. But when Sam touched him, instead of just feeling good, it felt *really good*.

Sam touched him more and more often, so apparently he liked it, too. Manfred loved how much attention he was getting from Sam. It made him feel like a giant, and he would get all big and stiff when Sam touched him.

One night, Sam was in the bathroom, holding Manfred firmly. He was thinking this must be what Heaven was like—eternity wrapped in Sam's hand—when there was a knock on the door. He heard the doorknob turning, but Sam had locked the door so it didn't open.

"Sam, I need to get in there," Sam's mom called.

"Tell her 'too bad,'" Manfred instructed.

To Manfred's surprise, Sam ignored him. After all, Sam seemed to enjoy this as much as Manfred. "Just a second, Mom," he called out. His voice was getting lower every day, but this time Sam's voice broke and he kind of screeched the words. Sam had Manfred in his underpants as fast as he could. Just like that, it was over.

So that's how things are, Manfred thought with agitation. *I'm still an embarrassment to Sam. What we're doing is wrong and he doesn't want anyone to know about it.*

It's because I'm evil. Everything is evil. I'm glad I'm a Christian, so I can be saved.

—m—

Evil was all around them.

Manfred didn't realize the extent of the problem until he found The True Christian Channel.

It started late one weekend night. They were lying in bed, Sam fondling Manfred absently, enough to get aroused but not enough to get him to pee the thick white pee. It was simply pleasant. Sam was trying to find something to watch and not having much luck. He went through the channels one by one, giving each a look for a moment and then trying the next one.

Manfred didn't find any of it interesting. He was spacing out when Sam stopped on a channel.

"Welcome back to The True Christian Channel," a soft-spoken man was saying.

"Oh, here you go, Manfred," Sam said with a laugh. Sam left it on for a few seconds, as usual, and moved to the next channel.

"Wait!" Manfred cried. "Don't change the channel."

"What?" Sam asked, caught off-guard. "Oh, I was kidding. You shouldn't watch this. Even if you are a Christian." He said that last part dubiously, which Manfred didn't appreciate.

"But I *do* want to watch it," Manfred insisted. "Just let me watch it this one time, please."

It took some convincing, but Manfred always seemed to be able to convince Sam of things when he really needed to. Sam said he would give Manfred five minutes, but he fell asleep, leaving Manfred to watch The True Christian Channel all night long. He learned so much that night.

The next morning he mentioned it to Sam. He told him how sinful everyone was, and how the world was going to end soon. Sam didn't want to hear any of it, dismissing everything Manfred said.

"Well, suit yourself. I'll go Heaven and you'll go to hell." Manfred thought he put Sam firmly in place, until he heard Sam's response.

"You're attached to me," Sam laughed. "If I'm going to hell, you're coming along."

Those words haunted Manfred for years to come.

—⁂—

Manfred didn't like Anne right from the start. He could never really put his proverbial finger on why. Sure, she was one of those college liberals who were destroying America, but, hey, so was Sam, and he liked Sam okay … sometimes. But when Sam was around her, he went out of his way to act like he didn't know Manfred.

Then there was that time Sam was giving Manfred the high-quality attention he deserved, but even as he cupped Manfred in his hand, he seemed distant. Manfred kept trying to engage Sam in conversation, but Sam didn't seem interested. An image popped into Manfred's head through his link with Sam. It was an image of Anne. Sam was giving Manfred hand, *but he was thinking about Anne*. Out of a need for revenge, Manfred learned he had the ability to "flip the switch" from white pee to yellow.

—⁂—

Manfred's first display of his new switch-flipping power wasn't enough to stop Sam from seeing Anne. When Sam and Anne were together, Manfred did his best to taunt Sam, goading Sam into paying attention to him rather than Anne. Finally, one day Anne proved to be the slut Manfred already knew she was, and lured Sam to her dorm room to get physical with him.

He was in a panic as Anne started unzipping Sam's pants. Manfred couldn't even count the number of things that terrified him at that moment. Would Sam ever pay attention to Manfred if he had an intimate relationship with Anne? If Sam was willing to engage in premarital sex, was there any hope of getting him to renounce sin and accept Jesus before they were dragged to Hell? *I don't know this hand! Where is Sam's hand? Get your dirty hand off of me! I have no idea where your hand has been! WHERE IS SAM'S HAND?*

He didn't want to be touched by this girl, and he only wanted Sam's hand. *But I'm not gay, I'm not gay, I'm not gay*, Manfred assured himself, but he was overcome with doubt. It was all too much for Manfred to handle so he did the only thing he could think to do: he flipped the switch to yellow pee.

Boy did that work. Anne reacted as if Sam had punched her, freaking out and kicking Sam out of her room. There was no way she would want to see him again, Manfred figured. Sure, Sam was mad at him now, but they'd make up eventually. They'd have to! What other option did they have?

Over the next couple of days, Sam was exceptionally mad at Manfred. Sam also started being hurtful, repeatedly calling Manfred gay. Manfred denied it vehemently, but there was still part of him left wondering if he was gay after all.

—∞—

The life drained out of him and Manfred felt relief. He was no longer attached to Sam. He was floating to Heaven and, predictably, demons were taking Sam to Hell. He would miss Sam, but Sam had been warned so many times. Heaven was going to be fantastic. Despite the pain, Manfred was as happy as he had ever been.

—∞—

Disappointment followed the joy. This wasn't Heaven. This was more of the same, except Sam wasn't even there. There was no point to any of it. There was no paradise to strive for. He was evil and nothing could be done about it. He would never see Sam's hand again.

The strangest thing about waking up in the future, detached from Sam, was that he could still see, somehow, even though his brain connection to Sam's eyes was gone. Furthermore, everyone could hear him when he talked. It was like he had a new brain connection with everyone. He had no idea how it happened. But, as it turned out, no one he met in the future was worth talking to, anyway.

Julio was a weenie shithead. He would sit down with Manfred for hours trying to teach him about being good. It was all so dumb and pointless. He was evil. Why didn't Julio get it?

—⁂—

Just when Manfred couldn't take any more of Julio's shit, a new home with some other penises opened up. Manfred had no idea such a world existed. He had never met another penis who could talk, as far as he could recall. Would he know if he had?

It didn't really matter now. These penises weren't attached to anyone and were all able to speak aloud to each other. But not having Sam around to move him from place to place was annoying. It took him so long to get anywhere!

Most of the other penises were friendly, but none of them were smart. He was happy to have peers (he made a joke to himself, calling them his pee-ers; he laughed about that one for days), but they clearly lacked leadership and intelligence. Manfred considered it his duty to step in and assert his authority. These penises needed moral guidance from a superior. The first step was to gain everyone's respect. Once he had that, he'd put them all in their place and make them his subordinates.

—⁂—

A man named Jim showed up. Manfred was able to convince Jim to pick him up, and being held in a hand brought back memories of Sam. It wasn't Sam's hand, but he imagined it was and it felt good. All his other pursuits faded out of his mind for that brief moment.

Then, for no reason Manfred could ascertain, the man threw Manfred and several of his pee-ers right into the archway thingie. It was a terrifying flight, and the next thing Manfred knew he was laying on hard dirt with a few patches of grass.

His pee-ers were laying on the ground nearby. "Zeus, what happened?" he asked, but Zeus didn't respond. Neither did any of the others. They were all just lying there—Zeus, Xerxes, Diesel, Bombo, Earthworm, Nightcrawler, Elvis, Skor, Vegemite, Moose, Loopy, sad little Waffles—limp and lifeless. For some reason, he was the only one to survive.

Manfred was all alone. Alone, again. He lay there crying. It was too sad to stay near his dead friends, so he began trying to crawl away from them.

And then the giant beasts came rumbling toward him. He looked up and the world ended.

CHAPTER 35

I smote you with blight and mold and hail to destroy every-thing you worked so hard to produce. Even so, you refused to return to me, said the Lord. (Haggai 2:17)

Manfred woke up in a white room. *That beast squashed me*, he thought. He must be back in the year 3542 with Julio. He must have died again.

"Welcome back," he heard Julio say.

His body felt strange, and he had a hard time controlling himself as he tried to roll over to Julio. He lost his balance and tumbled to the floor with a surprisingly loud thud.

"Whoa there," Julio said as Manfred tried to right himself. "Did you learn anything useful?"

What the hell was he talking about? *I was supposed to learn some-thing from being trampled by a gigantic mammal?* "Listen, Lopamoo," he said, still trying to squirm and logroll his body in Julio's direction, "I get that you want me to learn to be good and all that bullshit, but what was the point of throwing me into a jungle to be crushed and killing all my friends on the ride there?"

Julio didn't seem to have an answer. He said, "Are you all right down there? Let me give you a hand."

Manfred couldn't get his body to respond; it was too clunky for some reason. He managed to get his head around to see Julio holding out his hand—not reaching to pick him up—just holding his hand out tauntingly.

"Give me your hand, Sam," Julio said.

I don't have a hand! If I had a hand, do you think I'd give you or anybody else the time of day? Wait a second, you called me ... Sam? He contorted to see his hand. He knew that hand well. It was Sam's hand.

"What the ...?"

"Okay, take your time," Julio said. "Use your head and look at yourself."

Manfred did as he was told. *I used to look like this back when I was Sam,* he thought. *When I was Sam, I was trying to solve the problem of how to pull Manfred out of the past. But ... I'm Manfred and I'm already here.*

No, he realized, *I'm Sam.* It all came back to him.

"What happened, Julio?"

"Is that you, Sam?"

"Yeah, I figured out who I am," Sam said with a smile. "Do I get a chocolate?"

It was just a throwaway line, but a chocolate kiss appeared in Julio's hand and he gave it to Sam. "You deserve that. As for what happened, I tried to time things so the reincarnation would end right around the time Manfred died in the car crash. Since you never hit a hard stop, you didn't close out the experience, so you thought you were still Manfred. I take it the reincarnation worked?"

"I guess so, but what a waste of time," Sam joked.

"Didn't you get anything useful?" Julio asked.

"I got it all right," Sam replied.

Julio looked at Sam, but Sam stood there silently, forcing Julio to say, "Well?"

"I was never certain if Manfred understood Christianity at all," Sam began. "I think you know he had limitations in that area. Now I know he thought he was evil, and was relieved to learn he was *born* evil and couldn't help it. He saw all these other behaviors his religious leaders said were sinful, and he thought everyone else was born evil, just like him. But with Christianity, he could be as evil as he wanted to be, as none of it mattered because Jesus died for his sins. He could order anything off the evil menu; Jesus was picking up the bar tab. What's not to like, if you're Manfred?"

"So he believes himself to be completely evil, and he's acting on that now?" Julio mused to himself. "But how can we turn that understanding to our advantage?"

"We don't," Sam answered. "You're overthinking things. Sometimes a talking dick is just a dick."

"What does that mean?" Julio asked.

"I mean he's a dick," Sam explained, enjoying the fact that, for once, Julio was asking him questions and not the other way around. "He grew up with my hand. He loves my hand. All he cares about is handjobs. At the end of the day, everything else is a red herring."

"So the plan is to lure him out with your hand," Julio said matter-of-factly.

Sam grimaced. "I don't think it will be quite so easy. A promise of hand won't get the job done. He needs to feel like it did before."

"Are you saying what I think you're saying?"

Sam shrugged in resignation. "I don't like it, but we have to sew him back on."

"And get rid of your normal penis?" Julio asked.

"Obviously," Sam responded. "Manfred needs it to be exactly as before … though that's too bad. Imagine the possibilities with *two* dicks."

CHAPTER 36

No one whose testicles are crushed or whose male organ is cut off
shall enter the assembly of the Lord. (Deuteronomy 23:1)

Sam blindly trusted that by the year 3542, penis removal and attachment surgery was zero-risk and pain-free and he was right. Paradise, indeed.

Before the surgery, Julio had told him he'd wake up in Manfred's church sometime in the middle of the night. Meanwhile, Julio would be heading to the pre-Stonehenge rocks to make some adjustments. "The Druids who later build Stonehenge," Julio said, "will find rectangles and that's it." Sam didn't quite share Julio's passion on this Stonehenge topic, but so be it. In any event, once he was done, Julio would return to the viewing chamber to monitor Sam's progress.

Sam stirred under a tree, with a tree knob uncomfortably pricking into his back. He was naked. Looking around in the moonlight, he realized he was in Manfred's "church." The church wasn't a building, but rather a bunch of rocks arranged near a tree. There were larger rocks—boulders, really—making a rectangular perimeter with several rows of smaller rocks set up as pews. The tree was in the front, where the priest would stand. Many of Manfred's cross symbols dotted the landscape.

"Sam? Is that you? What happened?" came the voice that made it all real.

Indeed, looking down at his naked body, there was Manfred, attached without any surgical scars. Until now, Sam never realized how distinctive Manfred was, though he couldn't explain what made Manfred unique. But there was no mistaking him for a random, normal penis.

"Good morning, Manfred," Sam said pleasantly. He found himself oddly happy, having Manfred attached again. It did feel like old times, other than the fact they were sitting in a primitive church during the Pleistocene Era. That part was new.

"Why are you here?" Manfred asked. "It must have been a crazy dream. It went on so long." Manfred then seemed to clue in to their surroundings. "Wait, was it a dream?"

"No, it wasn't a dream," Sam answered. "We died in a car crash, we woke up to an afterlife in the year 3542, you were tossed into a portal to the past, you became a penis God to a tribe of stupid cavemen, and I came to find you so we could be reunited again." *Just your typical couple of months in the lives of Sam and Manfred,* he thought. "So here we are, together again. Welcome home! It's like you never left."

"Why are we back together?" Manfred asked. It occurred to Sam it wasn't quite like before because Manfred was speaking aloud. Sam imagined how much worse his life would have been if everyone had been able to hear Manfred, all along.

Sam had to gather himself before answering. He needed to get this right the first time, no mistakes. "I was lost without you." A couple of weeks ago, when he was playing with the sock puppet, that had been vaguely true. Now, the words felt like razor blades coming out of his mouth. "I just had to crawl back."

"You forgot two things," Manfred replied. "One, I hate you." Sam knew that was a lie. "Two, I love it here. Are you aware of what I've accomplished? I'm a God now, Sam. A God!"

Still concentrating on saying the right things, Sam replied, "Wow, I'm really impressed. That *is* something special. I can understand why you may not want to be with me again, but I'm hoping you'll take some pity on me."

"You want me stuck on you, is more like it," Manfred responded. "Now I can prove what I always suspected: you were the one holding me back. I have a whole herd of slaves now! What have you ever accomplished? Nothing! You've always been the zero in our relationship, not me."

"You're right," Sam replied. "I am nothing without you. But how have the cavemen been treating you, hand-wise?"

"I'm doing fine, thank you for asking!" Manfred responded in a huffy, uptight way.

"Being held in a hand is very different from being, you know, *rubbed*. These cavemen ... they have such rough, calloused hands. I can't imagine they'd do a good job with such an important task."

"No, really, why did you come back?" Manfred asked. "What's the deal? Does that Julio bastard want to destroy my little kingdom here? You pair of jealous fucks are sitting around lost without me, aren't you? Tired of sucking each other's dicks? Yeah: I'd get tired of sucking someone else's dick, too. Then again, I'm not you, and

I'm not Julio. It's hard to imagine either one of you getting bored of sucking dick. So, what's the deal? Why are you here?"

"Okay, okay, Manfred, calm down," Sam had some retorts he wanted to hurl at Manfred after that tirade, but fencing would be counter-productive. Groveling was a better bet; it would give him a base to work from.

Sam feigned despondency as best he could. "If you don't need me, I guess I can get Julio to separate us again." Here was the trap, to see if Manfred would take the bait.

"Well …" Manfred hesitated. Sam took Manfred gently in his hand, letting Manfred lie there while rubbing his thumb back and forth along the shaft. Manfred almost purred, and Sam knew he had him.

"Who you?"

In the dark, Sam hadn't noticed Zogla approaching. She should have been asleep, but here she was. She stared at him and he became aware of the fact he was still naked and she was staring at his penis. It was only fair, he supposed; he had to work to avoid staring at her bare *National Geographic* breasts.

"Oh, I'm, um …" Sam mumbled.

He was about to cover Manfred with his hand, out of pure instinct, when Manfred spoke up. "Zogla, it's a miracle!" he said with forced jubilation. "Through the power of the church, I have been resurrected as a whole man."

"Oooooooo," Zogla said, impressed. She stared at Manfred with wonder, and ran her eyes up and down Sam's body to take in the entirety of the miracle.

"Yes, it's a miracle," Manfred continued. "I am now three parts. I am the Father, Manfred. I'm now also the Son, which is the rest of this body in front of you. I'm also the Holy Ghost,"

Manfred paused and muttered uncertainly under his breath, "Holy Ghost ... I've never understood who the Holy Ghost is. Dammit." Then, louder and with more authority, he said, "Run, Zogla! Tell the others! But don't come back for at least 15 minutes."

Zogla stood there, looking uncertain. She studied Sam and Manfred intently. At first, Sam thought she was bathing in the glory of the miracle, but then he realized she was more likely trying to decide if this was good or evil.

"Run!" Manfred shouted, and Zogla responded this time, turning around and sprinting away. She looked back once with an uncertain expression, and she was gone.

"The number one thing we do after we establish this Holy Trinity story," Manfred said once Zogla was out of earshot, "is burn her for being a witch. She's an inquisitive pain in my ass. Maybe we'll eat her, too. Tasty witch ..."

He knew he was breaking character, but he couldn't help himself. "Fuck, Manfred, we're not Gods!" he yelled. "I don't want to be the damned figurehead of a new bullshit religion for cavemen! This is more humiliating than dying while getting a blow job from a meth whore!" He regretted the outburst. It wasn't smooth. He needed to be smooth.

"This is why I always hated you," Manfred said. "Here I am, propping you up again. I think we have a good thing worked out here, with the Father, the Son and the Holy Ghost."

"Who the fuck is the Holy Ghost?" Sam replied sharply.

"Uh, I always forget who the Holy Ghost is. And *you* certainly wouldn't know, *Jew*. I guess we're just the Father and the Son. That's still pretty cool. We can continue our dominion over these people."

"I don't want to fucking dominate here! It's pathetic. They're Neanderthals," Sam yelled.

"It doesn't matter if they're pathetic," Manfred responded. "It only matters that they're my slaves."

"Well, you can dominate without me," Sam said. He realized he was right back where he left off before Zogla arrived. "I'll have Julio separate us and you can stay here with your slaves. I'll go back to the year 3542, and be all alone."

Manfred was quiet and Sam steeled his stomach for the words he had to say next. "I just want to get you back into my hand again." Sam felt a vomit-like sensation rising in his throat. That last sentence was completely vile, like an insincere sappy love song, but Sam knew it would work for Manfred. "But I need to know who my competitors are. Who has been giving you hand here?"

"Don't you worry about it," Manfred replied smugly, but Sam could tell Manfred had a rather intense delight in the thought of Sam feeling jealous. *So gross*, thought Sam.

"Well of course I'm going to worry about it," Sam said, doing his best to sound like he was truly worried about who was touching Manfred where. "Are they any good? Let me tell you, I've learned some new tricks since you saw me last. If you thought my handjobs were good before, wait until you try one now."

This part was utterly sincere. Sam had given and received many handjobs in his reincarnations. Much more importantly, he had lived Manfred's life, so he knew exactly what Manfred liked. As Julio said: It was all about empathy.

"I've had all sorts of hand, and it's all been great," Manfred finally said, a transparent lie.

"If I'm not special to you, I'll just leave." *Vomit.* Sam stood up as if he were walking away forever, but quickly realized he *couldn't* walk away from Manfred since Manfred was attached.

For some reason, even though Manfred was coming with him as he walked, the walking had the desired effect. "Don't go!" Manfred whined softly.

"What's that?" Sam prodded.

"All right, all right, you win!" Manfred cried. "Your hand haunts my dreams! I want nothing more than your hand! I know you're a man. Maybe this makes me a fag. Maybe … maybe I've been a fag all along."

"Gay or not …" Sam began, "You seem more interested in being a God than in getting handjobs."

"That's just not true! I'll give you anything you want! Anything!" Manfred whined.

Perfect, Sam thought. "Well, I do need something from you."

"Anything," Manfred offered. "Give me hand now and we'll talk about it later."

"No, we'll talk about it now. I'll give you handjobs every day and you'll introduce morality into your stupid religion."

"What do you mean?" Manfred seemed sincerely confused.

"Well, let's start with this: Tonight, you don't burn Zogla for being a witch, but instead give her a job distributing that meat and fur you have on display for the glory of the faith or whatever bullshit, to the outcasts," Sam began.

Manfred made a groaning noise as if he had been punched in the penis equivalent of a gut, but said nothing.

Sam continued, "Tomorrow, we work on removing the idea of original sin. Also, no more Manfred statues. It's time for you to stop being an idol. Work with me on this and I'll give you handjobs galore." *Handjobs galore* was definitely not a combination of words he had uttered before. "Deal?"

"You'll give me quality hand?" Manfred asked. Sam nodded. "At least four times a day, exactly like before?"

"Yes, sir."

"Deal, deal, deal, deal, deal!" Manfred exclaimed. Then he added, "Wait, what's *original sin*?"

It was the code Manfred lived his life by, yet he had no idea what it was called. "You know: the rotten idea that everyone is born evil and Manfred needs to come along and save everyone from the Hell they deserve and take them to Heaven, and it doesn't matter what else they do. That nastiness."

"Oh," Manfred said meekly.

"We're going to preach good deeds matter and kindness matters. We'll change it so there are no blank checks for immoral behavior in exchange for accepting Manfred."

"I get it," Manfred said impatiently.

"We'll teach them that knowledge and science are good things, and sex is just *one* damn thing and not *every* damn thing, and …"

"Whatever. Whatever. Sorry I asked," Manfred interrupted. "Too many words. I said Deal and I meant it. Now, can we seal this deal with, you know, a handshake?"

Sam had more to say, but he decided against it. He'd make this one handjob the best Manfred ever had, and Manfred would be putty in his hands, so to speak. He reached down and grabbed Manfred, who responded as if he had seen Medusa.

Before Sam could really get into it, Manfred spoke up once more. "Hey, Sam," he said, "before we get going, can you go over to the pile of Manfred symbols and get a piece of vine?"

"What?"

"I was thinking it might be even better if you cut off my air supply," Manfred suggested with what actually sounded to Sam like some level of embarrassment.

Sam laughed aloud. How and why did Manfred think of this? Sam had been reincarnated as a musician who liked that stuff, so he had some familiarity with it, but how could he cut off the air supply of a penis with no respiratory system? What a silly idea, but he decided to not judge. "Whatever floats your boat, buddy." Sam walked over to a pile of raw materials for the Manfred symbol factory, and selected a vine.

"Let's get started, babe," Manfred said as Sam wrapped the vine around right below the head. That seemed like the most appropriate location. Sam was sure this would be the best handjob ever, even if the vine would only detract from it.

Sam sat down and sprawled back against one of the rock pews. This was too intense to stay standing. In a matter of seconds, Manfred was making grunting—or maybe choking—noises. "Are you okay down there?" Sam asked with concern.

"So great!" Manfred moaned. "So great, Sam, loving this …" He kept mumbling, but his sounds had devolved from words to happy grunts.

Sam kept going. He was careful to never let it get too far so he could prolong it, though he tried to be cognizant of the returning cavepeople. He'd have to finish before they arrived, but he had some time. When the pressure got to be too much he'd back off, touching something less sensitive for a while until Manfred cooled down just enough. *This is going to be easy as pie*, Sam thought. They'd have a much better, toned down religion within a week. No more bullshit. Then they'd get out of there.

"Holy Ghost!"

Sam looked up. It was Zog, there to ruin everything. Oxbo, Zogla, and the whole herd was there. It hadn't been fifteen minutes! Sam was a fool to have depended on Zogla's timekeeping skills. It's not as if she had ever seen a clock before.

"Oh, hello," was all Sam could think to say. He still had Manfred, as well as the vine, in his hand, all on display as he was sprawled out in front of them.

"What doing? What doing to Manfred our Lord?" Oxbo screamed, livid.

"Holy Ghost using vine to strangle Manfred!" Zogla exclaimed.

"Holy Ghost trying to kill Manfred!" Zog shouted. "Must save Manfred!"

"What, this?" Sam casually asked, trying to project that everything was normal. "It's no big deal. The vine is kind of novel, but Manfred wanted it." He loosened the vine to show Manfred safe beneath. "See? It's okay. Manfred's okay."

Cavepeople surrounded the church. There was nowhere to run. He stood up and moved to the tree, with some vain thought of climbing it and hiding. But he just stood there at the bottom of the tree, frozen. Unconsciously, he still gripped Manfred—hard as a rock—as if to protect him from a pending attack. Several of the cavemen were holding primitive weapons, while others grabbed some of Manfred's symbols, the crosses, which had pointed spear-tipped ends. They all moved in.

"Whoa, whoa, whoa, my friends. I'm not hurting Manfred," Sam pleaded.

Sam was of slightly below average height in his day, but he was much taller than all the cavepeople. A single caveman wouldn't worry him too much. But they were bulky, and they were many. And they were attacking.

Everything went out of control.

The cavepeople started yelling wildly. They ran at Sam, who held Manfred tighter than ever, corralling him near the tree at the front of Manfred's church. He felt several pointed ends of Manfred's cross plunge into him, delivering sharp pain.

"Oxbo, stop, it's OK!" he heard Manfred shout. "Holy Ghost was being good!"

The cavepeople backed away for a moment, and Sam added, "Manfred's ... okay ... look, listen to him. He's ... fine." Staggering, Sam tried to hold Manfred up to prove he was fine, but he stumbled and his hand accidentally slipped, yanking roughly at Manfred, and, somehow, like that, Manfred picked the moment to ejaculate, spraying white goo at the feet of the surrounding throng.

"NO TOUCH MANFRED!" Oxbo shouted.

"Stop trying to strangle Lord!" Zog screamed.

Sam fell into a fetal position as the cavemen attacked again. Blows were raining down on him. The broadside of one of the crosses hit his head.

"This is no way to get to Heaven!" Manfred cried out. "Oxbo, please, buddy! You were always my favorite! Stop!" But his voice was drowned in the chaos.

"Julio! Future people! Help!" But if he was hoping for Julio to appear in shining armor on a white steed with futuristic laser guns, it didn't happen.

One cross lanced through his side, filling him with incomprehensible pain. In that moment, he didn't comprehend why he had signed up for this shit. "Julio!" he cried, searching the horizon for a hero. "Julio ... why ... have you ... forsaken ... me?"

"I save Manfred!" Sam recognized Zog's voice and saw him holding a stone axe. The axe looked sharp, but not sharp enough.

Oh fuck, not again, Sam thought.

Perhaps seeing what was about to happen, Manfred called out, "Jesus! Jesus! I have sinned and I'm really sorry but I accept you as my Lord and Savior!"

Somehow, Sam found new clarity and forcefulness to yell, "Fuck you, Manfred! You didn't believe in Jesus five minutes ago! You said *you* were God!"

Seeing Zog charging, the surrounding cavemen secured Sam's bloodied arms and legs, pinning his naked body so Zog could get to his target. Sam was already in too much pain to fight, so he just watched it happen. Zog swung the axe, elevating the pain to staggering levels.

A single blow from the dull stone axe didn't do the job, so Zog kept swinging and swinging and swinging. Behind Zog, the other cavemen were screaming, "Save Manfred! Save Manfred from Holy Ghost!" There was a huge gash at Manfred's base.

Finally, on what must have been the twentieth blow, Manfred came off. Blood poured out of both ends. Zog grabbed Manfred and held him aloft. "I saved Manfred!" he shouted, as blood poured from Manfred onto his head.

More of Manfred's cross symbols started crashing down onto him again. With his last breaths, Sam looked to the sky and croaked, "Future people ... help ... me ..."

—⁜—

It was all gone.

The cavepeople, the church ... all gone. They were in pitch black darkness, with Sam lying on the floor. The pain was still there, but it wasn't quite so bad. Likely, he was in shock. He had lost so much blood, and he felt the familiar coldness of impending death. Beside him, he heard Manfred whimpering, calling out for Jesus.

As if in answer to Manfred's prayer, a beam of golden light appeared, shining down on Manfred. Familiar harp music began playing. But this time, it sounded distant and scratchy, as if it was coming from an old-time record player. Of course, there were two demons, like last time. The demon in the distance seemed to be enthusiastically boogying on some kind of raised platform, surrounded by multi-colored disco lights. The closer one was standing over Sam, but his dancing was perfunctory.

"Into the pit of Hell you go with the other non-believers," the Demon said in a perfectly normal conversational tone. "Hell awaits you. You will roast in the flames. Brimstone will sear the flesh off your bones. Eternal damnation. Lake of Fire. Add some more brimstone. Blah blah blah. Okay, I'm bored now."

The spotlight was still shining on Manfred, but this time he was flat against the ground, not rising to any golden gates. He was tone-deaf to the change. "Oh, thank you Jesus, thank you for my second chance!"

Julio pulled off his demon mask and turned to Manfred. "Manfred, you shit-stick," he said. "We've done this before! How many times do you need to learn the same lesson? Come on, let's go before you manage to screw something else up." Julio grabbed Manfred with his left hand and started to walk away, calling out,

"All right, get down from there, Hans. Let's go." The other demon jumped down from whatever he was dancing on. The lights went out, and he followed Julio.

Sam was still just lying there. He managed to get his arm off the ground, like a kid raising his hand in class to ask a question, and groaned, "Julio ... Julio? ... Pain ... I'm ... in ... Pain ... Help?"

—∞—

Zogla looked around. Everyone had calmed down. There was nothing else to do. They had tried to save Manfred, but he was dead. The Son/Holy Ghost was also dead, a bloody nub where his man part used to be. Something seemed wrong to Zogla. *Why is God man part?* she wondered.

Zog and Oxbo stood next to her. "Manfred dead. Go to Heaven," Zog said. He was looking at the ground in sadness.

"We believe. We go Heaven too," Oxbo said.

"God live in Heaven," Zog said.

"We be with God when we die," Oxbo said.

Zogla wasn't so sure. "Me no think Manfred is God," she said. "If he God, he no die. If Holy Ghost is ghost, he no die."

Oxbo and Zog looked at each other. Zog's lip curled. Oxbo spat.

Zogla added, "Manfred's words no make sense. Why have Manfred rules if not matter if follow Manfred rules? Me think no need church. No need display. Me think we need help outcasts." She paused, and then repeated, "Me no think Manfred is God."

Zog and Oxbo stared at her. They were angry.

"Zogla witch!" Zog cried. "Burn witch!"

312

Epilogue

*There are many servants today who are breaking away
from their masters. (First Samuel 25:10)*

"Well, that sucked pretty hard," Sam said, stretching his arms.

"Good morning, Sunshine," Julio responded. "It's nice to see you back among the living."

Sam was on the lone bed in the middle of an otherwise empty all-white room in Julio's facility. It seemed like yesterday he was here the first time, and yet, at the same time, it was lifetimes ago.

Sam tilted his head forward, looking down along his chest. Of course, he was still naked. When was the last time he had any clothes on? Strangely, he wasn't self-conscious about it. At this point, it would take more than nudity to make him feel self-conscious.

He glanced down and saw what he hoped to see: a normal, inanimate penis. What a relief.

"Well, I think I can forego the standard opening speech," Julio said. "I'll give you a few minutes to get yourself settled."

Julio floated out and left Sam all alone in the empty room. The first thing he needed was clothes. He was about to ask the omnipresent computer for some jeans and a T-shirt, when he decided to try something different today. He asked the nanofabricator to surprise him, and out came a fairly normal pair of brown pants, a billowy cream-colored poet shirt, and a huge, bright pink, starched Elizabethan neck ruffle adorned with gemstones. Plus socks and underwear, which were normal. He cracked up laughing as he put the clothes on. It was perfect. He could *almost* imagine going out in public like this, and providing others with amusement. But he ultimately reverted back to his first idea of jeans and a T-shirt.

He brushed his hair and his teeth, and stepped out the door to find Julio, whom he found lying down in the next room over. Julio didn't respond as Sam walked up, so Sam waited there. In less than a minute, Julio opened his eyes and sat upright.

"I just lived your last couple of months," Julio explained. "It's the first time I've been able to get inside someone's head after they arrived here, since no one has ever died a second time on me." He added under his breath, "Wish I'd gotten the chance to do that with Jim before it was too late."

Sam now knew who Jim was from Manfred's memory and hearing him complain about his wife before he flung Manfred into the portal. Sam, apparently, wasn't the only challenge on Julio's plate recently.

"Sorry. I think I failed," Sam said. He and Manfred had died before they had a chance to undo any of the damage. But at least Manfred was out of there. That was a plus.

"Well, we're still here, so that's good," Julio said, that constant smile as wide as ever. "As for any lasting impact, it's hard to know. Do you understand what happened?"

"I was there," Sam commented, but he knew that wasn't what Julio had on his mind. Remembering an earlier conversation, he had an idea. "You're talking about parallel universes, aren't you?"

"Well, consider this: is it possible we're now inside a parallel universe where the source of organized religion—and especially concepts like original sin—is a talking penis who lived fifteen thousand years ago?"

Sam let the thought sink in. It was a paradox—religion existed when Sam was alive, and that was *before* this caveman meltdown, at least in Sam's perspective—but Sam didn't have any real understanding of how time worked. He decided his next few reincarnations would be of physicists who tackled issues concerning space-time and parallel universes. Maybe then he'd be in a better position to consider the paradox.

"So, I have two questions," Sam said, jolting back to the here and now.

"Shoot," Julio offered.

"First question: when can I get my skeletal replacement and brain chip?" Sam asked.

Julio smiled and replied, "I wondered when you'd ask. I'd say you're ready. We can get them right now. We don't have waiting lines for medical procedures, you know." He clapped Sam on the back and added, "It'll be good to be able to count you among my peers."

The word "peers" reminded him of "pee-ers" and his second question. "Question number two: what happened to Manfred?"

Julio's mouth split into a devious grin. "At first I thought I'd try a resurrection in three days and re-introduce Manfred to their society so he could fix the damage. But I realized I couldn't trust him without you there, and since they just killed you, I doubt they'd accept you back. Sooooo ... after consulting with my colleagues, we've decided to continue trying to educate Manfred."

"Did you put him back with his fellow pee-ers?" Sam asked.

"Not exactly," Julio said. He started laughing, and Sam responded with a cautious smile.

"Come with me and I'll show you," Julio said. Sam followed Julio through the white halls of the retrieval facility. While they walked, Julio continued to explain, "We put the penis peer plan on hiatus. Instead, we're holding up a proverbial mirror."

With those words, they arrived in a standard empty room with a bed—Julio didn't make the mistake of using a viewing chamber room this time—to find Manfred sitting on a table. Except something was different about him ... he was now attached to two testicles.

"You already know Manfred," Julio said to Sam quietly, apparently not wanting to disturb Manfred. "Now let me introduce his new friends, Moonstar and Calliope." Julio pointed at each of the testicles in turn, with a sweeping arm gesture much grander than was called for given two small objects right next to each other.

"Please!" Manfred whined in an uncharacteristic monotone, a flat, dead voice. "I beg you. I'll do anything you want."

Sam initially thought Manfred was talking to him and/or Julio, and he almost responded in confusion. Then Manfred continued, "Please just stop singing that song."

"*Who Let the Dogs Out* by the Baha Men is our favorite song!" one of testicles responded—Sam couldn't tell which one—in a high-pitched, nasal voice. Sam had to wonder if Fran Drescher had been recruited for this purpose.

A second testicle voice, one that sounded somewhat like a frog, chimed in. "Manfred, what if we changed it up, so it wasn't about dogs? What if it was about cats getting out, and instead of barking, we meowed?"

"That's a great idea! We could do it for all different types of animals," the nasal ball concurred.

"Even snails. We should find out what sound snails make," said the frog ball.

Manfred screamed. "No. Dear God. Please no!"

"The Earth Goddess loves it when we express our joy in song," said the nasal ball.

"We're Wiccan. When you become Wiccan, you'll understand what joy is," the frog ball added.

The high-pitched voice somehow managed to shift to a tone of deathly seriousness "You have to convert to Wicca as soon as possible."

"I've been listening to your bullshit about Wicca for hours now," wailed Manfred, "and I'm absolutely certain you don't actually know anything about it! You're picking and choosing and making up shit as you go along, whenever you find it convenient for your current circumstances, and you're just …"

Sam couldn't help but laugh. *Reflect much, Manfred?* he thought. He didn't really know what to say about it, so he asked Julio, "Are you serious?"

"Very serious," Julio said, although his expression—a wide grin with his tongue sticking out a little bit—belied him. "That bastard has to learn somehow. I don't think we can send him on reincarnations, so we have to teach him empathy some other way."

"If you want to make him feel exactly like me," Sam said, "it looks like you've achieved your goal." Sam pulled out a bowl of cashews he got from the nanofabricator and offered some to Julio,

317

who obliged. They stood there snacking for a few minutes, enjoying the performance of Moonstar and Calliope.

Absorbed by the show, Sam almost didn't notice a man and a woman walking into the room, holding hands. "Hello Bob! Hello Mary!" Julio said. "It's about time you met Sam."

The man stepped forward first and shook Sam's hand. "Hello Sam, I'm Bob. I know all about you. I've lived your life. I really admire what you've done recently," said Bob.

"Mary and her first husband, Jim, were transfers of mine," Julio explained. "Bob was a doctor in his first life. He's now working as an intern on the Manfred Human Conversion Project."

"Human Conversion Project?"

"I helped give him the testicles," Bob piped in before Julio could respond. "If Manfred makes progress, he'll have an opportunity to earn legs and a head and everything else and become a normal person. No one will ever know he started off as just a penis!"

"Give him the hands last," Sam volunteered helpfully.

"Bob is so excited about this work," the woman named Mary said.

"Off topic, Mary and Sam have something in common," said Julio. "You were both killed in accidents with PT Cruisers."

"Oh, really?" Mary said with chipper interest. "Were you driving one or hit by one?"

"Please don't hate me, but I was driving one," Sam replied.

Mary made a playful disapproving sound. "Were you texting or just overpowered by the blind spots?" she asked.

"Texting? Absolutely not! I never texted while driving! I was never *that* irresponsible. I crashed while getting a blowjob."

After laughing about these grave details that no longer mattered at all in 3542, they broke back into the original pairs. Bob started talking to Mary about the technical details of the Manfred Human Conversion Project. Sam took the moment to ask Julio something that was bugging him.

"So, you suggested possible alternate universes before. Did you monitor what happened with that tribe of cavepeople?"

"Well, they didn't die off in a plague or a drought or anything advantageous like that," Julio replied. "They went on to interact with other groups. They procreated, and they passed down the horrible ideas they learned from Manfred. There's no way of knowing if there ever *was* a world in which Manfred *didn't* do that, or if we've diverged into a parallel universe. And if we did diverge, when did it happen? Was it when Manfred arrived fifteen and a half millennia ago, or was it when Jim hurled Manfred into the portal two-and-a-half weeks ago?"

"So, the paradox is that Manfred may have created the seeds of the religion he later adopted ..." Sam thought aloud.

"Maybe. Parallel universes are weird, if they exist at all."

Sam suddenly laughed. "So, those folks who believe in the talking snake were close. It was actually a talking *dick*."

"Hmm," Julio cocked his head to the side. "Well, yeah, that's sort of snake-like. Given the choices, I'd argue that a talking snake sounds less crazy than a talking dick. Nice approximation."

They didn't know. There was no way of knowing if Manfred had been a relatively unimportant bit of comic relief, the origin of religion, or something in between. They continued to munch on cashews, and with every bite Sam silently honored George Washington Carver's scientific discoveries with the crop. After they emptied the bowl, Julio asked, "Shall we go get your upgrades?"

"I'm as ready as I'll ever be," Sam replied. "Let's go."

As they headed towards the door, Bob stopped them.

"Julio, I need to ask. Is this really necessary? The whole, 'let's play the top 100 most annoying songs of all human history to Manfred repeatedly' part?" Bob inquired.

Sam and Julio stared at Bob in silence.

"What I'm saying is, I don't know if I understand the medical or psychological benefits. Is it really a critical part of the development plan? Couldn't we do without it? Again, is it necessary?"

Sam and Julio continued to stare as Moonstar and Calliope screeched the immortal words of Los del Río, *Hey Macarena*.

"Hell yes, it's necessary!" Sam and Julio managed to say in near-unison. They laughed and resumed their walk to the door.

As far as Sam was concerned, Manfred was getting off easy.